TROUBLE AT FIRST

THE DECKER CONNECTION

CHERYL CAMPBELL

ISBN: 979-8-9929865-0-1

2nd edition

To those who think it's too late to try something new and those who encourage you to do it anyway.

PROLOGUE

ASHLEIGH

———

"I don't know. Sounds a lot like blackmail to me," Trevor sighs.

"Is it really?" I mean, it's not like I'll actually do it. He just doesn't need to know that. Is that really blackmail, or more like influenced persuasion? It's all about perspective, right?

"Look, it's not like you aren't getting something amazing out of our deal. You get me and my services for free for a full summer as an intern to boost the Savannah Pajamas' social media presence. You know I'm about to graduate at the top of my class in my marketing and social media program. Add that to my baseball knowledge, and I'll make magic, I promise. And in return, I get a few months to prove myself outside of my family name. Is that too much to ask?"

"It could be." He takes a deep breath. "You know Alexander isn't going to like this." He sounds like he might be considering my proposition. Yes! I've got him where I want him. I refrain from throwing my hands up in celebration.

I'm not proud of my methods. I googled how to enter the

witness protection program, and unfortunately, being the daughter of a billionaire owner of a Major League Baseball team doesn't qualify, so on with plan B. Blackmail, I mean, persuade Trevor.

"Don't worry about my brother. I'll take care of him. I know he's your grumpy best friend, but I'll get him to understand why I need this. You understand, don't you?"

"No, not really, but I support you. You know I always have your back, Ashleigh." Trevor is just as supportive and overprotective as my two brothers. For that, I'll be forever grateful.

"Hey, and it's Leigh. Leigh Rutledge. Got it?" I've watched way too many episodes of *Undercover Boss* to know the importance of a new name and identity.

"Why that pseudonym? Where did Rutledge come from?"

"It's my middle name." My mother's maiden name, I think to myself, but laying that on him might be more guilt than I need right now.

"Ashleigh Rutledge Decker? That's a mouthful." He gives a familiar laugh. I can tell he's warming up to the idea.

"So let's say I agree to this. Do you have a place to stay, or do I need to arrange billet housing? Or do you want to stay with me?" As much as I'd love to stay with him, I'm trying to lay low, blend in, and be like everyone else. Staying with the team owner wouldn't exactly fit that narrative.

"Oh, I have it all worked out. I'm going to stay with Emma's parents in Tybee. If my BFF is thousands of miles away doing humanitarian work in Honduras, I'll borrow her bedroom and parents for the summer." I can't believe I will do this without her, but if I want to be independent, I might as well start here. No ride or die by my side.

"Sounds like you have a plan for everything."

"I do. You know I'm organized, thorough, and dedicated to a project. You and the Pajamas won't be disappointed."

"That's a pretty heavy-handed sales job, Ash."

I take a deep breath and appeal to him one more time. "You

know I'm not doing this on a whim. *I need to do this.* I need to figure out who Ashleigh Decker is, especially before I graduate. Besides, who knows how much drama and entertainment you'll get? And you with a front-row seat." Trevor is a drama junkie, after all.

"As Leigh Rutledge?" He questions.

"Exactly."

I let the silence hang between us. With each passing second, I start to deflate. He's not going to do it.

He startles me with a clap of his hands.

"Welcome to the Savannah Pajamas, Leigh. I hope this summer is everything you hope for and more."

CHAPTER
ONE

ASHLEIGH

———

I've been in Georgia for three days, and I admit, I feel lighter, more free, even with my hefty dose of nerves. Good, right? I turn up the tunes and bop my head to the song blasting through my stereo. Maybe this plan will work after all.

I need a fresh start, a little bit of freedom, and a summer of self-discovery. A chance to spread my wings and fly. That's what your college years are for, right? So here I am, the summer before my senior year, and I haven't spread my wings at all. My wings are clipped like a bird in a gilded cage. I feel like I have more oversight and security than the president.

How did I get to this point where I needed to go undercover to take an unpaid college internship? I'm no one special. At least, I don't think so. But my family thinks I'm special, so that's what matters. I don't mean the 'we are all special and unique as individuals' kind of special. As the only girl in an alpha male, testosterone-filled family, I'm special to them. It's a matter of my XX chromosomes versus their XYs. That makes me the lucky girl. Yay, me.

My phone rings, and it's Trevor. I answer with a sigh, using my hands-free.

"Hey, T, what's up?"

"Hey, Ash. Just checking in. Do you need anything from me before you start tomorrow?"

My irritation and nerves about tomorrow lie just below the surface. I haven't even started yet, and Trevor is already over-stepping. Damnit. He promised.

"Come on, it's Leigh, remember? And are you calling all the interns and your team to see if you can do anything for them before they arrive?" My tone is a bit harsh, and I know it's partially because I'm so on edge.

I grab the Savannah Pajamas baseball hat next to me and put it on, pulling my hair through the back. I tug on my long, blonde ponytail, tightening the hair tie. My friends know I'm frustrated when I start tugging on my hair. Good thing Trevor doesn't see my tell.

He chuckles. "Well, Leigh," he says, over-emphasizing my new name, "as a matter of fact, I do call everyone. I'm just that kind of guy. So see, I'm treating you like everyone else."

I roll my eyes, even though I know he can't see me. "Trevor, I really need this." I know I'm sounding whiney now. I never said I wouldn't use all the tools in my arsenal to make this happen. "I want people to know me as me, not as a Decker, you know?"

I hear him sigh and can picture him rubbing the back of his neck. "I know, Ash. I get it. I do. These players would go nuts if they learned your dad owns the Carolina Reapers. I promised I would keep your secret, and I will. I know how important it is to you. I mean, it will be hard enough to keep them from lining up at your door, and I don't need the added Decker connection sweetening the pot. I got you."

I give a half-hearted laugh. Guys lining up at my door without my family connection? Doubtful.

My father, Sullivan "Sully" Decker, owns several companies, but his primary focus is his beloved baseball team, the Carolina Reapers. Owning a Major League team has always been his dream, and when he was awarded a franchise twenty years ago, he was like a kid with Willie Wonka's Golden Ticket. He loves baseball and the business behind it. He's made the Reapers one of the best teams in the League and one of the most profitable too.

His love of baseball is a family affair. Both my brothers played ball in college. I grew up in baseball stadiums, trailing after them. I never knew anything else. Baseball is in my blood. I love it, and I won't deny it. I love everything about the sport. The talent, the psychology, the averages and statistics, the fandom. It's everything, and it's a big part of me. That saying about diamonds being a girl's best friend? They meant baseball diamonds, right?

"Thanks, T. Really, I appreciate it."

"But..."

"But, what?" My nerves are on edge again. My lighter-than-air mood sinks like a lead balloon.

"I'm not telling all the other interns that their brother is in town. So heads up." I can hear the wince in his voice. I feel a little guilty knowing he's caught in the middle.

I scream in frustration. I'm at a stop sign, and since it's late May in Savannah, I have the top down on my Mini Cooper. A lady walking her dog gives me a disapproving look at my outburst.

"Damnit! He promised!" I knew Alexander wouldn't let me around an entire baseball team without his watchful eye. It's not that he doesn't trust me. It's the guys he doesn't trust. I may be twenty-two, but I'm still his baby sister. Ugh! I hate that term.

"I know, I know. Calm down. I'll do my best to keep him on a tight leash. I didn't want you to be surprised."

"What's he doing here?" Like I don't know. I'm going to kill him.

"Well, he's using the scouting excuse. But I told him to stay away from you. I'm doing my best here, Ash."

Yes, my oldest brother, Alexander, is General Manager and part-time scout for the Reapers. Of us three siblings, he's the most like my dad. He's stoic, protective, a man of few words, who usually keeps his emotions contained. When they surface, it's like a tsunami, all rushing out from behind the wall he's kept them behind. Most people think he's grumpy, but he's not. He's just always on high alert, keeping a watchful eye out for his family and friends.

I feel like Alexander wants me to have a vanilla life, and I hate vanilla. It's so safe. Boring. Sometimes, I get sprinkles, but they are only under supervision. What if I want rocky road instead of vanilla? His answer? You might not like it, and you could get hurt. I want the best for you. Stick with me, kid. I'll take care of you.

I. DON'T. WANT. TO. BE. TAKEN. CARE. OF! UGH. It's maddening.

I want to succeed because of my hard work, not because there is a building named after my family or other promises they can make. I mean, of course, I want my family to support me but get out of my way. Is that too much to ask? Apparently so. When it comes to me, they can't help themselves.

Alexander is ten years older than me, but that doesn't mean we aren't close. I grew up attending his baseball games and was essentially the team mascot, the little sister to all the guys. Oh, it's not a complaint, exactly. I have dozens of guys who love me, just not in *that* way. It also means he has a network of friends literally around the world keeping an eye on me. Overprotective, remember?

I couldn't make up the stories if I tried. I've had his friends show up at restaurants when I'm on a date, had chance encounters while I'm on vacation, and even had one show up at an airport in a foreign country when I mentioned a mixup with my ticket. Seriously. They are everywhere. It's like Alexander runs his own Secret Service or something. Except his Secret Service agents are smoking hot guys who are high-powered executives, professional athletes, and even a Hollywood movie star. Yup. Legit superhero movie star.

"Dammit!" I slam my hand on the steering wheel. Another disapproving glare from the dog walker. I give her a fake smile and wave. I turn left at the stop sign and head home instead of hitting my favorite boutique.

"I'll deal with Xander. Thanks for the heads up." My mind starts to think of ways to get rid of him. Most ideas involve baseball bats and kneecaps. Fortunately, my bark is much worse than my bite. I love my brother to bits. I just had a script for this summer written in my head, and it's already getting edited and modified. I can feel the disappointment growing.

Trevor laughs. "Yeah, good luck with that. Anyway, see you tomorrow, Leigh. Don't be late. Need to impress the boss." He disconnects, and my music plays through the speakers like that call didn't ruin my mood. Even Five Seconds of Summer can't perk me up from Trevor's news.

I pull into the driveway of my home away from home and smile. My teal car matches the white and teal of Emma's house, and for some reason, that calms me down just a little. The combination of white and teal reminds me of beaches and happy memories and soothes my soul.

I take several deep breaths, inhaling the fresh salt air. It's so peaceful here. The palm trees sway in the breeze, the seagulls call to one another, and the surf breaks in the distance. I look up, watching the clouds hurry across the skyline like they have somewhere else to be. Sixty seconds of Tybee Island meditation is what I need to calm my anxiety.

I pull my phone out of my purse and text my other brother, Julian.

Get the shovel ready because I'm going to kill him.

JULES

What did he do now?

He's here!!!!!

JULES

Does that really merit 5 !!!!!

Yes. Yes, it does!!!!!!

JULES

You knew this would happen. This is a big deal
for him. Let him have it.

Let him have it? Wow. I didn't expect this from Jules. Even though Julian is eight years older than me, he and I have a special relationship, and he always takes my side. Always. Until now. Maybe he's not a fan of this summer plan, either? Come to think of it, he's been unusually quiet lately.

Where Xander is uptight and overbearing like Dad, Jules is more laid back and relaxed. Both brothers are highly driven, but their personalities make them seem like night and day. Jules is more like Mom, sharing her dark blonde wavy hair, blue eyes, and a smile that lets you know it will all be okay. He has a casual way about him. Give both brothers a thousand-dollar suit, and Alexander is the buttoned-up, boardroom boss, power look all the way. That same suit on Jules? He looks casual, flirty, and approachable. They couldn't be more opposite.

I tend to favor Jules in appearance, but everyone says I look just like my mom. I don't see it because, unlike Mom, I usually keep my blonde hair long and up in ponytails, braids, messy buns, and baseball hats. I'm more of a sporty, low maintenance, because why bother with two brothers who are determined to keep me locked in a tower kind of girl. Why wear dresses when leggings are so comfy? I practically keep the athleisure industry in business.

While Xander makes no secret of his overprotectiveness, Jules is more discreet. As one of the most successful sports agents in the country, his friends are more likely to invite me to parties to watch me in plain sight. Too often, I've met a guy at a function, and by the end of the evening, one of Julian's friends will ensure I make it home safely and alone. I'm not sure if they report back to Jules, but I assume they are watching over me. Nobody touches the Decker little sister. Nobody.

And THAT is why I need this summer. I need to stretch my wings before I graduate and fulfill my destiny to work for the family team. I have a job waiting for me that I didn't really earn on my own merits, but I get a VP title because I'm a Decker. Honestly, I just want to be like everyone else. I know, poor little rich girl. Well, it's not easy because I never know if people are being sincere or using me for my connections. I'm hoping this summer will give me the answer I'm looking for.

Et tu Brute?

What have you done with Jules?

JULES
Trust Trevor. He's got your back. Gotta run. Got a player with a Vegas crisis. Let me know how it goes tomorrow.

Another one? When will they learn? Good luck!

As their agent, Jules is a babysitter to a group of wealthy, young guys with more talent than sense. He's fantastic with the PR stuff, but I don't envy him. He should ban them all from Vegas.

Ugh. I grab my stuff and go into the house, where I'm greeted with a hug by Mrs. Jones, my best friend's mother.

"What's wrong, Ash? You looked stressed."

"Xander," I growl the one word that explains everything.

She gives me a sympathetic look as she rests her hands on my shoulders.

"Why don't you take the kayak out before dinner and relax, work out the tension and nerves."

"That's a good idea. You sure you don't need any help with dinner?"

"No, I'm enjoying *the mom with kids in the house* again role, so be prepared for a summer of meals and treats and chats." She gives me a side hug. Her smile assures me of the support I need and am lacking from my family at the moment. "I'm so glad you are here, Ashleigh."

"I'm glad I'm here too." And I am. "I miss Emma."

"Me, too. But this gives us time for you to spill all the tea about her." She laughs.

"And on that note, I'm out. The kayak is a good idea." I make my way to the dock, where several kayaks are in the boathouse.

Their house sits on the river dividing Tybee Island from the mainland. It's a different vibe than the beach side, and I'm looking forward to the serenity it brings.

I usually enjoy the outdoors and the fresh air. It settles me and grounds me when I'm feeling overwhelmed. I'm not a workout kind of girl, but I enjoy being active. I love food too much not to be active, and the compromise I've made with myself to keep eating what I want is to exercise doing things I enjoy with others. My five-foot-eight frame is proportionate, but a few weeks of Emma's cookies, no exercise, and my hips quickly get a little extra padding. So I'll run with Jules, go to the gym with Xander, take a bike ride with Emma, but do something by myself? It's a new experience for me.

Emma and I usually kayak together when we are here. Alone time is one of many new experiences I will surely have this summer. I usually have someone around all the time. Emma and I are practically joined at the hip during the school year. For now, I need to focus on relaxing and letting my anxiety go.

I lean into thinking about my summer as Leigh Rutledge. WWLRD? I decide she'll deal with it tomorrow when it comes.

I've been out on the water long enough that my arms burn

from the exertion, and the sun starts to lower on the horizon. When I'm focused on a task, I lose track of time. I guess focus is a Decker trait I share with my siblings. Maybe we aren't as different as I'd like to believe.

The solitude and quiet of the tidal salt marsh, especially as the sun begins to dip below the horizon, is a spiritual experience. This evening Mother Nature is showing off. The sky explodes with brilliant colors of pink, orange, and purple, blended against a dimming blue sky. It's breathtaking.

I love paddling on the river, taking in all of nature's glory. I'm close to home, so I slow the kayak, not quite ready to go in. I allow my mind to drift, thinking about how much love I have for my family compared to the amount of frustration. Love wins out every time. I have a hard time staying mad at them.

I also consider Emma's family and how their dynamic is different from mine, with family vacations and holidays spent together. My family was more like theirs when I was younger, often taking family vacations on Tybee. We used to have a house on the island near Emma's house. I think back to the last time we were here as a family.

Mom used to insist on family time, baseball be damned. She'd work hard to get us all together as often as possible. I remember one trip during the summer All-Star break when I was ten. Mom and I sat at the edge of our dock, feet dangling over the water, drinking ice-cold sweet tea. We sipped on our drinks and talked about school, my love of baseball, and art.

Mom loved to talk about art the most, and I hung on to every word. Painting with her was one of my favorite things to do. She waxed on about the colors in the sky at this time of day. The sky's canvas would swirl, giving us a magnificent show like this evening. Maybe that's why my thoughts drift back.

Those times on the dock were our special girl time. We left my father and brothers to fend for themselves for an hour or so every evening. It was our island thing.

I smile wistfully at the thought of that dock, Mom's toes

skimming the water, creating ripples that would extend into the calm water of the river. I let my fingers skim the water, recreating similar ripples lost in the memory.

I couldn't wait to grow up so I could touch the water with my toes, just like my mother. "Promise me you won't grow up too fast, Ash. You have plenty of time," she whispered. I looked at her like she'd crushed my dreams. I wanted to be like her now.

"Maybe next summer will be different," she added. She squeezed my hand, and we watched the sunset together.

Has it been twelve years?

A tear slips down my cheek.

Yeah, the next summer was different, but not because I grew four inches and could finally touch the water. No, the next summer was the first summer without my mom. Only seven months after that sunset, she died from an aggressive form of cancer. Cancer sucks.

Dad sold our island house, and we hadn't gone back again as a family. Dad just couldn't do it. When she died, a part of him died too. He never dated or remarried after her. I think she was his one true love, his soul mate. Love is beautiful. Until it's gone. I wonder if that's why my brothers haven't married yet. It was hard to watch my dad pull into himself. That's when my brothers stepped in and stepped up.

I don't usually allow myself to play what if, but I slip into thinking about all the what ifs now. What if Mom was still alive? What would my life look like? Would I still be painting? Would I be as close to Xander and Jules as I am now? Would they be as overbearing and protective in my life, or would Mom have kept them at bay?

I shake my head, letting those thoughts go.

Here I am. No sense playing what if. I'm in the real world now. And I'm back on Tybee Island for a whole summer on my own. All grown up.

I take a deep breath, letting the fresh air fill my lungs. I close my eyes and hear the cicadas play a loud melody, drowning out everything around me.

I clear my mind, attempting to quell the anxiety in my stomach. My internship starts tomorrow, and despite my desire to do this, I'm nervous. I'm the kind of nervous that feels like butterflies in my stomach are having a dance party. I hate this feeling.

Deep breath. It's going to be great. It's what I want. I'm standing at the threshold of a new opportunity. I mean, this summer could be life-changing. Come on, Leigh Rutledge. You've got this.

CHAPTER
TWO

COLE

———

"I can't believe this is our last summer here," Matt says as we cruise down the highway from Charleston to Savannah. I'm driving my old Jeep Wrangler, the best beach car in the world. Matt's surfboard strapped to the top, my guitar in the back seat with the doors and soft top, and our bags crammed in the back, full of bats, gloves, and board shorts.

"I know, we are at that stage of lasts. Remember when that happened senior year in high school? It became a bit much," I say.

Matt laughs. "It's our last home opener. It's our last home game. It's our last beach party. It's our last time together," he says, mocking. "Remember when we thought life couldn't get better than that? Man, were we wrong."

"But it wasn't our last beach party, was it? And we thought it was our last prank on Hobbs, and it wasn't. Hell, we still get him every time we play against him. I'd like to think this isn't the last. Maybe it's really a beginning."

I laugh at myself. The truth is, Matt's right, but I play it all off before I get emotional and let my mind spiral into the future. We are college seniors. It is our last. It's our last shot at the dream. At the draft. This time next year, we will have gotten the call. Or not.

This summer will be full of scouts, stats, and baseball. If we are going pro, this is make-or-break time. We've always wanted to play pro ball, and honestly, I don't have a plan B. Everything is riding on this summer and next season. This is our chance to have fun, enjoy the game we love, and impress the scouts.

Matt and I have known each other since we were eight. He played for the Hardware Aces, and I played for the Brixx Bombers, rival Little League teams. I had stolen third base and started talking smack to the third baseman, Matt. I was relentless with my eight-year-old smack talk. He asked me to stop. Politely, I might add. Matt has impeccable sportsmanship. Well, most of the time.

I told him he had three seconds to shut me up, and I started counting Mississippis. He punched me in the mouth after two. We've been best friends ever since. Best friends don't really cover it. We are brothers.

After that season, we were inseparable, whether travel ball, high school, or college. You want Matt Hartman? Cole Davidson comes along too. You want Cole? Well, be prepared to take Matt too. We are like a buy one, get one special. But the truth is, plenty wanted our extraordinary duo when it came to college offers. We play like one on the diamond and have the power behind the bats to match it. We feed off each other's energy and keep the team pumped up. Not to sound cocky, but we are the whole baseball package.

We picked NC State for the great baseball program and coaching staff, plus it was on the east coast, just a short distance from home. Whether or not we want to admit it, Matt and I are Mama's boys. We love our hometown of Charleston and go home when we can during the off-season. Matt needs a hit of salt water periodically, or he'll die. I've always said he's part sea creature. That's partially why we spend our summers near the ocean in Savannah.

I glance over at Matt, the all-American, clean-cut guy. Intelligent, talented, loyal, and the best friend a guy could ever ask for. His smile fills his face, his golden retriever energy radiating off of him. He's the team captain, the leader, the unofficial dad of the group—the responsible one.

I guess I have a few of those traits too, but I'm a little more hot-headed. I'd like to call it passion, but my mom calls it a temper—tomato, tomahto. My dark hair is a little longer, curly around the edges of my ball cap, having perfected the ultimate hair flow. Where Matt shaves daily, I may let my scruff go for a few days because it's easier and maybe a little sexier.

Matt tends to be proactive, thinks it through, and avoids issues before they occur. I'm more reactive, a fix something after the problem evolves kind of guy. That means I'm a pretty good problem solver because I tend to find myself in messes of my own making more often than I'd like to admit. I'm working on it.

Where he's the poster child for team leader, I tend to be the prankster, not to say he doesn't participate. Matt keeps me from going over the top because my passion and focus can take on a life of its own. I tend to go all in when I do or want something, like baseball. I'm going to get drafted and be a Carolina Reaper. It's what I've wanted since I was a kid. All my energy is focused on that. No plan B.

And that's why we've come to Savannah for the past three summers to play in the Southern Coastal League for the Savannah Pajamas, the best and, more importantly, fun baseball team in the collegiate summer leagues.

The Pajamas have a bit of a non-traditional reputation. They are like the Harlem Globetrotters of baseball. Their coaching staff is of the highest caliber, and they assure the college coaches they will send us back to school in the fall stronger and better than when we arrived. When you spend the summer as a Pajama, your stats will increase the following season, guaranteed. And there are plenty of Pajamas who get that draft call. That will be us this time next year. I know it.

The other thing the Pajamas guarantee is that you will have fun and put on a show as a team. They have data to prove that if the fans have fun, the players have fun, then the performance on the field improves. And outrageous fun is the way the Pajamas play. We are the first team ever to play a complete game in night-shirts. And win! We have dance parties outside the dugout, lead singalongs with the fans, and play dizzy bat during the seventh-inning stretch. It's a blast.

Not gonna lie. Playing Division One level baseball is intense. Baseball is a team sport, but it's also individual. It's your stats that get you the call. It's conditioning and hours in the batting cages. I've seen lots of guys crack and lose it all. Most lose the love of the game. That's a damn shame.

I've always had a bit of a reputation as a class clown, and this team allows me to focus on that too. Whether it's chirping at the other team, putting slime in a locker, or stealing a mascot, it's about opening the pressure valve. I believe laughter prevents cracking. The Pajamas are a natural fit for me.

And the fun isn't just on the field. It's off too.

The Pajamas put us up at billet homes in the area. The hosts are all super cool and tons of fun, just like the people of Savan-nah. It's a party city with a lot of history. It reminds me of Charleston, with a little more quirk.

The hosts encourage us to make ourselves at home and let loose. This is our time to play ball, have fun, and not worry about balancing a strict student athletic schedule and academics. We train daily and play four games weekly with the Pajamas, often traveling several hours to other cities. We also spend team time at the beach, riding jet skis, taking ghost tours through the Savannah streets, and building friendships that will last a lifetime.

I also love the summer because I can spend some of my

downtime playing my guitar and writing songs. It's just a hobby, another way to relax and unwind, but something I wish I had more time to mess around with during the school year.

"I'm glad the McIntyres aren't sick of us yet. I love staying with them. Do you think Mr. Mac got that new pinball machine he was eyeing for the game room?" Matt asks.

"I hope so. One last epic pinball tournament sounds like a great way to end the season."

The McIntyres live in a vast six-bedroom house on the beach side of Tybee Island. They are the primo Pajama host family, and anyone placed with them is extremely lucky. All the host families are great, but the Macs? In a class all by themselves. The McIntyre kids left the house ten years ago, so they say they enjoy hosting us for the summer. It's nostalgic for them. They used to try to spread the love and only host rookies each year until they hosted Matt and me two summers ago. Now, it's us and two rookies each year. They have become a surrogate family for us. They even attend a few of our games in Raleigh each season. You can never have too many people to look out for you and be part of your support system. We are lucky guys.

And for that, I'm damn grateful. Mrs. Mac is a great cook and feeds us well. She is a part-time party planner and the perfect Southern hostess. She loves to take care of people, especially with food. I'm guaranteed to gain a few pounds every summer because of her fantastic cooking, and I'm not complaining.

I'm looking forward to her special shrimp and grits tonight. OMG, my mouth is watering just thinking about them.

Mr. Mac is some tech wiz who made his money in the early Silicon Valley tech boom. I think he hung out with Steve Jobs or something like that. He cashed out and retired at forty. Now he is like a personal Go Fund Me page for small businesses and start-ups. His real love is old-school arcade games and baseball. He has a huge room that would rival any Dave and Busters. And his baseball memorabilia is nothing to sneeze at, either.

"What do you know about the rookies staying with us this

year?" I ask. Matt always pays more attention to that kind of stuff.

"We've got Brady, a sophomore shortstop from Notre Dame, and Drew, a junior pitcher from Vanderbilt. I started a group chat with them, and if you paid attention instead of sending GIFs, you'd know a little something about them." He shakes his head like he's disappointed in me, but he knows me by now. Group texts drive me crazy.

"I know they'll be great. The Pajamas pairing system never fails. They do a better job than any dating algorithm."

We pull into the driveway and see Mrs. Mac unloading groceries from her car. Matt jumps out before I even put the Jeep in park and grabs the bags out of her arms, always the gentleman. Unfortunately for him, that leaves her arms open for me.

I reach down, scoop her up, and swing her around in a huge hug.

"There are my favorite boys! I'm so glad you are here," she exclaims. I put her down, and she reaches up on her tiptoes to kiss Matt on the cheek. I chuckle as I watch him blush. He's such a softie that way.

"Hey, Mrs. Mac, it's good to see you. You go inside, and we'll get these groceries right in for you. We want to teach these rookies how to treat you right," I say with a wink. Matt and I know where our bread is buttered. We grab the groceries, and our summer begins.

CHAPTER
THREE

ASHLEIGH

———

My kayak drifts through the water, and I hold my paddle still while a blue heron watches me as I pass. I pull out my cell phone to capture it on my camera. I wish I had my Nikon, but my phone will have to do for now. I doubt either device can capture the magnificence of my surroundings, but I want to document this moment. I'll post it on my new IG account. My Leigh Rutledge account.

A dolphin swimming beside me for the last few minutes pops up, startles me, and I jump. As my kayak wobbles, I laugh at myself. "Flipper, if you splash me, I'm having dolphin for dinner," I tease. I steady the boat and take one more panoramic picture.

As I swivel in my seat to get the 180-degree picture, a jet ski comes flying through the water, causing my kayak to rock in the wake. I let out a yelp and try to steady the boat.

Everything moves in slow motion. My phone slips out of my hand; as I reach for it, between the wake and my weight shifting, I capsize, rolling the kayak over like a turtle.

Don't panic! I will myself to think. With my legs still secured in the kayak, I try to remember the instructions for righting it in the water. Damn, it requires the paddle, which is not in my hands. I can do this.

Suddenly, strong hands grab my upper arms, and I'm flipped upright. I gulp in a big breath of air and look around, getting my bearings. I'm still sitting in my kayak, almost like nothing happened. Unfortunately, the sopping wet clothes and lack of a phone remind me it's all too real.

An abandoned jet ski floats a few feet away. I look down into the water next to my hip and find a dark-haired stranger smiling up at me. The air leaves my lungs again, this time in a loud sigh. He's hot. Like dark-haired, hazel-eyed, chiseled jaw under a few days scruff, could be a cover of a romance book, hot.

"You okay?" His face is full of concern. His eyes scan my face, looking for a sign of injury.

His strong Southern accent is smooth and deep. Of course it is. He reaches for my paddle before it drifts away. He hands it to me, and I take it, still processing what is happening.

A wet curl falls across his forehead, and water drips from his long eyelashes. Why do guys have the best eyelashes? They frame his captivating green eyes. The red of the kayak appears like dancing flames in his pupils. He continues to scan my face, searching for something.

His muscular shoulders move with the slow movement of his arms as he treads water beside me. I am completely captivated. Then, as my brain catches up, my temper kicks in.

"I was just fine until someone tipped me with their wake!" My hair is stuck to my face. I pull the ponytail and wring it out, pulling a piece of reed out and tossing it his way.

"Sorry about that," he says sheepishly. "I was rushing to get back for dinner and didn't see you. I'm really sorry." He gives me a lopsided grin, turning on the charm. "But I came back to rescue you," he says with a wink. Did he really just wink at me? If I weren't so angry, I might actually swoon.

Flipper decides it's playtime and pops up between us, spraying me with water from his air hole. Ugh. Dolphin phlegm. The guy in the water laughs as he floats back toward his jet ski, lightly kicking his legs below the water.

My frustration and anxiety about Alexander, and the confusion I'm feeling toward this guy, morph into a fit of displaced anger. "Well, thanks to you, Flipper here gets to enjoy my sunset picture and my phone! UGH!" It hits me that I'll start my first internship day without a phone, and my frustration escalates. I slap the water with my paddle. "And I don't need to be rescued. I'm quite capable of taking care of myself. I'm no damsel in distress!"

Do all guys think they have to be my knight in shining armor? I came here to get away from my brothers for this very reason. Is that part of male DNA?

I watch his arms and abs flex as he pulls himself up on the jet ski. I can't deny he has a muscular, toned body. Water flies off his curls as he shakes his head like a dog after a swim. That's right. Think of him like a dog. A mangey, flea-ridden dog that isn't cute at all. But then my eyes focus on drops of water slowly making their way down his washboard abs. Dammit. I am mad. He is a jerk. Look away, Ash, look away.

He smiles, and a dimple pops on his left cheek. A damn dimple. My kryptonite. My stomach tightens, and a smile tries to break free. Be strong, Ash. Remember, even hot guys can be assholes. And here's another one. What a shame, really. It would be great if I had a summer fling too. I hadn't even thought about that possibility until now. Maybe a fling would be good for me? But not with him. I'm still angry. And wet. My clothes, that is. And my phone is somewhere at the bottom of the intercostal waterway.

With that reminder, I come to my senses. What an arrogant,

good-looking, ignorant, fit, irritating, gorgeous ass! And that ass? Yeah, I notice that too.

"Is that your way of saying you don't want to give me your number?" he asks, giving me a playful splash.

"Seriously?" His persistence and charm baffle me. I just pulled seaweed from my hair. I'm sure I'm a hot mess, and, wait, did his smile get broader? His lips part a bit, and I wonder what they would feel like against my skin. Focus, Ash, focus!

"Look, sweetheart, a polite thanks for the assist would suffice," he says as he starts the jet ski. The idle of the engine disrupts the peacefulness of the marsh. I'm supposed to thank him for the predicament he put me in?

"I wouldn't have been in the water if not for you. I don't need a rescue." I have to yell louder to ensure he hears me over the jet ski engine. Apparently, he hears just fine because his chest shakes as he laughs at me. I feel my cheeks flush, and the heat rises throughout my body. I'm not surprised if steam rolls off me at this point. I tell myself it's because I'm mad. That's it, right? Anger is making me react this way. I mean, I've been mad before, but this feels different. I don't think I've ever reacted to someone like this before. It's confusing.

"Well, I'll make sure my armor is polished, just in case, damsel," he replies as if my anger amuses him. His eyes lock with mine, and after several seconds, I look away, the intensity of his glare unsettling. I bite my bottom lip, debating if I should engage with him any longer. I need to get away, but part of me wants to stay and continue our banter.

It's unfortunate for him, but my frustration with Alexander is channeled toward this guy. Well, directed mostly at him. I'm also getting mad at myself as every second ticks away. Quit being that girl! You are strong and independent. Who doesn't need rescuing, remember?

"Do you need a tow home?" he offers, evidently trying to make amends.

"Nope," I say in a huff. I turn my shoulders straight ahead and begin to paddle away. Unfortunately, my dock is less than fifty feet away, and my exit isn't going to be as dramatic as I hoped. I slide the kayak beside the dock and hold it for a minute. Getting out of the kayak isn't exactly graceful on a good day. I'll just pretend he isn't here. I pull myself out and tie up the boat as quickly as possible. I stomp away toward the house, feeling a little like a toddler having a temper tantrum. I know my wet tank top is clingy, and my tight bike shorts give him more of a show than he deserves.

I pause at the top of the dock and turn back toward the water. I just can't resist. Is he still watching me?

Yep. There he is, in all his hotness glory, sitting on the jet ski, a stupid grin on his face, watching me walk away. Damn, he caught me. I turn quickly and march back to the house, successfully resisting the urge to turn around again to see if he is still watching. I don't hear the jet ski engine gun until I reach the back door. Yeah, he was still watching. I can't help the slight sense of satisfaction in that fact.

———

"Ashleigh, what happened? Are you all right?" Mrs. Jones asks as she takes in the wet clothes and the pissed-off glare on my face.

"I'm fine," I growl. "Some asshole on a jet ski made me capsize. And I lost my phone."

"Well, I'm sorry, but I'm glad you're okay," she says with a little chuckle. I'm sure I look like a drowned rat. My hair is no longer in a cute messy bun but is more like a wet mop stuck to my forehead. The other half is in a ponytail, still in the hair tie.

"I'll tell you what," she starts, "I just upgraded my phone and still have my old one. Let's see if we can't set it up for you. You can have it until you get a new one. I think a quick call to the carrier and they can transfer everything over. It won't be shiny and new, but at least it's a working phone." Mrs. Jones is exactly what a mom should be. She's kind, thoughtful, caring, and knows exactly the right thing to say, exactly when you need to hear it.

She looks at me with a slight smile and continues with the most mom-like line of questioning. "So, was he cute?"

"Um, yeah," I say before catching myself. "But a total asshole. So no, not cute. His rating went from a ten to a two when you take away his personality points," I counter. That's how it works, right? He goes from hot to not, just like that.

"A ten, huh? Wow. Sorry I missed him then," she says as she grabs a towel and throws it my way. It's a subtle hint that I'm dripping on the kitchen floor.

"Why don't you go take a shower, and I'll see what I can do about your phone. And let's get that smile back. I can't have you grumpy for your first day tomorrow."

"I'll be fine as long as I don't run into him again," I grumble. I stomp up the stairs to take a shower and wash that boy right out of my hair.

CHAPTER
FOUR

COLE

————

The first day back with the Pajamas is always one of my favorite days. Everyone reports to the stadium, the veterans reconnect, the rookies get razzed, the coaching staff has one-on-ones, and the administrative staff gets to know the team. We become a summer family on day one.

I'm so excited to be back that I'm at the stadium an hour early. Coach Grant gives me a firm handshake and a few good back slaps. "Glad to see you, Cole. You had a great season. You're going to be on the scouts' lists this year," he says.

"I sure hope so. This is the year to find out if my dream comes true or if I scramble for a plan B."

"Well, you've got the talent and work ethic, that's for sure. You gotta stay healthy and focused. You know we appreciate your leadership and love of the game. I can't wait to tell people I knew him when he was a Pajama." He chuckles. I know Coach Grant is sincere. He has pictures of former Pajamas that were drafted lining his office wall. His wall of fame.

"Being a Pajama is one of my favorite baseball memories thus far. I'm looking forward to this summer. It will be epic."

"That it will. We have a great group of guys this season. Where's Matt? You two not fighting over something stupid like a girl or anything, are you?"

"Nah, you know us better than that. Girls mess with your game too much. He couldn't pass up the waves this morning. He was showing the new guys a thing or two. They'll be here on time, without a minute to spare."

Coach laughs. "That boy sure does love the water. If I didn't know his dad, I'd think his father was King Neptune."

Matt's dad was our high school coach and well-respected in the region. He'll come to watch us a few times this summer, and he and Coach Grant will probably throw back a few after the game, talking old-school baseball days.

"Yeah, don't go questioning his parentage, or his mom will have your hide. And don't tell Matt you think he's royalty. He's hard enough to deal with." Honestly, Matt is the most laid-back, most straightforward guy you'll ever meet, but I still like to bust his balls. That's what best friends do.

"Hey, do you mind going to the admin offices and grabbing a copy of the agenda for the day? I want to post it in the locker room this morning. We may have fun, but we need to stay on task, right?"

"Absolutely. I'll be back in a flash."

I walk down the administrative hallway, enjoying being in this historic stadium. I can't help but smile, and I begin thinking up new celebration dances for the summer.

I'm startled when I hear raised voices drifting down the hall. Yelling isn't typical in PajamaLand. Everyone is generally happy being here.

"Come on, honey. You know you can't say no to this. I promise you will love it," the male voice says, practically pleading.

"I can say no and have said no, multiple times. Now please. Just stop," she says, her voice firm but shaky.

"I'd hate for your future to be impacted by this choice," he says, a bit of harshness in his tone.

"Yeah, me too," she says, sounding almost tearful.

As I round the corner, I can see them in the glass conference room, the door ajar. What the fuck? What is this guy trying to pull with her?

The guy appears to be in his early thirties, and even in his expensive-looking tailored suit, I can tell he has a toned, muscular body. Definitely a gym rat. He's standing too close to her for my liking, crowding her, using his body in a threatening manner.

Even though I only see her from the back, she's tiny compared to him, and her shoulders are drawn in, making her smaller than she is. The power dynamic is evident, and it fires me up. I go from happy-go-lucky to I'm-going-to-fucking-kill-him in less than two seconds. I'm so angry I'm shaking.

Mom was sexually harassed by her boss once, and I hated watching what it did to her. She blamed herself and tried to devise ways to make it better when he was in the wrong. Men should not have that power over women, especially in the work-place. Women are to be valued, cherished, and protected - not dominated. They don't have to change their dress so that guys will behave. No way. This guy is a total D-bag, and I want to ensure he knows it.

I can't see the girl's face from my angle, but based on her long, loose braids, khaki shorts, and polo shirt, I assume she's one of the college interns. When the guy reaches out his large hand and grips her upper arm as she tries to leave, I have seen and heard enough.

I charge into the room and shove the guy away from her.

"Get your hands off her," I shout. "Didn't you ever hear, no means no, asshole? And she said no. So leave her the fuck alone and find someone your own age to harass!"

I put my body between them, still not looking at her but staring the guy down. My hands are in tight fists, tapping against my thighs. My adrenaline is pumping now. If he wants a go at me, I'm ready.

The man's face shifts from shock to deadly. You know that saying, 'If looks could kill?' I think they were talking about him. But I've got one of those looks, too, and I'm giving it right back.

"Excuse me? Who the fuck do you think you are?" the man says, closing the space between us. We are chest to chest, eye to eye. I can smell the expensive aftershave, and if I weren't about to throw down, I'd ask him what he's wearing. It smells nice. But he's an asshole who is inappropriate with women, so I won't.

I'm a six-one, strong as fuck baseball player who has a big mouth. My mouth gets me in trouble on the regular. Man, can I chirp at a batter and rattle the best of them. I also tend to stand my ground and push my luck. Backing down isn't in my play-book. So learning how to throw a punch is also part of my base-ball arsenal. It's an essential survival skill, right up there with knowing whether to use ice or heat on an injury. I wasn't plan-ning on pulling it out today, but a guy's gotta do what a guy's gotta do.

Even though this man has about twenty pounds of muscle on me, I'm not backing down. We are the same height, so as our stare down continues, I notice the man's dark blue-green eyes darken and narrow, attempting to make his look more menacing. He's trying to intimidate me, but it won't work. I just smile at the motherfucker, never breaking eye contact.

I feel a soft hand touch my shoulder from behind, and the man's eyes glance at the movement. A look of concern passes across his face, but he quickly redirects his glare back to me. That's right, asshole, you are dealing with me now, not her.

I feel the delicate fingers pinch my brachial plexus, causing a slight pain in my shoulder. What is she doing? I snap my head toward the girl. "Are you attempting the Vulcan Nerve Pinch on me?" What the hell is going on?

Did the guy just snort? I glance back at him briefly, his stone face watching me. I focus my attention on her. And I really look at her. Damn. It's the kayak girl. The girl who starred in my dreams last night. The girl I thought about in the shower this morning when I took care of myself. She has one hundred percent of my attention now.

I take in her tall, athletic body. This boring intern uniform isn't as revealing as those wet clothes yesterday. Up close, I can smell the intoxicating light scent of citrus from her shampoo and see the shades of blonde in her braided hair. Those loose braids hang over each shoulder. When I follow those braids down her shoulders, they stop right above her perky breasts, like arrows, pointing them out in case I hadn't noticed them. But I have noticed them.

I can't be objectifying someone I'm defending from sexual harassment, so I snap my eyes up to her adorable face. Her sapphire eyes sparkle, even under the fluorescent office lighting. She has that same determined look she had yesterday, like she's trying to be mean and tough, but it's not really her nature, so she's trying extra hard to be menacing. It doesn't work because it comes off cute.

A small smile creeps from my lips, but I reel it in. Now is not the time for this.

"I'm going to repeat the question, who do you think you are?" she says, accentuating each word. I hadn't been close enough yesterday to notice the gold specks in her blue eyes, but now, as they narrow at me, they hold me captive. Her eyes are the most intoxicating shade of dark blue, and her blue eyes are my new favorite color.

What? I'm confused. Is she mad at me? For stepping in to help her out? Again? This guy is clearly threatening her. Does she want to be sexually harassed? Why is she yelling at me? Is she 'with' this douchebag? Is she still mad about yesterday?

I blink a few times, hoping that will clear the confusion from my brain. Our eyes stay locked on one another. She attempts to give me one of those 'if looks could kill' glares too, and the similarity to Mr. Asshole over here is another checkmark in the confusion column. Honestly, her's is a little more terrifying because she looks like, 'I'm thinking of how to dispose of your body, and no one will ever find it.' Women scare the shit out of me. They are not to be underestimated.

Our stare-down continues, and her cheeks flush as her breathing becomes shallow. She squeezes my shoulder tighter, like she knows my mind has drifted to impure thoughts.

Maybe she's still scared from her encounter with this asshole. I try to soothe her, like I would approach a wounded animal. Hands up, I say, "Can you stop pinching me, please? You might hurt yourself."

She squeezes harder. So I guess that was the wrong thing to say. I reach up gently to remove her hand and get a tingle, practically an electric shock, shooting down my arm. I don't think it is from her pinch. It's strange. In a good way. In a weird way. Like my entire body is filled with bees, I'm buzzing.

Her cheeks go from light pink to a darker red, and her eyes narrow. She is trying to make herself look threatening. She's too damn cute to give a mean look, so it's just contrary.

She releases my shoulder and stomps her foot, anger visibly coursing through her body. Did she really just stomp her foot? It's kind of adorable, like when she stormed off yesterday. Her angry girl vibe is turning me on. I can't help but grin at her.

"I told you I'm not a damsel in distress! I don't need a knight in shining armor to rescue me. And you." She focuses her attention on the other guy. "Just stop. Don't bring it up again." She looks like she's about to cry. "Please," she says quietly, almost pleading.

She turns quickly and runs out of the room. Her sudden spin causes one of her braids to hit me across the arm. It's soft, and I get a quick hit of that citrus-smelling shampoo again, my new favorite scent. I don't know what it is, but it's sweet. And has a bite to it, just like her.

I consider going after her, but I hear the asshole clearing his throat. I turn around to deal with him. He's scowling at me. What's up with all these looks today?

"I suggest you choose your next words carefully, kid. And they should start with *I apologize*." The man crosses his arms across his broad chest and leans into my personal space. I don't know who this guy is, but I really don't like him. Even if he does smell good.

My mouth, which often works faster than my brain, decides this guy needs to be put in his place. "I apologize for your inadequacies, motherfucker. You must have a tiny dick if you can only get a woman's attention by touching her without her permission and threatening her job." That is the only apology he is getting from me.

The guy cocks one eyebrow at me and shoves me away. I step back and open my stance, glaring back at him. I'm not backing down.

"You have exactly three seconds to get out of my face, or I'll be rearranging yours," the guy replies, any ounce of amusement gone from his tone. I guess the dick comment hit a little close to home. Ouch.

I stand there and do the only thing that makes sense. I shrug and start the countdown. "One Mississippi, two Mississippi...."

In a flash, the guy swings, making good contact with my jaw. Son-of-a-bitch, that smarts. It knocks me back a few steps, and by the time I am ready to return the swing, the guy casually strolls out of the room. "Hope that doesn't leave a mark," he says as he reaches the door of the conference room and goes into a nearby office, slamming the door.

I work my jaw back and forth, running my tongue over my teeth to ensure nothing is loose or broken. It's going to hurt tomorrow. I won't be chewing gum on that side for a few days. Worth it? Probably.

With the immediate situation resolved for now, I leave the conference room and try to check on the girl, but I have no idea

where she ran off to. Looking in all the girl's bathrooms is definitely not the right move, so I head back toward the locker room,
finding an icepack in the training room on the way.

I hope I see that bastard again. He won't sucker punch next
time.

I walk back into the locker room and find most of the team
introducing themselves and finding their lockers. Matt is introducing Brady and Drew to a few of the guys from last year. He
looks at me, notices the ice pack, and says, "What the hell
happened to you?"

"He didn't wait until three Mississippi." I shrug.

Matt shakes his head and laughs. "They never do, bro. You
think you'd know that by now."

Well, I've had an eventful first day, and it isn't even
lunchtime yet.

CHAPTER
FIVE

ASHLEIGH

"Em, you don't understand!" I whisper shout into my phone. "It's my first day, and it was just, just, UGH!" I'm so exasperated. I tried to explain what just happened to me, but she sighed. Frickin' sighs into the phone. From another country.

"He sounds nice," she says.

"Are you not listening to me? I don't know which arrogant asshole I'm more mad at."

Emma is quiet. I can tell she thinks I'm being dramatic. But I'm not. I'm really not. Really.

I can't stand the silence, so I continue. "I mean, why is he here? And who in the hell is this guy getting in my way whenever I turn around? It's like he's my personal demon, just stirring up trouble for me," I say. Her silence is like a wet blanket to my fire.

"Maybe he is," she says.

"He is what?" I'm almost at the point of frustrated tears.

"Trouble for you. But maybe the good kind of trouble."

What the hell is she talking about? Good kind of trouble? Who needs that? I have goals for this summer. And they don't include the good kind of trouble. I can't deny this feeling, something I've never felt before around anyone else. My stomach gets butterflies when I think about him. It must be nerves.

"I'm sorry, Em. I'm just so nervous. And I miss you. How are things at the orphanage?" Emma is definitely the better human of our duo.

"It's great. We have a new brother and sister here today, so I'm helping them settle in. They are so sweet. Edgar is only eight, and he's so protective of Anna. Overprotective big brothers aren't just a you thing, I guess. Anyway, Anna is four and has the cutest giggle, so I keep making her laugh so that I can hear it. I might have to bring them home with me."

"Well, your mom would love them, and she'd take over, so maybe you shouldn't get too attached."

"I know making her a grandma is high on her wish list. Just need to find that boyfriend first."

"Your mom is the best, Em. I'm so glad I get the spend the summer with her." She's like a surrogate mom to me, and I'm so grateful for her. "The only thing that would make it better is if you were here."

"The only thing?" she asks.

"Well, not the only thing. I need Trevor to keep his promise and this boy to stop being so damn cute."

"Well, good luck with that, Ash. Keep me posted. I've gotta run. I have a little girl I need to make laugh."

"Bye, Em. Love you."

"Love you too. And you know what? Why don't you give trouble a chance?" I sputter to respond, and she hangs up. Give trouble a chance?

I make myself take several deep breaths, square my shoulders, and resolve to take on this summer as Leigh Rutledge. And you know what? Leigh is a badass, independent woman. She's got this. Trouble? Fine. Bring it on.

———

"Damn," I mutter, realizing I only have five minutes to be at my first official Pajamas meeting. Don't panic. And don't be late. Blend in. The Pajamas are big on team and not just for the players. In Trevor's words, everyone is the talent. Everyone is vital when it comes to the show.

I have enough time to text Trevor quickly, reminding him of our agreement, and head outside. People are taking seats in the grandstands behind home plate, everyone mixing and mingling. The excitement in the air is palpable. I can already identify some players and see they are mixed throughout the group. Interesting. They really do blend everyone together.

I take a seat in the back of the section and slide in. I pull out my camera and start snapping pictures for future posts. Everyone is animated and fresh. This job is going to be so much fun!

Trevor gets in front of the group and shoots a confetti cannon to get our attention. "Welcome to the Pajamas!" Trevor shouts. Everyone claps and cheers. "We are going to jump right in because that's what we do here. We work hard and play harder."

Someone up front yells, "Hell yeah!"

"So, the first order of business," Trevor says. "Let's get to know each other. Everyone on the field, now." We all go on the field, and he gives us our instructions. "Everyone take ten Post-it notes and a sharpie. Mix and mingle. Meet everyone. Here's the catch, you can't talk to anyone for longer than ten seconds, so keep it moving. When you think you have a sense of who they are, write one word on a Post-it as a first impression and stick it to their back. Try not to duplicate words. When you are out of Post-its, sit back down."

The game begins, and I'm greeting people and assess everyone quickly. It's moving really fast. And it's fun. I'm making quick, witty judgments, and I like everyone I talk to, even if it's only for ten seconds. I have one Post-it left and turn to find someone I haven't talked to yet. As I turn, I feel someone place a sticker on my back. I turn to see who it is and turn right into Mr. Knight in Shining Armor himself. Did he put a sticker on my back without talking to me for ten seconds? I look up into his mossy green eyes and immediately notice his cheek is swollen. Shit. I've seen that damage before. He goes to say something to me, but I'm faster. I look down, write one word on my last Post-it, reach around, and slap it on his back, and without saying a word, I head back to the bleachers to sit down. I can't help but smile to myself as I walk away. Two can play that game.

Now it's time for the introduction and reveals. Trevor calls each person up to the front, where they give the standard information: Name, hometown, school, and role on the team. Then it's Trevor's turn to share and reveal the first impression stickers. He reads all the stickers on their backs. Some are funny. I suspect many are spot on. Almost everyone walks away with a nickname.

It's Mr. Knight's turn. The gorgeous, asshole, knight, pain-in-the-ass stands up next to Trevor. He has a casual smile and connects to several people in the grandstands as his eyes sweep the section. He spots me, and once he finds me, he makes me his target and has me on missile lock. I'm waiting for the beeping to start any second. I shrink down a little in my seat and try to hide behind the guy in front of me.

You can tell he's confident. His megawatt smile enhances the sunny morning. And he's definitely a player. Baseball, for sure. The other kind? Probably.

"Hey! I'm Cole Davidson, a senior at NC State from Charleston, South Carolina. I play first base, and this is my third year with the Pajamas. Brace yourself for the best summer ever." And then, he winks….at me? "Okay, Trevor, let me know what they really think of me," he says with a grin. He's definitely relaxed. Maybe it's because he's been here before. He seems comfortable, and Trevor seems to like him too.

Trevor looks at his back and laughs, slapping his hand on

Cole's shoulder. "Yeah, dude, they pretty much have you pegged. Let's see. Kind. Meh. Leader. Friend. Outgoing. Yeah, yeah, yeah." Trevor looks at the group. "Why are you guys sucking up to Cole here? What kind of blackmail does he have on you?" Everyone laughs, and at the mention of blackmail, Trevor looks at me. "Let's see. Someone thought Cole is cocky. Musician. Athletic. Player. Bruised? Well, if that one isn't descriptive?" Trevor gives another laugh, this one sounding a little nervous. "Want to share with the class?" he asks.

"Nah, does one of those stickers say clumsy?" Cole banters back.

"No. No, they don't, Cole." Trevor shakes his head and follows Cole's line of sight straight to me. Trevor takes a deep breath, and stage whispers to Cole, "The last one says trouble."

Cole slowly nods and walks back to his seat, getting high fives and fist bumps as he passes teammates. "Yep, you have no idea how true that is," he says.

I'm so screwed.

CHAPTER
SIX

COLE

————

So she thinks I'm trouble, huh? That had to be her word. None of the others seemed like something she'd say. I wonder what she means by trouble? Like I'm in trouble? Am I not worth the trouble? Will I get her in trouble? I can't explain it, but I like it. I'm okay, as long as I'm her trouble.

Come on, Trevor, get to her row. My leg is bouncing with excess energy. I need information. I need it like a junkie needs a fix. What's her name? What's her story? What is it about her that consumes my every waking and sleeping thought? I've never had a girl get under my skin like this, and it's only been twenty-four hours.

I mean, sure, girls are around all the time. I go to parties. We hang out and fool around some. But it's a symbiotic relationship. She gets a little, and I get a little. But I've never made girls much of an investment. I have to focus on baseball. Girls require time, and that's a luxury I don't have. Especially at school. And I don't like being a trophy boyfriend, someone who can fill up a girl's Instagram feed so she can say she's dating a ballplayer. That's not my scene. So I keep it casual. Laid back. I don't lead them on. They know I don't date. It's just not worth the hassle and distraction. I wonder if that's because I've never met someone worthy of the investment. But this girl?

Finally! Trevor pulls her up next and stands slightly too close, stepping into her personal space. What is it about these guys getting so close to her?

I like Trevor. He's friendly, and I've never seen him be inappropriate with anyone, especially an intern, but he gives her a little wink, and she takes a small step away and smiles at the group. "So tell us about yourself, *Leigh*." It sounds like Trevor said her name with a weird inflection. Maybe I'm just hearing things. So Leigh. Her name is Leigh. That's a start.

She looks around the group and gives a big smile, a little wave, and her face lights up. That's a look I haven't had the pleasure of seeing yet. I can't wait until one of those smiles is directed at me. What will it take for her to smile for me?

She looks around the group, and if I didn't know better, it feels like she's making eye contact with everyone but me.

Matt elbows me in the side.

"What?" I ask, a little sharper than I should.

"Is she the reason for the ice pack?" he asks, cocking his head toward Leigh. "And the stupid grin on your face?"

"Shhhh. I need to learn everyone's name." Matt smacks my leg to get me to stop bouncing.

"Hi, Pajamas! My name is Leigh Rutledge. I'm a senior at Meredith College, and I'm from Charlotte, North Carolina. I'm going to be focusing on the Pajamas' social media accounts. So get ready to be filmed and asked to do some fun and crazy things. I'm going to make ya'll TikTok stars."

Meredith? She goes to school in Raleigh, just like me. I wonder why she picked an all-girls school. My curiosity is peaked.

"That's what I'm talking about," Trevor says. "Leigh is going to share you all with the world. So get ready! You've been warned."

She smiles at Trevor. "So what do they think of me now? I'm sure if we do this exercise at the end of the summer, they'll have new words for me." Everyone laughs with her.

Trevor peeks at her back and starts reading off the tags. "Well, Leigh, you sure did make some interesting first impressions. Here we go. Ready?" She nods her head and bites her bottom lip, appearing nervous.

"I'm ready, I think," she says, wincing.

"Beautiful. Stunning. Sparkles. Really guys? Sparkles?" Trevor gives a slow shake of his head and continues. "Gorgeous. Adorable. So apparently, you only talked to the players?" Trevor asks.

She shrugs and blushes. "No, I didn't think so." She is embarrassed and tugs on her braids, looking down at her shoes. "Are you done?" She takes a step away, back toward her seat. He grabs her by the hand and pulls her back. Again, a little too intimate for my liking. What about this girl makes everyone want to get handsy with her and makes me go all caveman?

Trevor chuckles and continues. "Not quite. There are a few more. Let's see, fun. Passionate. Cute. Darling. Well, and um...." Trevor casually puts his hand on her back and takes a Post-it off.

"What?" she whispers.

"The last one says, um, smart. And that you are. Welcome to the team, Leigh. I'm ready for you to make this team famous. Let's have fun."

She smiles at him and says, "Let's do this!" He gives her a high-five and transfers the sticker to her hand during the slap. It was a subtle move, but I caught it. She starts to walk away from Trevor and looks down at the paper. She stops in her tracks and slowly looks up, her eyes narrow, which is becoming a familiar look for her, and she zeroes in on me. Everyone turns to follow her glare. She looks irritated. That warm, happy smile is gone.

I grin because I know what the sticker says.
It says *MINE*.

CHAPTER
SEVEN

COLE

———

We take a break for lunch after the meet and greet. I grab my burger and take off to sit by myself to do a little recon. This should be easy. If social media is her thing, I'll just cyber-stalk her a little, find some inside scoop, and our next encounter will be golden.

I start with Instagram. Leigh Rutledge. There are a few accounts, and after clicking, I find hers. It's set to private, so I request to follow her. Same for Twitter and Facebook. Well, unless she accepts my friend requests, this was a strike-out. I don't use my social media much, primarily to share baseball stats, reposts, and that sort of thing. Curious why someone into social media would be private?

I scan the picnic area and see her chatting it up with a few other interns and Brady, my new housemate. I watch as Drew and Matt join their table too. Matt sits next to her and reaches over to shake her hand. What the hell is he doing? She must say something funny because Matt throws his head back and laughs. Quite obnoxiously, I might add. Really, Matt?

Trevor and Coach Grant come and sit at my empty table.

"Cole, Cole, Cole," Trevor says, shaking his head at me. "So many questions, I don't know where to start." He's doing one of those silent laughs. What's so funny?

I choose to ignore him. "Hey, Coach, I'm excited to get some wins this season. What are the chances of taking the conference this year?" Baseball. Stick to baseball. Always a safe place.

Coach Grant has a mouth full of burger, so he chews before answering. Thank goodness for that. But instead of waiting for his response, Trevor jumps in.

"Yeah, we'll have a great team this summer. That kid Brady is quite the hotshot. And a ladies man too. Looks like he wants to add becoming a TikTok star to his resume."

I don't know what the hell Trevor is trying to do, but he's yanking my chain. And it's working. I've enjoyed getting to know him the past few summers. He's quite an interesting guy. He has built a business focusing on the fans, kind of a modern-day P.T. Barnum. Even though he focuses on baseball, he also consults with several Fortune 500 companies to help create their corporate culture. I think he's even written a book or two. He's a great guy and someone I admire for their business sense and love of baseball. However, my opinion of Trevor is declining by the minute.

"Want to talk about your face?" Trevor continues. "You can't be the face of the Pajamas if you keep walking into doors. What's that all about?"

This seems to be a topic Coach Grant is interested in too. Of course he is. While he's all about performance and feeding the fan frenzy, he's also about getting us to the next level. He knows fighting and personal issues can kill a player more than a batting slump.

Coach Grant nods at me and says, "So let's talk about what's going on. You didn't have that this morning when you came in.

Something going on with another one of the guys I need to be aware of?"

Man, my face is a little tender, but it must be swollen or purple or something to get their attention. I need a mirror to assess the damage. I use my phone in selfie mode to get a look. Ugh. He got me good. Damn. No easy way to downplay this one.

"It's nothing. None of the players. They are all cool. I think this could be our best team yet. You did a great job pulling us together." Yeah, that's it. Suck up. Change the subject. Move on.

I hear Matt's obnoxious laugh again and swing my head in that direction. They are having quite the lunch party there.

"Something going on with Matt?" Coach Grant continues, following my line of sight. He's not letting this go. The question about Matt catches me off guard.

"What? No, no. We're great. All good."

Coach Grant lifts his eyebrow at me. Trevor slowly shakes his head and takes another bite of his burger. He's watching this like some damn telenovela. That guy sure does thrive on entertainment and drama.

I need to clarify and get Matt out of my shitshow. I need to rescue him, even though he doesn't know he needs it. Because that's what I do. I'm a chronic rescuer, apparently. Even when the damsel doesn't want to be rescued, her words rattle in my head.

"I came over here to send an email. That's why I'm not over there. We are still amigos, bros, compadres. But I'm glad to see him branching out and making friends. He can't depend on me forever." I swallow hard. I'll need him forever. He keeps me balanced and my mouth out of trouble most of the time. He's the best friend a guy could ask for, and I'd do anything for him, no questions asked. I'm the one who tends to be the more outgoing one of the two, so I'm usually the one to break the ice and take the lead. But Matt isn't shy and can hold his own. I wonder if I keep him from taking the lead. And when, if we get drafted, there's a good chance we won't be going together. That's not something I'm looking forward to at all. I sigh.

"What's the sigh about?" Trevor asks, pulling my attention back to him.

"Just thinking about us getting the call. Pretty sure that will be when we go our separate ways. The chances of us going to the same team are almost zero." And that's the truth. It will be a bittersweet day. One we are both looking forward to, but I know I'm secretly dreading it. Matt is my best friend and my other half. He knows me better than I know myself. We'll still be friends, but we'll lose the proximity. And worse yet, we'll be competitors.

Coach Grant pipes in. "Speaking of the call. There will be a good number of scouts here this summer. I know they have their eyes on you. I've even talked to one today about you. So, keep your bat hot and your glove solid, and it won't be a question if you get the call. It will be a matter of which single-digit round it will be."

Seriously. I knew this. Well, I hoped for this, but Coach Grant has confirmed it. Stay baseball focused, and your dreams will come true. What team was he talking to about me?

"Really, Coach. That's great to hear. I promise to give you one hundred percent. But why was a scout here already? We don't have our first game for a week?"

"He's my best friend, and we don't get much time together like we used to. So he'll be here hanging with me for the next few weeks, scoping out practices, observing, that sort of thing," Trevor says.

At that moment, I see someone walk up next to Trevor, and as I look up to see who it is, I see the guy responsible for my face this morning.

"Hi, Cole," he says, extending his hand to me. "I'm Alexander Decker, General Manager with the Carolina Reapers."

Oh, fuck me.

CHAPTER
EIGHT

ASHLEIGH

―――

FML.

Today was supposed to be the first day of the rest of my life or some bullshit platitude like that. Seriously, it was supposed to be fun and freeing. But instead, it starts with Xander showing up at my freaking internship on day one, I might add. Then Mr. Knight, because that's what he's going to be called in my head, shows up. Obviously, Xander's fist met Cole's face after I left. I have no idea what was said or how that ended up being the result.

Then Mr. Knight turns my insides out with his label. What the hell did he mean by MINE? Clearly, Trevor didn't like it. I'll give him props. He covered it well. But Mr. Knight has no idea the kind of shitshow he's just walked into. My own three-ring, try to keep all the plates spinning, walk on a tightrope, get shot out of a cannon, shitshow. And I'm the star of all three rings. Not a ticket worth having, that's for sure.

So pile on with the Xander thing, then add in Trevor, who

may be playing along with me this summer, but he's also a protective brute like my brothers. He won't like someone sniffing around me, especially not a player.

I need everyone to LEAVE. ME. ALONE.

I feel a little sorry for Mr. Knight. Really, I do. Maybe just a smidge. He's still a stick-his-nose-where-it-doesn't-belong-ass who may be sexy hot, but still. He must be a decent guy because, if I'm honest, he was trying to defend me from a situation that probably looked pretty bad out of context.

But I'm sure he's like every guy here, with his hopes pinned on getting drafted. And if Xander blackballs him, his dream will be crushed. I can't let that happen to him. I won't let that happen to anyone. At least, not because of me.

I'll have to deal with Xander. And Trevor.

So, *MINE*? I don't think so. That will be a guaranteed way to get him a good ol' nine-to-five desk job for twenty to life. That's no sentence a draft-bound college player wants to serve.

I shoot a text to Xander.

> Why did you punch him?

X

He deserved it.

> Why? He was actually doing a pretty stand-up thing defending me. Even if I didn't want his help.

X

Yup

I'm not even sure what that means, but I don't really care. I need him gone. And to back off.

> You promised to let me have this summer.

X

I did. And you will. You know I keep my word, Leigh.

Ugh. I don't like that.

I sigh.

> Just give him a chance. Please.

X

Yup.

Well, that might be the best I will get from him for now. I try another angle and text Trevor.

> Please make X behave.

TREV

Not sure that's possible, Ash. 🏔️ 🐦 But you probably should avoid trouble if you catch my drift. 💀 🔒

> Message received, I think. Just don't let X ruin any futures this summer, please. That includes mine.

TREV

I swear. Trevor is the most emoji-using guy I've ever texted. If I only understood half of them.

Well, that's the best I can do for now. I'll have to hope they can both stay somewhat professional regarding Cole.

I sit with two other girls at a table, and a few players join us. Conversations flow naturally, and everyone is throwing out ideas for videos. I'm loving it. The focus is on the team, the media, and the fun. This is what I wanted my day to be. I relax my shoulders and lean into the conversation.

Drew, a pitcher, is willing to shave his head for a Major

League parody. That's commitment, ladies and gentlemen. But I won't let it go that far. I tell them I see skirts and a little "there's no crying in baseball" video in their future. They are very open to skirts. Wow. They are a different breed of baseball players, that's for sure.

The player sitting next to me is Matt Hartman, and he's adorable. And downright charming. Oozing with charm, actually. The fact that he also goes to NC State with Cole "Mr. Knight" Davidson doesn't go unnoticed by me.

Matt appears to be Cole's opposite. Where Cole has this casual, I just rolled out of bed, needed a haircut three weeks ago, sexy curly locks, Matt has a more conservative, clean-cut look about him. His dark brows frame his chocolate eyes, and his kind, caring personality seeps from every pore. He's a great listener and an obvious hype man, encouraging everyone.

I can tell Matt and I will be fast friends. He's the kind of guy I'd love to hang out with. I tend to get along with guys since that's most of my social circle, with Emma being the exception. There's no spark with Matt, and he's not throwing any. Maybe that's why I like him. He's not looking at me like a date. He's moved to the top of my summer friends list.

"Yeah, the four of us are staying on Tybee with the Macs," Matt says.

"The four of you?" I ask.

"Yeah, me, Brady, Drew, and Cole. What about you? Where's your host house?" Matt fires back.

"I'm on Tybee too. I'm staying with my roommate's family."

"That's awesome," Brady interjects. "Is she here this summer too?" He wiggles his eyebrows in an attempt to be suggestive.

"No, she's much more altruistic than me. She's in Honduras volunteering at an orphanage."

"Wow. She sounds great. Sorry I'm missing her," Drew says. I look at Drew closely and think Em would like him too.

"We're having a beach party tonight before we get too hard into the season. You have to join us," Brady says, directing the invitation to me. "All of you," he says to Jane and Mandy, the other two interns at our table.

"That would be great," Mandy says. "We are in Midtown Savannah, but the drive to Tybee isn't that bad. We're in!"

My gaze sweeps over to Cole sitting with Coach Grant and Trevor. Cole seems uncomfortable with their conversation. His eyes keep looking around, and he appears nervous.

"So what about you, Leigh? Are you in?" Drew asks. It takes a nudge from Matt to realize they are talking to me. I'm not used to being called Leigh. I'll need to work on that.

"Um, yeah, sure. I'll come for a bit, I guess." It totally makes sense that they are on Tybee too. Cole and the jet ski. How could I forget?

I look back over and see Xander walking up to Cole's table. I must be staring because everyone at our table stops and looks too. I'm holding my breath.

"Who is that gorgeous hunk of a man?" Jane asks. She puts her chin on her hands and sighs, like something from a stupid sixties beach movie. I'm waiting for her to say he's just dreamy or some crap like that. And this, right here, is why I'm Leigh Rutledge this summer, not Ashleigh Decker. I made the right call. Yep. Right call, indeed.

Matt says, "I'm pretty sure that's Alexander Decker. He's with the Reapers organization. Cole must be shitting himself right now. Oh my god, he's wanted to play for the Reapers since we were kids."

"Don't we all," Drew comments.

"THE Alexander Decker?" Mandy asks. The guys all give her a questioning look. "One of the most eligible bachelors, according to *People Magazine*, Alexander Decker?" Again, the guys just shrug and get back to the party planning, but Matt keeps glancing back at Cole. I can't help it. I'm staring.

Matt leans into me and whispers, "You think he's hot, don't you?" He gives me a wink and a shoulder nudge.

Who, Xander? Ewww, he's my brother. Cole? Oh yeah. I'd

even use the word dreamy, which makes me feel a little guilty about judging Jane that way. Not sure who he's talking about. I just go with the tried and true shoulder shrug.

"You know, if we could get Alexander in a video, I'm sure we'd go viral," Brady adds. "Do you think we should ask him, Leigh?"

Between being riveted by the interaction between Xander and Cole and not being used to the name Leigh, it takes another shoulder bump from Matt to get my attention.

"Hum, what? I'm sorry," I say to the group.

"What do you think about asking Alexander to be in a video with us, Leigh? It would be sure to get views and start our season off right," Brady says.

"I don't know," I say slowly. "I'd hate to take the focus off of you guys. It may not send the right message." But unfortunately, Brady is right. It would be genius and sure to go viral. But Alexander usually hates social media stuff. He doesn't have any public accounts and hates the spotlight.

I also know that if I ask him, he will do it. I know he'd do anything for me. Well, almost. Everything but leave me alone this summer.

Matt chimes in. "I'll share the spotlight, for sure. I think we need the right video. Maybe a mock rose ceremony, a la *Bachelor*? But we give out teddy bears instead?"

"That's pretty funny," I say, returning my attention to our table. "Let me see how I can work that out." Maybe I should take this opportunity to drop in on that conversation over there. "I'll go see if he's open to it." I start to get up, and Matt stands up too. I give him a half smile.

"What?" he asks. "Just thought I'd introduce myself too. Cole and I are a pair. You can't get one without the other."

"Is that so?" I ask. Well, that makes this summer even more complicated. I've got two futures to protect.

We make our way over to the table, and I stand next to Xander, gently placing my hand on his shoulder to get his attention. Matt is between Coach Grant and Cole. Cole's eyes go to my hand, and I immediately move it like Xander's shoulder is a hot iron. Trevor seems to watch it all with great interest. Damn drama queen.

"Sorry to interrupt, gentlemen, but we have an idea we want to present."

"We?" Xander asks, cocking an eyebrow at me.

"Um, yes. Alexander Decker, this is Matt Hartman, the third baseman for the Pajamas this summer," I say.

Xander reaches out and shakes Matt's hand. "It's nice to meet you, Matt. You've got some great stats. I look forward to watching you this summer," Xander says. I watch Cole smile with pride at the compliment to Matt, but he's still watching me.

"Thanks," Matt says. "I hope I don't disappoint. But Leigh and I came over to ask you a favor."

Xander raises one eyebrow and gives me a smug look. "Oh, you have something you want from me, Leigh? What could that be?"

Xander can be a real bastard, and right now, he's teaching how to perfect the behavior. He's baiting Cole, and he knows it. Cole glares at him, his eyes no longer on me. I think Trevor is starting to put the pieces together because his face brightens like a lightbulb went off. A smile stretches across his face as he leans in, putting his elbows on the table.

Coach Grant and Matt are both missing the backstory, and it's evident at this point that there is one. As they look around at everyone, their eyes settle on each other. They shrug and wait to see what happens next.

"Why yes, *Alexander*, I would like to ask a favor of you," I say with a hint of sarcasm. "If you will be around for another day or so, we'd like to ask you to participate in our kickoff video. We figure with your, um, notoriety, it will help get views and possibly go viral. That would be a great way to start our season, don't you think, Trevor?" I need Trevor's buy-in here. And his promise to help reign in Xander.

Trevor shrugs like he could care less and eats his french fries like a bucket of popcorn at the double feature.

"Well, Leigh," Xander says, with mocking consideration, "I will be here for the next week or so. I might consider it if you agree to discuss the details and script over dinner tonight." The gleam in his eye is evident to everyone. To me, he's being evil. I'm sure to the others, it looks like he's asking me out. Trevor and I know he's challenging me to break my secret identity. Think fast, Ash.

"That sounds great!" I fake enthusiasm. "Matt and I had already made plans, but he can come, too, and we'll pitch our idea." Cole snaps his head, his look of *what the fuck* directed at Matt. Matt casually puts his hand on Cole's head and points it back toward me.

"Um, sure," Alexander says. "I'll meet you at Wolfie's on Tybee at seven-thirty. Does that work?"

I just glare at him. Wolfie's is the best white tablecloth, take a date to place on the entire island. Cole looks confused and a little angry. Poor guy. We are going to send him to an early grave.

"Yep," I say, popping the p. "Perfect." I pull out my phone and act like I'm putting it on my calendar.

> You are such an ass!

Xander casually looks at his phone and laughs.

"Well, it sounds like I've got work to do. I'll see you all later." I turn to leave when I see the text on my phone.

X

> But you love me anyway. Good move bringing the best friend. You are a tricky minx.

I stop a few steps away to reply.

> You promised.

X

Your secret is safe with me. I always keep my
promises.

———

I'm in the intern bullpen watching *Bachelor* highlights. I hate that
show because it makes women look so desperate. But then, they
do that to themselves, right? I hate to admit that I watch it sometimes. It's like a train wreck, and I can't look away. I have a
moment of self-hatred every time I turn it on. Emma tries to find
redeeming qualities in each person, but it's hard for me. The
people on it seem to be attention-seeking, petty, and shallow.
And looking for love? Doubt it.

The contestants are like the women I see Xander and Jules go
out with. They want that boost to followers more than to get to
know my brothers. It breaks my heart because they are great
guys and deserve someone who will love them for who they are
as people, not for their money or fame. I know, hard to believe
I'm actually a romantic at heart. I'm open to unique ways to
meet people, but I think there is either a connection or there isn't.
You can't turn it into a competition.

That horrible show has pursued my brother, Julian, to be the
bachelor for the past two years. I don't think he would consider
it, but he loves to push my buttons and act like he might. I think
Jules will get a kick out of Xander doing the video. Maybe I can
get him to make a guest appearance? It would be a way for Jules
to give the show the middle finger and hopefully stop the
pursuit. And maybe he'll get Alexander to go home.

Hey! Where are you? Want to come to
Savannah tomorrow to shoot a Bachelor
parody with X and the Pajamas?

JULES

Xander didn't tell you? I'm joining you for dinner tonight. Sounds like you've had an interesting first day.

No, he didn't tell me. But you're in?

JULES

Yep. I want to be the host.

You owe me all the deets. I want your version. Xander's version sounds.....concerning.

No need to be concerned. You have to trust me.

Matt strolls in and takes a look at my messy desk. It's cluttered with Go Pros, battery packs, and other equipment. He grabs a selfie stick and looks at me. Cole walks in just as Matt's knee hits the floor.

Palming the selfing stick with both hands and holding it over his heart, he says, "Leigh, will you accept this selfie stick?" I'm glad he can mock the show too.

I look at him, give him my best dreamy look, and grasp his hands. I'm sure I look ridiculous.

Using my best Scarlett O'Hara Southern accent, I say, "Why yes, dear Matt, whom I've known for a hot minute, I can't wait to accept your marriage proposal after you made out with all these other girls at the same time over the past four weeks. I'm so grateful you picked me. Thank you for thinking I'm worthy." Of course, this is all said, dripping with sarcasm. I dramatically bat my eyelashes at him and wink. Cole laughs and gives me a slow clap.

"Smooth operator," Cole says as he slaps Matt on the shoulder.

We all crack up. "Give me a sec, guys," I say to Cole and Matt as I grab my phone to read the text that just came in.

JULES

I'll try. Love you

Love you more

As much as my brothers drive me crazy, I do love them. They have the biggest hearts on the planet.

"A boyfriend?" Matt asks as he motions to my phone. "That text sure did put a smile on your face." Did he see what I texted?

Cole seems to be holding his breath. Would it be easier if I made myself unavailable? Even though I'm full of half-truths this summer, I can't lie. And like I'll ever let him cash in on the whole *mine* thing. Nope. Not gonna happen.

"No, it's my brother. I miss him," I say honestly. Jules travels often and spends most of his time in New York. He's one of my favorite people on the planet. I'm excited to see him tonight. It's been months since we were in the same place.

Cole gives me a half smile. "A brother, huh?"

"Actually, I have two older, very overprotective brothers, if you must know. I'm the annoying little sister."

Cole's smile stretches, going all the way to his eyes. "I have one of those too. A younger sister. Darcy."

Matt jumps in, "But she's not annoying. Darcy's great."

"She really is," says Cole. "But still, a guy has to watch out for his little sister. She's precious, you know."

Precious. Yeah, I know a thing or two about that. Big brothers. A blessing and a curse.

"So I take it you two are close?" I move my hand between the two of them. "I mean, since Matt is so quick to defend your sister's honor and all that."

"We've been best friends since we were in third grade," Matt says.

"Cool. Lifelong friends are special. So…. what brings you to the bullpen? You lost? The locker room is in the other direction."

"I wanted to see if you need me to pick you up for dinner tonight or, um, if you wanted to meet there?" Matt seems a little uncomfortable. He wasn't like this at lunch. Why is he acting stilted? Is this because of Cole? Their friendship is an interesting dynamic.

"You know what, why don't we meet there," I say. "That way, I'll have my car and can follow you to the beach party afterward."

"You're still coming to the party?" Cole asks. He seems surprised.

"Sure, why wouldn't I?"

"No, no. I'm glad you're coming. It'll be fun."

Matt is watching us with a smirk on his face. This is amusing to him. Well, you know what, Matt? Let's double down.

"Hey Cole, why don't you join us tonight? Let the Reapers buy you the first of many dinners," I suggest.

"Oh, I can't, um…"

"Sure you can. It'll be fun. We'll all work on the video ideas, and Alexander can get to know you both on a more, um, personal level."

Matt puts his hand on Cole's shoulder. "Count him in. Come on, let's hit the weight room before we head out."

"See ya' later, Matt," I say. "Trouble," I mumble.

They turn to leave, and Cole looks over his shoulder at me as I pick up my phone and send another text.

> Sounds like you need to add one more to the reservations for tonight.

X

See you at dinner, you minx

CHAPTER
NINE

COLE

————

"Tell me this isn't a mistake, Matt. Maybe I should stay home and help the rookies get ready for the bonfire?"

Matt looks over at me from the passenger seat and laughs. "Dude, you won't tell me what happened today, but I think I'm putting some things together."

"Oh yeah, what have you figured out?" I'm curious to hear his theory because there is no way he can be even close to the tangled mess that is my life right now. Let's see how close he gets.

"You like her."

"What? That's what you put together? Hope you didn't overwork any brain cells to come up with that." I scoff at him. Yes, scoff. Seriously Matt. Don't be lazy. Work on this a little more.

Make it more like the real story. Alexander fucking Decker, of the Carolina Reapers, my dream team, has a relationship with Leigh. He punched me after I questioned his manhood, and he probably hates me. I've blown my shot to get a chance to play for my dream team. Maybe the entire MLB. This fucker's connected. I know that. Why didn't I know who he was when I saw him in the conference room? Oh, that's right, because he was grabbing her. And I saw red. Then there's the fact that she may or may not be with him. Something's there. She's not afraid of him like I initially thought. And she seems to know Trevor better than the rest of the new interns, and he seems to give her looks. Is it because of her thing with Decker? Then there's the fact that half the team has voiced their intentions to ask her out. And the most fucked up piece of all of this? I want to make her mine. Add me to the long list of possible suitors. Shit.

"Yep. I haven't figured out who's fist kissed your pretty little face, but I have a guess, and I'm fairly certain it was because of her. And if I'm right, this will be anything but a simple summer. But regardless, YOU. LIKE. HER." The bastard almost seems smug. Like he knows something else and isn't sharing.

"Well, half the team likes her. Seems she's the talk of the locker room. She's fucking adorable. Don't deny it. You like her too." Yeah, Matt, don't think I didn't watch you at lunch. Well, this is new territory for us. We've never liked the same girl before. Let's add this to the complicated mess of my life right now. I'm going to compete with my best friend for a girl. And hell, when my career goes to shit because I pissed off Decker, it will be a whole *Pearl Harbor* movie ending where she gets with my best friend, and I have to watch. Ugh. I should just drop him off and bail.

"Yeah, I like her," he says. "She's great." I turn my head to look at him, and he has that look. I know that look. It's the look he gives runners when he knows they will try to steal third, but he won't let them. It's the look of, come on, asshole, I dare you. And it's a rare day when someone steals his base.

Matt just keeps rambling on. "She's a sweet girl. And funny. She seems pretty sheltered. Not a party girl. I'm a little surprised she agreed to come to the beach tonight, if I'm honest."

Sweet? Funny? Yeah, I could see that. But my encounters

with her have all been sassy. And I like it. I like that she has a temper. And a fiery streak. I like that she stands up for herself, and I promise to let her do that.

No more rescuing, even if it goes against my genetic makeup. With a single mom and younger sister, that's my job. My purpose. Women are to be cherished and protected. But I'll work on giving her space. But if Decker touches her, I can't promise I won't lose my shit.

"Why are you surprised? She seems pretty social. She obviously wants to get to know everyone so she can do her marketing thing." Tell me more, Matt. I need to fill up my database of Leigh knowledge.

"I think she prefers to be behind the scenes. I don't think she's shy, just not a scene-stealer. She loves baseball and knows the game better than most. But she's absolutely not a cleat chaser."

"And you got all that from lunch?"

"Yep."

"Well, that's all interesting. You gonna ask her out?"

Matt smiles as he looks at me.

"I already did." I turn and look at him so fast that I jerk the car to the right. He laughs so hard that his hand hits the dash. I give him a *what the fuck* look. "Yeah, asshole. But I'm letting you crash our date. So behave yourself, okay? Don't embarrass me."

So he is going after her. Well, isn't that just fan-fucking-tastic.

As I pull into the parking lot, several sweet rides are parked along the front row. For some reason, I am drawn to the little teal Mini Cooper, top-down, sandwiched between the Mercedes AMG-GTR and a retro McLaren. It's a sassy toy car hanging with the supercars. It doesn't seem like it can compete but don't count it out due to its spunkiness. Honestly, it's kind of a cute picture. I am also aware that those expensive cars are a stark reminder that if I don't fix this mess with Decker, I may be driving this Jeep for another decade.

Matt gives out a low whistle. "Sweet. Which one would you pick?"

"The McLaren, definitely the McLaren. You?"

"The night edition Mercedes. It's stealthy."

That's true. Matt tends to lean toward the classics, the subtle. I like the more temperamental and exotic. So the fact we both like the same girl? A bit unusual. But maybe she's a little bit of both?

Then I share before I can stop myself. "But I'm drawn to the Mini."

Matt laughs and slaps me on the back. "Tell me something I don't already know."

———

We walk into the restaurant, and I scan the room. I see our group at a round table in the center of the dining room and let the hostess know we can seat ourselves. Their conversation appears animated and relaxed, but as Matt and I walk up to the table, all conversation stops. My eyes go straight to Leigh, who is flanked by Alexander, and another guy who appraises me head to toe. They both straighten their backs and sit a little taller. The empty chairs at the table are beside them, with Trevor between us. Wow. A little intimidation tactic, perhaps. Split us up, and they flank Leigh. Well, I'm not intimated. Not really. They may be rich and famous but are too old for her. And from what I can tell, she's too good for them both.

I walk over to the guy I don't know and extend my hand. "Hi, I'm Cole Davidson."

He stands up and, wow, is this guy tall. He must be at least six-foot-four.

He leans down a little and says, "Nice to meet you. I'm Julian Decker. Thanks for letting me crash your party tonight." He turns to Leigh and winks. What is it with everyone winking at this girl? Mine.

"Ah, so you must be Alexander's brother," I say. I may have done some cyber stalking this afternoon to learn more about Alexander and looked into his brother Julian too. Julian played college ball before an injury took him out for good. Tough break. He was a top prospect pitcher too. Injury or not, he still has the build of a professional athlete. He apparently doesn't let his office job keep him out of the gym.

He's one of the top-performing sports agents in the country. He represents guys like Tripp Stevenson of the Reapers, Chance Fuller, the best forward in the NHL, and most of the top quarterbacks in the NFL. He's known for getting high-paying contracts and keeping scandals at bay. He's got quite an impressive roster of clients.

Julian smiles in contrast to Alexander's scowl. He appears to be more laid back than the high-strung Alexander fucking Decker. His demeanor is that of a frat boy hanging out with his guys. I immediately see why people like him. He gives off that vibe like he's very unassuming, quick to gain your trust, then when he's close enough, he goes for the jugular. I mean, that's what I'd want in an agent if I were ever lucky enough to need one. Also, I'd always want him on my side. If Julian Decker is against you, you might as well hang it all up.

Matt stands next to me and extends his hand. "Matt Hartman. Glad to meet you, Mr. Decker."

"Please, we're all friends here. Call me Julian. You guys have a seat."

I claim the seat next to Julian, putting Matt between Alexander and Trevor. I want to stay as far away from him as possible. We say hello to everyone else and take our seats. Fuck, this is stressful. Now I'm having dinner with a team owner, an MLB representative, and one of the top sports agents in the country. Oh yeah, and a beautiful girl with ocean-blue eyes who won't even look at me.

The waitress appears and asks for our drink order. A quick scan of the table tells me alcohol is on the menu for everyone, and I order a bourbon. Everyone takes a second round except Leigh. It doesn't look like she's touched her white wine.

There is an awkward silence as we all seem to mentally assess the table. Finally, Julian slaps his hand on the table, startling us all. "Can we just talk about the elephant in the room?" We all look at him. Are you kidding me? There is a fucking herd of elephants charging straight toward me. Which one does he want to tackle first?

Alexander scowls at his drink like it also accused him of having a tiny dick. Matt looks between Leigh and me like he's watching a damn tennis match. Leigh is watching Julian and twirling her wine glass like it's a member of the ice capades. Then Trevor claps his hands together like a giddy teenage girl right before the *Gossip Girl* reveal. XOXO motherfuckers.

"What was that, Cole?" Julian asked.

"Hmm, what?" I look at him. Did I miss something?

"Something about Xs and Os?"

Oh shit. Did I say that out loud? Now everyone is looking at me.

Julian continues, "Let's just throw it out there. We are all dazzled by the amazingly talented Miss Leigh Rutledge right here. We are all here to share a meal because of you, darlin'. You have all of us wrapped around your finger." Julian raises his glass to toast her.

Trevor cracks up and lets the release valve off the pressure cooker I live in. "Abso-fucking-lutely we are. Dazzled and wrapped." He raises his glass and takes a drink too. "So, Leigh, tell us about this TikTok video you want to make and how you will make people go wild for the Pajamas."

The waitress takes our order, and Trevor encourages Leigh to continue.

"Oh, well," she starts. Her blush is a deep red, and it's doing something to me that makes me grateful I'm sitting down with a napkin over my lap. I don't think I've ever reacted to a woman like this. I want to go all caveman and grab her, throw her over my shoulder, and take her away from these other guys. Who am I? Never. Not once have I ever had this undeniable urge. Get it together, Davidson.

"I thought we could introduce our starting lineup with a parody of a rose ceremony," she says, finally finding her voice.

"Only we use Teddy Bears," Matt interjects.

"Right, Teddy Bears." She smiles at Matt. "I thought it would be funny if Alexander is the bachelor and Julian, you can do a surprise cameo as the host. With your involvement, it's sure to go viral. I mean, two of America's most eligible bachelors are spoofing the show. It's TikTok gold."

Now that she's wound up, she's going strong. Damn, she's beautiful when her eyes light up like this. This is her passion, and she's good at it. She talks about cross-marketing and translating views to merchandise sales and added boosts for the players for name recognition. When you hear her talk about it, it's more than a silly video. And I'm all in. Of course, I was all in before dinner. But now I'm really all in.

Our dinner is served, and Julian encourages Leigh to discuss business strategy and social media. It's fascinating, really.

As she reaches for the bread basket, her white, loose summer sweater drops off one shoulder, revealing her sexy collarbone and no bra strap. Is she not wearing a bra? Ah, hell. I inadvertently take in an audible gasp. Alexander looks at me, and that icy glare is back. I clear my throat and gulp my bourbon.

Julian nods his head as she talks. He's totally engaged. We all are. He puts his arm behind her chair and gives her a little side-shoulder hug. And swiftly but casually, he brings her shirt back up over her shoulder. That was a little intimate, and I'm wondering how many guys regularly touch her inappropriately. I know I said I'd leave it to her, but seriously Leigh, I'm sorry you have to deal with this.

Julian squeezes her shoulder and brings his hands back to his lap. Good move, frat boy. "Love it. Girl, you are going places. Great idea. I might need you to help me with some of my clients on their social media game. Stevenson needs to quit making videos of his cat. It's disturbing."

We all laugh at that. Tripp Stevenson, starting pitcher for the Reapers, has become a meme because of his fucking cat videos.

"I don't think anyone can help Tripp. He may be a lost cause," she says with a giggle. The sound of her laugh makes my balls tighten. What is she doing to me?

"I hear he even had socks made with him and the cat on them," Alexander adds.

"Yeah, they were custom-made, one of a kind, I hear," Julian replies.

"Were they?" she whispers. I am hanging on to every word she speaks, even though it's often confusing as hell. I feel like I'm missing the key to translating this conversation.

Trevor chimes in. "I love it. I'd like to see at least four videos a week. Is that doable, Leigh?"

"Sure. It's not as easy as it looks, but with the great team you've assembled, we can create the content you are looking for. But with the team travel schedule, we'll have to do a good bit of the filming in advance. Maybe start to get some this week before things get hectic?"

"I'll help," I volunteer before I know what I'm saying. "Matt too. We'll help get the guys on board and help with the logistics. We can even film things for you on the road. I mean, if that would help. Sometimes the team can be tough to wrangle when they are off the field. And we do some crazy shit on the bus."

Matt nods his head in agreement. "Absolutely. Anything you need, Leigh."

Trevor, Julian, and Alexander all pledge their help. I think this may be the formation of the Leigh Rutledge fan club right here. Or maybe it already existed, and I'm the newest member? Doesn't matter. I'll do anything I can to become president.

After the initial testosterone pissing contest, everyone chills out, and we have a pleasant evening. Julian tells lots of stories about his clients that keep us in stitches. Trevor shares a few stories about his college days with Alexander. I didn't know they were roommates and best friends, but now some puzzle pieces are clicking into place. They all ask lots of questions about Matt and me. They ask us to critique each other's strengths and weaknesses on the field. When Matt or I ask a question of Leigh, one of the other guys deflects or asks a different question. I want to learn more about her, but I don't glean much. It's like they play major defense where she is concerned.

I know a few things. She wants to work in sports marketing after graduation. Her favorite sport is baseball, followed by hockey.

When she says she has a crush on Chance Fuller of the NHL Raleigh Renegades, Julian almost chokes on his pasta. She just giggles and takes a sip of her wine. Chance Fuller is one lucky son of a bitch if Leigh crushes on him. And she thinks I'm trouble?

"Don't you think he's a little old for you?" I ask. I can't help it. It makes me think of Decker sitting there, and I wonder if she has a thing for older guys.

"Why would you ask that?" She has an edge in her voice.

"Well, I know he's established in his career, and Julian here makes sure he's bringing home an enormous amount of money. Is that the appeal of a guy like him? Is there a reason you go for older guys?"

"Are you calling me a gold digger?" she asks, clearly getting pissed off. Alexander appears amused. He leans back and crosses his arms with a smug look. I want to punch him. Trevor watches with rapt attention.

"What? No. No. It's more like a hypothetical. I'm asking why Chance is someone you would crush on. I just want to know. What is it about guys a decade older than you that you find appealing? For someone so adamant about not being rescued, you sure do gravitate to, to, to…that." I can tell I'm digging my own grave, but I can't stop myself. I keep on digging deeper.

"I kind of have a crush on him, too, if I'm honest," Matt

chimes in, trying to be a good wingman and dig me out of my mess. It's always my mouth that gets me in trouble.

Julian laughs. "Yeah, he's my best friend, and I kind of crush on him too. He's such a cinnamon roll kind of guy. The appeal is just Chance. He's awesome. So I get it, Matt. I'll see if I can't set up a meet and greet in Raleigh. I'll make that love connection come true for you." Julian holds up his drink and gives Matt a slight toast.

The look of pure loathing is rolling off Leigh, directed at me. I can't tell if she's pissed about the comment, about the conversation being hijacked, or just angry at me all the time. Her fingers begin to drum on the table. The redness rises up her neck and darkens her cheeks. Her eyes become a darker blue, and a little crease forms between her eyes. Watching her get mad turns me on a little, and that can't be good.

Matt looks a little awestruck. "Seriously? That would be great. Not the love connection part, but just getting to meet him and watch him play."

"Not a problem. Just consider it part of my bachelor host role. It will be one of those fantasy date things." Julian and Matt laugh, ignoring the tension between Leigh and me.

Leigh keeps a steady glare at me, and I watch Alexander lean over and whisper something in her ear. She gives him a death glare too. I'm not sure if I find that amusing, comforting, or scary. Maybe a little of all three.

"I think I'm going to skip the party tonight. I've had a long day," Leigh says, ending our dinner. "Matt, I'll have to take a rain check." She makes that comment to him, clearly sending a message that she's done with me.

As we walk outside, Alexander opens the driver's door to the Mini, helping Leigh into her car before getting into the Mercedes. I'm not surprised to see Julian claim the McLaren. Yep. Just like at dinner. The two big dogs flank the cute and spunky one. And me leaving with my tail between my legs.

CHAPTER
TEN

ASHLEIGH

———

It's been a long day, and I'm spent. I feel like I've been on a crazy roller coaster all day. The scene with Xander and Cole. The mixer with the Pajamas. Mine? I can't even begin to process that. And then that testosterone-fueled dinner. It went better than I thought it would, all things considered, but I won't deny it was stressful.

I want to go to my happy place, so I pull out my Kindle. Getting lost in a book helps me escape from my world.

I curl up in bed and open my latest romance novel when my phone rings with a FaceTime request. I hit accept and let out a big sigh.

"Yeah, I figured you might feel that way," Jules says.

"What way is that?"

"Like you might need a little girl time with your big brother," he says with a wicked grin. "What are you reading?"

Our sibling book club started with *Twilight* when I was in middle school. We both read it and debated every nuance for hours. I was Team Edward, and Jules was Team Jacob. Since then, he has kept my Kindle loaded with books he thinks I'll like.

I hold up my Kindle so he can see my latest title, *Puck Off - A Hockey Romance*. He knows I love sports romances, and he reads them too. I used to think it was so we had something to bond over, but I suspect there's more to the story.

"I'll be curious what you think of this one. It's getting lots of five-star reviews on Amazon." That makes me smile and shake my head at my brother.

Jules is the opposite of Xander in many ways. Oh, he's still uber-protective and can be an ass, but he's also easy to talk to about anything.

Girl time was something we started a few years after Mom died. He was in college and had a bad shoulder injury that required two surgeries and months of rehab. It ended his competitive baseball career. While he was home recovering, we binged shows like *Dawson's Creek*, *Gossip Girl*, and *90210*. He realized girls needed to talk about things like emotions. He researched female psychology and discovered that girl time was essential for healthy emotional development. While he was home with me, he found out I didn't have girlfriends I could trust, so he decided to fill the role.

Now, we have girl time at least once a month. Because of school and his travel, we have to do it virtually most of the time. I'll get the most random gift boxes with scented candles, face masks, cute nail polish, or a great bottle of wine. After the box arrives, I usually know girl time is a few days away.

Nothing compares to girl time when we are together. He'll ask me to give him a facial, and we'll eat ice cream straight from the carton while we watch chick flicks. I'm not sure who enjoys girl time more, me or him. I love the vulnerable and sensitive side he only shares with me.

"I wish you were here right now."

"Yeah, wasn't sure what Emma's parents would think if they saw me in a face mask getting a manicure." He chuckles.

"Oh, I'm sure Emma has told them all about our family rituals. But I'm just really happy you were there tonight," I confess. "It was a crazy day. I couldn't decide if I wanted to cry or laugh or hit something or run away. And honestly, I still haven't settled on one of those yet. Maybe all of them?"

"Yeah, I heard a little bit of Xander's version. You want to give me yours?"

Not really, I think. But maybe Julian will have a male insight and help me untangle my mess. Once I get started, I give him the whole rundown. "Well, um, I don't even know what happened. Xander showed up and surprised me. I should have known he wouldn't leave me alone here. But, Jules, I really want to do this, you know? I want to make friends because of me. I know you get it. People always want to be close because of WHO you are but not because of who YOU are. I need to know people will like me for me. And I thought this would be a way to build those relationships and see if I'm good at what I do or if people blow sunshine up my ass because I'm a Decker." Tears slide down my cheeks, and I get mad at myself for the tears.

Lucky for me, Jules is well versed in Ashleigh girl-speak and isn't phased at all.

"Ash, let's break this down. First, you are awesome. Do you hear me? And people do love you for you. Emma doesn't give a shit about baseball or money or what you can do for her. She knows you and loves you for you. And you know Xander and I do, too, not because we have to but because we can't help it. You are smart, fun, spicy, and so fucking amazing. No one tonight was giving you platitudes over your marketing strategies. We were all hanging on every word. And I'm sincere when I say I could use your talents with my clients."

I drop the phone to grab a tissue.

"And I'm not finished, so get back here," Jules yells. I pick up my phone and prop it on my nightstand as I lay down and hug my pillow.

"That's better," he says. "Let's see, where was I? Oh yeah,

how awesome you are. And I get the name change, probably better than most." He winks. "But promise me you won't change who YOU are, okay? Changing the label doesn't change the contents. Promise?"

My heart swells. I know he's right. I'm just tired and a little freaked out. "I promise. I'll just be an expensive bottle of wine with a Two-Buck Chuck label."

We both laugh. "Oh, Ash, I promise you could never be mistaken for Chuck. But you get what I'm throwing?"

I nod. "I do. Now, can you tell me why Xander punched Cole? That is what happened, right?"

"Yeah, let's talk about your player's issues. It looked like you were ready to punch him too. Maybe he's just a punchable bastard?"

"He just pushes my buttons. Every encounter sets me off. And you know I don't usually react like that. So I can only imagine what happened with Xan."

"Well, according to Xander, Cole stepped in the middle of something he probably misinterpreted but stood up for you. He admired him for it. Then you snapped at Cole, and Xander figured there was more to the story. So that put him on alert. And then……"

"Then what? What in the hell happened after I left? I can only guess what Cole thought he walked in on. And I haven't done anything to change that narrative. He probably thinks Xander and I are, um, involved. Tonight Xander kinda kept playing that role too. And then Cole says that about Chance. UGH. He just, he just…" I shudder at the thought. "If I tell him who I am to Xander, then my summer will be shot. So I need him to keep thinking whatever it is he thinks. But then he thinks I'm a gold-digging jersey chaser. Whatever. I can't deal with that right now. So how did Xander go from admiration to assault?"

It takes Julian a minute to catch his breath from laughing. "Well, apparently, Cole insulted Xander's manhood."

"What do you mean?" His manhood? What does that even mean between guys?

"He accused Xander of having . . ." He is laughing again. When he composes himself, he looks into the camera with a deadly serious look. "He told Xander he had a tiny dick." Julian cracks up again.

"Are you serious? That was all it took for Xan to hit him? There has to be more than that!" I'm stunned. Cole must have been pissed and said some colorful words to Xander. And I know he wouldn't take that well. I swear, men have the most enormous egos when it comes to their dick size. I guess my brother is no exception. And I don't even want to think about my brother's manhood. Ugh. Boys are dumb.

"Nope. But I think it was also his sense that Cole was throwing off some serious pheromones. Like you are his to protect or mark his territory or something. You know Xan can go all mama bear when it comes to you." Oh, I'm very aware.

Like I'm his? All I can think of is the label. *Mine.* Do I like that idea? Maybe. But the idea I belong to anyone pisses me off too. That's the whole point of this summer, right? To be independent, to be my own person. It's got me all tangled up.

"So, what did you think at dinner?"

"About Cole?" he asks. "Well, I agree with Xander's assessment. He's a smitten kitten."

"A smitten kitten? Seriously, Jules. I know Xander didn't use that term. Do you not cringe when you say things like that? Does your manhood not shrink a little?"

"Nah, not when I'm in girl-time mode with you, Ash. I'm secure enough with myself. "

"So, back to Cole?" I'm dying to know his thoughts on this guy who has done nothing but turn me into an angry harpy ever since I met him.

"Okay, so look. I won't pull a Xander, but I will play the big brother card here for a second. I know you put yourself in dating time out for a while now. And even in high school, you didn't have the regular freedoms that most young ladies have as they figured all this out. And now here you are 'on your own' surrounded by a bunch of college baseball players. It's like going from zero to sixty in two-point-three seconds. I'm not sure you are ready for all this attention. I don't want you to be hurt. So, Ash, just be careful. Trevor told me about your mixer labels. Of course, they all think you are beautiful. He was a little concerned about the one that said MINE. And maybe I am too."

"Uh, yeah. The thing is...."

"You know who wrote it, don't you?"

I feel my face get warm and bury it in my pillow. "Maybe?"

"Want to share?"

"Nah, I'm not sharing, but I hear you. I'm not naive. And I'm pretty good at shutting guys down. This time, I'll move them to the friend zone quickly. I've got a job to do here. And so do they. But do you think Xander can look past it and evaluate Cole as a ball player? I can't have his dreams dashed because of a run-in with me. Apparently, his childhood dream is to be a Reaper."

Jules considers my question. "I don't know, Ash. But he's good about putting the Reaper's needs above anything else. But when you are added to the mix? All bets are off. But I'll keep in touch with him and try to keep him objective. I'm headed back to New York in the afternoon after our video shoot tomorrow, and I'll do my best to keep Xan away from Savannah for you. But I think keeping Cole at a distance from you is probably his best shot at cleaning up this mess with Xander."

I think about what Jules is telling me. He's probably right. The best thing for Cole is to stay away from me. It is best for his scouting prospects and his future. It is probably best not to get any more tangled up in my crazy mixed-up family. And it's probably best for me, too. I feel my stomach tumble a little. I need to focus. Set boundaries and professional objectives. I can hold trouble at bay.

"Yeah, you're probably right. Hey, Jules?" He bats his big aqua eyes at me. "I'm lucky to have a big sister like you."

He chuckles and blows me a kiss. "Get some rest, *Leigh*. You've got a big day tomorrow." He hangs up, and I immediately get a text.

JULES

I'm the lucky one. 🤍

I am the luckiest girl on the planet.

CHAPTER
ELEVEN

COLE

———

The video shoot was a blast. Leigh did a great job, and the video has over half a million views and climbing. It was even featured on ESPN. The guys are all hyped about the exposure, not only for the team but for themselves as well.

Baseball is a team sport. It takes a team to win, but the team doesn't get the call. Individuals do. It's incredibly competitive amongst the teammates to shine, stand out, and be the reason for the team's success. The business of baseball is also evolving. It's not just about stats. Teams want personalities. Images. Brands. Buzz. Followers. Followers translate to fans, ticket sales, and the pot of gold: merchandise sales.

The guys on the team really like Leigh. I mean, what's not to like? Her beauty and charm are enough, but add her social media prowess, and she is a commodity everyone is clamoring to get a piece of. That bothers me more than it should. Mine.

It's been over a week since our dinner, and I only want to talk to her. I want, no, I *need* to apologize. However, she's avoiding me. When I see her looking my way, she turns her head. Or she's always in a group. I guess she thinks there is safety in numbers, but I'm about to blow that theory out of the water.

Practice is over, and we have our first sold-out home game tomorrow. I want to clear the air with her. She's in the stands with a few other media interns, probably discussing roles for tomorrow. No time like the present.

Matt grabs me by the shoulder. "Good workout. You were hitting the leather off the ball. Working off something?" He follows my look and laughs. "Oh, well, good luck with that. I'm hitting the showers. I'll catch a ride home with Brady."

"I won't be long," I say.

While all the other guys head to the locker room, I make my way to the stands. My cleats crunch on the cement stairs as I walk, keeping my approach anything but stealth.

Josh, one of the color commentators for the Pajamas, greets me first. "Hey, Davidson, hot bat today. Think that will translate into points tomorrow night?"

"I can only hope. I like it when they go over the fence. Then I don't have to run as fast," I respond, looking for a laugh.

"Yeah, jogging the bases is one way to avoid cramps," he chuckles.

"What are you guys working on up here?" I ask.

"Talking about creating baseball cards as a giveaway," Jane chimes in. She bats her eyes at me and tucks her hair behind her ear. Possible cleat chaser vibes are coming my way. I make a note to ask Matt about her. He's good at spotting that kind of thing. I don't care because I've come for one reason, and she appears to be ignoring me.

"That would be sweet. I'd love it. We could sign them for the fans as they leave or something."

"I bet everyone would be in line for your signature," Jane says.

Leigh scoffs, her back still to me, refusing to allow me into their chat circle.

I lightly touch Leigh on her shoulder to get her to look at me. "Hey, can I talk to you for a minute?"

"Don't you need to hit the showers?" she says with a little edge.

"I do. I will. But I needed to get your help with something real quick. It will only take a minute."

When she doesn't move or acknowledge my request, I follow up with a "please?"

She shakes her head and gives an audible sigh. "Sure. I'll be right back, y'all."

We walk a few steps down, and I motion for her to take a seat in the bleachers. She sits down and folds her arms, my eyes noticing how her folded arms accentuate her breasts. Um, that little action. I mean, her arms go and cross right there and lift them up a bit. I'm a human man, after all. Give me a break.

I sit next to her, effectively blocking her escape. Desperate times, desperate measures, and all that. Now that I have her, I'm not sure how to start. I take my cap off and run my fingers through my sweaty hair. Playing baseball in Savannah in the summer is no joke. Maybe I should have hit the shower first. Oh well. I'm committed now.

"You're a hard girl to talk to."

"Eyes up here, Davidson." I look at her face, and she's fighting a smile.

Shit. Right. "Sorry. I, um, look, I just wanted to apologize."

She raises one eyebrow at me. No verbal response, just that little facial moment. I know she's probably making a list of which infraction I'm about to apologize for. I'll start with the worst and work my way backward.

"I feel bad about our dinner last week, and I want you to know I don't think that you are, well, I know you aren't that kind of girl. I mean, I know how I sounded, but that's not what I meant. It seems you don't like me, and I just want a chance to redeem myself."

"And exactly WHAT kind of girl is that?" Her face is not cracking the slightest smile. She's like stone.

I know she can smile. I've seen her smile with Matt and the other guys. I'd give my left nut for her to give me one of those smiles.

"I know you aren't a jersey chaser." Her eyebrow arches in my direction.

"And how, pray tell, do you know that? Maybe all I want to do is hitch my wagon to some rich and successful athlete's star. Maybe I want to be a kept woman who enjoys the perks of someone else's success. How do you know that isn't my deepest desire, Cole?" Her look is stern. And earnest. I'm not sure if she's seeking an honest answer to this line of questioning, but I'm about to give her one.

"Well, I've got several points that validate my conclusion."

"You sound like you are working on a research paper."

"Would you like me to submit it in written form using proper APA format? I can do that, Leigh. I would do that for you." I give her my most sincere tone. I mean it. I'm not used to people not liking me, and her cold shoulder drives me crazy. The corner of her mouth turns up just a bit. I'm cracking her stone wall. "I was thinking, well, no, I was hoping, I, um, I could take you to dinner tonight. But if you'd rather me write the best fucking paper I've ever written, I'll stay up all night working on it. It's the first step of my apology plan."

She gives me a confused look. Maybe amused. Not pissed. Well, not totally.

"And why would I want to go to dinner with you, Davidson? Why should I put myself at risk for additional insults and judgments?" Calling me by my last name. That's a distance thing, but when she does it, it kind of melts my heart.

I clasp my hands and hold them to my chest. "Ouch. You wound me. Although deserved. How about I give you the high points of my thesis?"

"Like you have enough data to form a thesis?" She gives a small scoff and shakes her head.

"Hey, Leigh," Josh yells. "We are going to call it a day. We're all headed to The Thirsty Turtle for drinks if you want to join us. It's open mic night. Always a good time. Do you want me to wait for you?" I want to knock that hopeful look off Josh's face, but probably not the best move right now.

Leigh looks over at the group. Everyone is focused on her. They all want to be around her. Everyone is drawn to her. She's magnetic. Well, except for Jane. Jane's previously friendly look has a shade of green. Jealousy is not a good look on anyone, especially Jane. No need to consult Matt now. She's a one-hundred percent cleat chaser and quite probably a mean girl.

Leigh looks at me. My dinner offer is hanging out there, and now this group offer. She looks like she's debating over her answer. I desperately want to spend time with her, so I help her out.

"Hey, Josh," I respond. "We'll meet you there."

Now the glare is back and directed right at me. "Now you respond for me?" She starts to stand up.

I gently put my hand on her thigh, trying to ask her to stay with me. Her body stills, and I realize what I did and where I'm touching. I pull my hand away like I touched a hot stove.

"Sorry. Really." Her look softens, but not much. "I want to spend time with you. If it's in a group setting, maybe that's better for you. I didn't mean to speak for you. I just really, really want to be friends. And friends don't let…"

"Let them what?" She gives me a smirk. I'll take that smirk. She's toying with me.

"Deal with mean girls by themselves?" I go with that? What? Where did that come from? I swear, this girl is messing me up.

She gives me an amused look. Okay, I'll take that. It's promising.

"Am I the Regina George here?"

"What, no, no way. You are totally Cady Herron. Jane is Regina. Or am I misinterpreting that?"

She leans in a little, even though no one is around. I can smell her perfume, and it's fresh, like lemons or citrus. I want her to stay close to me, just like this.

"You might be right," she says conspiratorially. "I don't think she likes me much."

"I knew it!" I slap my knee. "Let me take a quick shower, and I'll take you. I didn't like the look Jane was giving you. It's the quiet ones you have to watch. I'm playing tomorrow, so no drinking for me, so I'll be your DD. How's that sound?"

She hesitates and thinks about it, biting her bottom lip in contemplation. "Want me to invite Matt and some of the other guys? Safety in numbers?" I hate that idea. But whatever it takes to get her to say yes.

"Sure. That would be fun. Now go shower. You, um, smell like a baseball player."

"Like strong man, cut grass, and summer?" I wink at her and give her my most charming smile.

She laughs, and I swear, my chest constricts. I've earned my first laugh from her, and I feel invincible.

"No, like sweat, dirty socks, and agony. Go shower, Davidson."

"Yes, ma'am. I'll meet you in ten."

I take off for the locker room, shooting a quick text to Matt asking him to meet me at the Turtle. Operation Charm Leigh is in full gear.

CHAPTER
TWELVE

ASHLEIGH

———

Cole Davidson drives me crazy. He's cute and cocky. But something makes me want to hear his thesis on why I'm not a jersey chaser when he practically accused me of that last week. What changed his mind? I have such a push-pull with Cole. I think there is more to him than the cocky baseball player. Around me, he's a walking contradiction. He's bold but sometimes vulnerable. Funny but serious. Protective, but trying to tamp that down.

While I wait for him, I shoot a text to Jules.

> How do guys identify jersey chasers?

JULES
> Trying to go incognito?

> Haha. Just trying to figure out the signs.

JULES
> They have a smell.

> Like a pheromone?

JULES

Like desperation.

Guys don't want to be the hunted. Are you deciding to give it a try? Don't tell me you want me to call Chance. 😕

> Would you? 🙏

JULES

Never.

> That's OK. I've got his number. I can call him myself.

FACETIME REQUEST FROM JULES

I'm laughing as I answer. "I thought that might get you."

"Why do you have Chance's number?"

"I don't know." I shrug and give him a smirk. "We text sometimes."

"You DO. NOT." Jules is distraught.

"We do, actually. It's usually after a particularly popular Insta post or something. He seems to notice when I don't like his posts, and he wants to know why."

"He pays attention to your likes?" Jules is getting red in the face.

"Calm down. There's nothing going on. I'm his best friend's kid sister. I don't even think he knows I have boobs or anything."

"Trust me, Ash, anyone who has ever seen you knows you have boobs."

"And on that note, I gotta bounce. Hitting The Thirsty Turtle for drinks with the gang."

"Bye. Love you!"

"Love you too!"

Cole walks up just as I hang up.

"Boyfriend?" he asks.

Haven't we gone down this road already?

"Brother."

"That's right. No boyfriend. Just brothers."

"I never said no boyfriend. You seem to always catch me talking to my brothers." Both of them.

"Oh. So…..boyfriend?"

I decide not to answer. Let's keep that option open.

"So, Mr. Knight in Shining Armor, let's get going."

We walk to the parking lot, and he leads me to a red Jeep with the doors and top off. For some reason, it fits Cole. He's adventurous. Casual. Hard-working. Fun. Unpredictable.

"Knight in Shining Armor?" He quirks one eyebrow at me. "And how did I get that moniker?"

"You always seem to want to rescue me. As I've stated previously, I don't need rescuing, Mr. Knight."

"Yes, you've made that perfectly clear. And for the record, I've never seen you as someone who needs rescuing. But my upbringing by a single mother, a VERY STRONG single mother, I might add, taught me to respect women and be a gentleman. I don't mean to rescue. I mean to support. Do you believe that?"

Wow. That is like a punch in the gut. No jokes. No cool guy. Just sincere words. He's telling me he's one of the good guys. Can that be true? Can his protective streak be like my brothers'? But I don't need another protector in my life. I have more than enough. This got deep fast.

"I do. So just you, your mom, and your sister?"

"Yep. Both are very independent, strong women. But it doesn't mean I can't be helpful to them. And yes, they may see it as protective at times. Especially Darcy. But I look out for my people. I do the same for Matt. I have his back. And he has mine. If loyalty is a crime, I'm guilty."

"I guess that's, um, noble. My family can be a little smothering."

"I can see how you could feel that way. Darcy tells me that, too, especially when some guy comes sniffing around. But I know how guys can be. I just don't want her to get hurt."

"But isn't getting hurt part of the process? So she'll know what to look for the next time?"

He shrugs. "I suppose." He's quiet for a minute.

We both buckle up, and he starts the car. "So, boyfriend?"

I just smile. Nope, not going to respond.

"Tell me one point of your thesis. How do you know I'm not a cleat chaser? How do you know I don't have a vision board on how to capture an athlete with my feminine wiles?"

He glances over at me and slowly nods his head.

"Okay. So I'm not saying you don't have a vision board. That's the kind of thing focused girls do. And you are definitely focused and driven. But I think your vision board isn't about sinking your teeth into a jersey. And I'm not saying you don't have feminine wiles because, um, have you seen how all the guys react to you?" His eyes travel from the top of my head to my toes. My cheeks blush. He clears his throat and focuses his attention back on the road.

He continues his thesis. "But here's what I do know. I think you support people you care about. Like I do. I think you celebrate their wins and want them to be successful. But I don't think you share in their accomplishment, even if you had something to do with it." He pauses and seems to think about what he wants to say next. It's cute. Cole Davidson is cute.

He stops to let pedestrians cross. He looks at me. I see my reflection in his sunglasses, and I look like I'm interested in what he's saying. I can't believe how desperately I want to hear his thoughts. He clears his throat and continues. "I think you need your own accomplishment. I think you have dreams and want to make them happen. On your own terms." The car behind us honks, and Cole looks away and starts driving again.

What the fuck? Where did this come from? How does he know that's exactly what I want? Cole Davidson piques my interest. It wasn't an out-of-the-park homer response, but a solid double.

I give him a slow clap. He looks my way and smiles. His smile lights up his face, and he looks happy.

"What?" he asks. "You have a vision board?"

I laugh. "Several," I respond. I really don't. But he doesn't need to know that. Maybe I should make one? "But I tend to consult my Magic 8 Ball for guidance. It seems to be most reliable, don't you think?"

He laughs. "What did the Magic 8 Ball say when you asked about me?"

"Reply hazy. Ask again."

"So that means you asked about me. I'll take that." He got me there. His quick wit is another attractive quality.

I roll my eyes hard at him. "I swear, you drive me crazy."

"Crazy in a good way?" He looks at me and wiggles his eyebrows.

"My Magic 8 Ball would say definitely not. So tell me something about Cole Davidson not everyone knows."

"Oh, so now we're friends and telling secrets? Are we going to braid each other's hair next?"

"I was thinking pedicures, but sure." I like the fun and easy back and forth, so I let my guard down. "Tell me something, Cole. You're up to bat. Two outs. Bases loaded. Full count. What are you going to do? Take the swing or let the pitch go?"

He seems to think longer than I thought he would. "Swing," he says. "Always swing." He pulls up to the front of the Turtle. Chatter, laughter, and music drift into the parking lot from the patio. He turns the car off and turns to look at me. "So, something not everyone knows. Well, I'm a pretty open book. Not a big secret keeper. And Matt knows just about everything. So it's a difficult ask. But here's a confession."

A confession. Holy shit. I'm not sure I like where this is heading. And it's all my damn fault. I was flirting, or at least attempting to flirt. I'm so bad at it. And then he took it to a serious place. Cole Davidson, you are twisting me all up inside.

"I cyber-stalked you," he says.

"What?" That catches me off guard. Oh shit. What did he find? Is that why he's changed with me? Does he know who I am?

"Yeah, and for a social media guru, you are pretty private. And you haven't accepted my friend requests. What gives?'

I saw his requests to follow. I went private for the summer and set up new accounts under Leigh Rutledge. Leigh posts a lot of nature pics and retweets a lot of baseball accounts. I had to make sure my real accounts are private so no one could deep dive and see the numerous pictures of my family and friends.

Cole nudges me on the shoulder. "You aren't in the witness protection program or anything, are you?"

I know he's joking, but he doesn't realize how close to the truth he is.

"Um, no, not exactly," I hedge.

He cocks his head to the side, looking like a confused puppy. He gives me a little nod, encouraging me to continue my thought.

I go with a version of the truth. "Well, I decided to go private and shut them all down for the summer. This is a once-in-a-life-time opportunity for me. And a little time for reinvention, you know? So I didn't want my past to dictate my future. Does that sound crazy?"

"Not crazy, but it makes me want to ask a million questions."

"Fair enough. But you promised me a drink, so it's time. Let's go."

We find our group out on the patio. Josh waves as we walk in and motions us over. He greets Cole with a fist bump and me with a half hug. Jane hops up and hugs Cole and ignores me. Oh, okay. Definitely Regina George. Matt, Brady, and Drew are here, too and greet us warmly. I get a full-on hug from Matt, and he, in turn, gets an icy glare from Cole. It makes me laugh. Matt and I already know we're just friends. But evidently, Cole hasn't gotten that message. Let's keep him on his toes, shall we?

A rousing game of *Would You Rather* starts, and we all have a good time. The players aren't drinking, but it doesn't keep them from laughing and playing right along.

I must have missed Cole leaving the table. I look around for him and hear his voice from the sound system. I look to the small stage in the corner and find him standing in front of a microphone holding a guitar.

"Glad everyone is having a good time this evening," he says.

I look at Matt, and he leans back in his chair with a massive grin. "This should be fun," he says to himself.

"What is he doing?" I ask Matt.

Matt gives a knowing shrug.

"I heard tonight was open mic night. I'm not ready to play anything original right now, but I thought I'd play a little song for you guys tonight. Feel free to sing along." He gives the crowd a wink, and our group gets loud.

Then he plays the guitar and sings, giving Charlie Puth a run for his money with his version of "One Call Away." It is a total panty melter. Women are literally clutching their hearts as he sings. He is a natural on stage.

Of course, I'm not surprised about his stage presence. But his voice? Wow. I could listen to him sing all day. His tone is pure and deep. He has a singer-songwriter vibe, but I bet he could belt a country song too. Damn, that's hot. And what's really hot? I swear, he doesn't break eye contact with me. At all. He's totally singing it to me. When he gets to the line about wanting to see you smile, he breaks out a grin that I know is only meant for me.

Matt leans a little closer and whispers in my ear. "I think my boy has it bad. You gonna break his heart?"

Cole finishes his song to loud applause and cheers from the audience shouting encore and one more song. I'm captivated by Cole's talent and stunned by Matt's comment.

"What?" I turn to look at Matt. "He does this all the time, right?"

"Nope," he says. "He plays in his room, sometimes after a few beers around the fire, but in front of a group like this? Never seen it." Matt has this grin that looks like the cat that ate the canary. This revelation catches me off guard. I can't take my eyes off Cole on stage. He's looking at me like he's waiting on my response or permission before moving.

I give him a big smile and a "one more song" shout, and he seems to exhale. I swear, this guy. My heart skips a beat at the smile he sends my way.

"Okay, okay, settle down," he says into the microphone. "One more song. This one requires some audience participation, so please sing along. And I need my boys to complete the band." Brady and Drew high-five, and Matt gets up reluctantly. As they head up to the stage, the bachelorette party in the back encourages them to take it off. Brady whips his shirt off without a second thought. I laugh until I snort. Jane glares at me. Whatever.

Cole strums the guitar with one simple chord and breaks out with "Oh! Darling" by the Beatles. Again, he's singing to me like I'm the only girl in the room. But this time, he moves around a little and even leaves the stage when people start singing along. The next thing I know, he's at our table, being overly dramatic and overly loud on the line about never doing harm. Brady, Drew, and Matt are great backup singers. It's the Pajama Beatles, and it's hysterical. The entire audience is eating this up. I realize I need to get this on film. It's a perfect TikTok. I pull out my phone and leave my chair to film the fab four and the crowd's reaction. Maybe this show can be their off-season gig?

He's making me ask myself some serious questions. Who the hell is Cole Davidson, and what am I going to do to keep his dream safe?

———

The Pajamas' schedule is busy, but they give the guys time off each week. They don't take the entire team on away games, and with the rotations, they get a day off to relax.

For some reason, Cole has decided to spend his day off in the intern bullpen with me while I edit film from last night's game for a YouTube highlight reel. He's sitting in my cubicle with his feet on my desk, juggling baseballs, playing with my camera equipment, and peppering me with questions. "Of all the things to do in Savannah, this is how you chose to spend your time?"

"Yep. I figured I better learn the business behind baseball in case I don't get the call. Thanks for teaching me." He gives me a wink, resulting in one of my award-winning eye rolls.

I'm not sure about my teaching him. He's asked a million questions but more about my taste in music and movies than marketing.

"Cole, would you like to learn from me?" Jane asks from across the room.

Cole takes his feet off my desk and slides closer to me, practically putting his head on my shoulder. His breath tickles my ear, sending shivers down my spine. I still, my fingers perched above the keyboard. I'm frozen in place.

He's pretending to be interested in something on my screen. "Jane, I'm not sure what you could teach me."

"Soooo many things, Cole," she purrs.

He removes his NC State ball cap, runs his hand through his hair, and puts his hat on backward. I've watched him do this numerous times. It's his tell when he's nervous.

That's just one of the things I've learned about Cole this summer. He's talented in both baseball and music. He's kind. And sweet. And a little overbearing. A good friend and teammate. He makes people laugh. And when he's nervous, he takes his hat off, runs his fingers through his hair, and puts it back on backward.

I mean, Jane is gorgeous. She has that perfect body guys seem to like. Big boobs, tiny waist. Her hair always has those perfect waves. Frankly, I have no idea how she does it in this heat and humidity. Honestly, that's what I wish she would teach me. Jealousy sweeps through me. Any guy would want her, yet most players stay away from her.

Then there's me. Here I am with my dark blonde, straight hair in two loose braids to keep cool. I don't have any makeup on except sunscreen and mascara, and I'm wearing a baggy Pajamas tank and a modest skort. We work in an old building in Savannah. It's hotter than a hooker in church.

Then there's the other thing. My body isn't voluptuous. I'm more like Sporty Spice to Jane's Posh Spice. My five-eight frame is trim, and I stay in shape, but I'm low on the put-together and sexy scale compared to Jane.

Cole exhales loudly. "Sorry, Jane, but I think Leigh here needs my help. She may never get it done if I don't rescue her from this project."

Cole's words trigger me. Help? Rescue? Please.

"No, really, Mr. Knight, I've got this. I don't need to use my phone-a-friend lifeline. Go help Jane. I'm sure she has something you could do so she doesn't mess up her manicure."

He whispers, "I like it when you get feisty."

Jane is beside my desk before I can react. She reaches for Cole's hand and pulls at him.

"Come on, Cole, help me with something in the team store." She bats her eyes at him. Who really does that?

"Yeah, Cole, go help her," I say. I'm flustered and need a moment, not caring if I'm sending him to the lion's den.

He tilts his head like a puppy trying to figure something out. It's endearing, and for a moment, I feel sorry for him. But Jane has her claws in him now, and I'm feeding a mean streak I didn't know I possessed. This is a summer of self-discovery, after all. I learn something new about myself every day.

"Oh, go and practice defense. It'll be good for you." His eyes plead with me for help. "Don't be a baby. Go help her out, and

I'll be done when you get back. Then we can go hit River Street or something."

"Seriously?" He smiles ear to ear. When his face lights up, he is irresistible. He turns around and grabs Jane's hand, dragging her away. "Come on, Jane, let's make quick work of this!"

I can't believe I offered to hang out with Cole solo. What was I thinking? I don't have much experience dating. For the first time, I think a guy might like me for me. He doesn't know about my family, which can be a blessing and a curse. Because what happens when he does find out? But still, I wanted this summer to be about having relationships with people because of me, not who I am or my connections.

Hanging one-on-one with Cole is a new experience, and I admit I'm nervous and anxious.

I give myself a pep talk. I can do this. I'm fun. I'm witty. I can hold an intellectual conversation. At school, everyone wants to know if I know Tripp Stevenson, one of the best pitchers in the MLB. Of course I know Tripp. We drew names last Christmas, and he was my Secret Santa. He got me the most fantastic pair of comfy socks I've ever had — with pictures of him and his cat on them. It was hilarious. One of a kind, apparently.

As a direct result of my testosterone-filled contact list, I gave up on dating. I even changed schools during my freshman year. I thought being at a large co-ed school would make it easier to be anonymous, but I was wrong. It just made me more popular. All the girls wanted me to rush their sorority, and half the baseball team managed to sit near me in our big auditorium, freshman English class. I became a bitter hermit. I didn't want to go to parties or hang out at the union. I didn't trust anyone, and I became depressed.

When I transferred to Meredith College, a small, all-female school, I thought it would be easier to make friends. No baseball team. No guys at all. Unfortunately, it just made for different problems.

While the transfer eliminated the potential bad dates, it

didn't stop the girls all wanting to hitch their wagon to one of my connections. Before I knew it, I had more friends than I could handle. Then they would ask to meet players or other athletes I knew, and I realized they weren't my friends. I had no idea how many cleat chasers there were at an all-girls school, but it was eye-opening. Shocking, really. Do they not realize most players are on the road, many are too busy to invest in a relationship, and most are players on and off the field? I love my brother's friends, but I'd never want to date them.

This is why Emma is my ride-or-die. We were assigned as roommates when I transferred mid-year at Meredith, and she wasn't even mad to lose her private room. She loves me for me. She doesn't fangirl over my brothers or their friends. I practically have to drag her to games or events.

I make the final edits and upload the video across multiple social media accounts. I notice Emma commented on the latest Twitter post a few minutes ago, so I pull out my phone and call her. She must have Wi-Fi today.

She answers almost immediately.

"Hola, chica! Como estas?"

"Hey, Em! I miss you! How are you?"

"I'm good. Exhausted but good. How about you? How's PajamaLand?"

"Oh, it's good. I'm enjoying the work. And everyone is great." I hear Jane giggle from down the hall. I wonder what Cole said to get that reaction from her. "Well, almost everyone is great."

"Oh no. What's wrong? Project Undercover Boss isn't foiled, is it?"

"No, not that I know of. I feel a little guilty for the lie, but it's the right thing." I hesitate for a second.

"Ash?"

"No, I'm good, really. I'm thinking about giving trouble a try."

Emma catches on quickly. She lets out an ear-piercing squeal.

"I'm so excited. You should. Go for it. Now which one is it? I'll need to rewatch your videos to check him out. Tell me it's the adorable third baseman. Ohhhhh, or that hottie on first?"

I suck in a deep breath. I close my eyes and confess. In a whisper, I say, "First. And he goes to State." I know my entire body tenses up waiting for her response.

"So he's in Raleigh?" I can visualize her jumping up and down. Emma is a tiny ball of energy. "Girl, I say follow your heart. You may not have this chance again. I'm so excited I can't stand it!"

"But what if…"

She doesn't let me finish my question. "No! No what-ifs. Just enjoy the summer, Ash. Kiss the boy. Maybe more. Hell, just enjoy it. Xander has backed off, right?"

"Yeah, I haven't seen him in a few weeks. He's been remarkably quiet." Honestly, I'm a little unnerved. Maybe Jules got him to back off?

"Don't question the gift. Enjoy it. Do you have a game to work tonight?"

"No, it's an away game. I told Cole we could go to River Street tonight. It'll be our first one on one."

"Ohhh, just like on *The Bachelor*. Or more like *The Bachelorette*, because you have all the power. Don't forget that. You get to decide if he gets a rose at the end of the night. Just go and have fun. And text me all about it tonight, k?"

Talking to Emma makes me feel better. All the second-guessing I've been doing is gone. She's right. There's no harm in getting to know someone.

"I will. I miss you so much."

"I miss you too. We'll be back at school before we know it and start our senior year. It's the big one."

It is. I know Dad and Xander want me to work for the Reapers after graduation, but I'm not sure I want to work for the family business. After getting a taste of working in an environment where no one knows my family, I feel more fulfilled and am doing some of my best work. The added pressure to maintain the facade of the owner's perfect daughter expectation is heavy. Trevor even mentioned last week that I seem more relaxed and content here. When he said it, I realized I feel authentically happy.

"Yeah, I can't wait to see you again. You've only got another three weeks there, right? Or are you going to do the extension? I have four more here. Why don't you come here that last week before heading back to school? I'll even give you your room back."

"I'll let you know. Being here is amazing, but I do miss Mom's cooking. And a good washer and dryer."

"I never thought laundry would be your breaking point!" I'm laughing out loud when Trevor walks into the bullpen. "Hey, Em, I gotta run. T just walked up." Trevor takes my phone from my hand before I can hear her response.

"Hey, love," Trevor says to Emma. He nods his head and smiles at me. I have no idea what she's saying to him, but he is smiling like the cat that ate the canary.

"Yeah, yeah. Got it." He's laughing at whatever she said. His tone changes. "Hey, listen, you take care of yourself. Stay safe, love." He looks at me. I'm wondering what's up with this tone. He adds as an afterthought, "Our girl is going to need you."

He disconnects the call and lays my phone down.

"What the hell, T?!" He didn't even let me say goodbye. All of my brother's friends know Emma because, for the past three years, she's been my sidekick. We are together all the time, so of course, Trevor has spent time with her. But this conversation sounded like they knew each other better than I thought.

He gives me a shrug and starts to walk back toward his office.

"Oh no you don't!" He doesn't get to walk away from me. "What was that about?"

He stops at Jane's desk, looks at the pink sparkle desk accessories, and scrunches up his face. "Not sure what you mean," he says. He twirls a pen with some puff ball on top between his hands.

"What did you mean I'm going to need her?" Yeah, the conversation was weird and more friendly than I was expecting. But that parting comment was concerning.

He looks toward the hall where Jane's shrill voice pierces the quiet of the bullpen. "Didn't mean anything by it. Just that she's your BFF. Isn't that what you kids call it these days? I'm sure you'll have lots to catch up on after this summer." He gives me a wink, puts the pen down, uses the hand sanitizer from the wall, and leaves.

Ugh!

I hear shouting from the hall. "Leigh, quick, grab your stuff!" The footsteps are getting louder. Someone is running. Cole bursts in the doorway, headed straight toward me. "Come on, we gotta go," he shouts. He's grabbing at my hand. "Get your purse! We have to make a break for it."

I'm confused by his urgent request. He looks a little more disheveled than when he left, but maybe that was from moving boxes or something. Then I see the lipstick on his face and burst out laughing.

He's pulling on my arm, and I'm not budging. He drops his hand and puts his hands on his hips, looking like a disappointed mom. I decide to humor him, so I grab my phone and purse and shove him in the shoulder.

"Come on, trouble, let's go." He links his elbow to mine and practically skips out of the bullpen.

"Oh, girl, you haven't seen trouble yet." I don't think I've seen lottery winners smile this much. Man, I hope I don't regret this.

We skip by Trevor's office, and I hear him say on the phone, "Yes, I promise she's fine." I'm willing to bet that's his daily check-in with my brother. Well, maybe I'll give him something to report next time.

CHAPTER
THIRTEEN

COLE

———

We get to the parking lot, where our cars are parked next to each other. I don't want us to drive separately. I need every minute with her I can get.

"Hey, wait here a minute. I have an idea." I hop in my Jeep and drive toward the entrance to the stadium. I park my Jeep in the field maintenance area where it can sit for the night, locked up tight. I run back to Leigh. She's leaning against her car, doing something on her phone.

She looks up and screws up her mouth, giving me a funny look. "I thought you might have changed your mind."

"Never, just getting our transportation taken care of. I figure we'll take your car, and I'll get my car in the morning."

She gives an uncertain laugh. "Oh, in the morning, is it? That's pretty presumptuous, Davidson."

"Well, yeah. I want you to be in charge. If you want to leave me, you can. And if you drink, I can drive you home. Seemed like the best choice."

"That's awfully thoughtful of you. Come on, get in."

She unlocks her car, and I open the door for her before going to the passenger side. I fold myself into her tiny car.

"Is this a yoga pose? I only ask because my knees are bent at a strange angle." Of course, I'll subject myself to any form of torture to be next to her.

She looks over at me and laughs so hard she cries.

"Are you done laughing, sweetheart? Because I know other positions too."

My innuendo seems to stop her laugh. That wasn't the effect I was going for. I love her laugh, and if it's at my expense, it's a price worth paying.

"Move your seat back, trouble. I'll drop the top to give your big head more room." Once I'm situated, this tiny car is larger and more comfortable than I thought.

She looks at me from head to toe, a slow smile forming on her face.

"Like what you see?"

She puts the car in gear, and we take off toward downtown. The stereo blasts some song with lyrics repeating *everything about you*. It's a One Direction song, I think. I'm no boy band expert, but I file that information away. She said her roommate loved boy bands, but I think she meant to say she likes them too.

"Meh. Just not sure that shade of lipstick is right for you."

What? Lipstick? Oh damn! I forgot about that. I pull the visor down, hoping this toy car has a mirror, and see the remnants of the horror show on my face.

We pull up to an intersection, and she pulls a wet wipe from her purse and hands it to me.

"Thanks." I start to clean my face. She cuts her eyes my way but focuses on driving. "Is that like a Mary Poppins bag?" Girls never surprise me with stuff they can pull out of their purse.

"Maybe." She shrugs again. Her air of indifference isn't fooling me. I know she's dying to know about the lipstick, but she won't ask.

"So, what shade would you recommend?"

"What?" She looks at me, confused. I've caught her off guard.

"Shade of lipstick? Would your shade go better with my coloring?" I give her a wink and a grin.

Her cheeks turn pink. It's cute. I like making her blush. Still no response. The need to push her becomes compulsive. "I mean, I prefer something with a little flavor too."

"So you're a bubble gum lip gloss guy? What are you, twelve?" Her side-eye game is huge. Getting a rise out of her is my favorite pastime.

"What can I say? I like what I like."

"I'll pass that information on to Jane." Oh, she likes kicking me in the balls too. Game on, sweetheart.

"I'm sure it's in her basket of mean girl props. But do you hate me that much? I thought we were friends." I sure as hell hope we are friends. I'd like more, but I'll take what I can when it comes to this girl.

"Jane's the perfect girl. I thought you'd be flattered to be attacked by her." Her tone is flat, almost indifferent. But it's not indifferent. There is a hint of curiosity and maybe jealousy. The jealousy is probably my wishful thinking.

"Why would you think she's perfect?" She shoots me a look that says, get real. "No, seriously, I want to know. What about her says perfect to you?"

She rolls her eyes. I'll wait until I hear her answer because I want to know what she thinks is a perfect girl.

"Well, for starters, she's gorgeous. Her hair is a magnificent shade of auburn with luscious curls that I couldn't keep if I sold my soul to the devil. She has huge boobs that guys seem to like. Her makeup is flawless. And her flirting game is on point."

"And you think that's a perfect girl?"

"You don't?"

"Nope. Not even close. You want to know what I see when I look at Jane and girls like her?" I get a half-shoulder shrug. I guess that's an affirmative, so I continue.

"It's all fake. She's a predator. You know, like in nature. Scary creatures make themselves attractive on the outside because once you are within striking distance, they kill you. I bet that hair was made in a salon. And those boobs? Not every guy is about that. It's all trappings. She needs the makeup. It can't hide her ugly personality. And she, my friend, is not pretty on the inside."

She lets out a gasp and looks at me like I'm lying.

Leigh pulls into a parking space on the street and puts the car in park. I reach over and tug on one of her braids. She turns her head toward me and looks down. I put my finger under her chin so she looks up at me.

"Let me tell you what a perfect girl looks like. She's kind. And has a killer smile. And she's so beautiful and confident she doesn't need makeup. Her hair is adorable in a messy top knot, braids, or down around her face. Perfect girls give off a vibe so intoxicating that everyone clamors for their attention. Guys will do anything to just spend time with them. And they don't need to throw themselves at guys because guys are waiting for their attention. That, Leigh, is what a perfect girl looks like."

The corners of her lips turn up. The pink returns to her cheeks. I think her blush is my new favorite color. I start to lean over and kiss her, but a big raindrop lands on her nose, breaking the moment.

"Oh no!" She reaches up to press the button to raise the top before the sky opens up. Big raindrops splat against the windshield. "We'll have to make a run for it!"

It takes me a minute to unfold myself from her car and run until we reach her destination, Spanky's. I purposely let her pick where we went because I want her to have control. I get the idea from what she said that she doesn't always feel in control of her life. Maybe those overprotective brothers are too overbearing? I make a mental note to chat with Darcy to make sure she doesn't think that about me.

"Is this okay?" she asks before I head inside.

"It's great. Like I said, a guy will go anywhere and do anything just to spend time with the perfect girl."

"I'm far from perfect," she mumbles.

"Sweetheart, I'm never gonna lie to you. Ya hear me?" I reach out and take her hand. "Never." I put our hands over my heart. "If I think you are wrong, I'll tell you, just like now. And if I think you are wearing the wrong shade of lipstick, I'll tell you. I'll always be honest with you."

She bites her bottom lip and gives me an indecisive look. She is not buying it, but that's okay. It's a promise to her that I intend to keep, whether she believes me or not.

"Come on," I say. "Let's get some chicken fingers and drinks. After dinner, we're going ghost hunting."

She knocks her shoulder into me, silently setting the boundaries for us. I hear her without her having to say anything. Friends. And for the perfect girl? That's good enough for now.

CHAPTER
FOURTEEN

ASHLEIGH

———

Cole is sincere when he says he'll always be honest with me. I believe him, and unfortunately, that's not something I can reciprocate. I think about telling him my truth, but I can't. I'm falling for this guy and can't be honest about who I am. I'll tell him when I know for sure it won't matter. Yeah, I'll tell him. Eventually.

We grab a table upstairs on the deck under the awning. The rain lets up, and I can see a blue sky in the distance. That's the magic of coastal weather. Storms roll in fast but leave just as quickly.

My insides are in a twist. Cole's declaration is a lot to digest. I'm unsure if my lack of dating experience, insecurities, or wishful thinking is winning the battle for my sanity. He thinks I'm the perfect girl. Ha. Far from it.

The waitress brings water to the table.

"What can I get you two?"

I watch her eye fuck Cole, and I feel this surge of jealousy. I don't like her. What is this strong reaction I'm having? I'm baffled by my feelings and honestly a little confused. I react, and on impulse, I grab his hand. He looks up and gives me a mischievous grin. He's undoubtedly entertained. He kisses my hand, and my heart skips a beat.

"What's your poison, sweetheart?" He looks at me like he's daring me to let loose.

"I'll take a top-shelf margarita, an extra shot of Patron on the side, and an order of chicken fingers. What about you, trouble?"

"I'll have a blonde IPA and chicken fingers. Thanks." He never looks at the waitress as he gives his order. He's made it clear he's not looking elsewhere. At least for now.

She walks away, and I pull my hand away. He captures it and holds it on the table.

"So, tequila, huh? Color me surprised."

"Why does that surprise you? You said you would drive, I've had a day, and you've threatened me with ghosts. It just feels right." It actually doesn't feel right. I need to keep my wits about me, but I want a little liquid courage, too.

The waitress brings our drinks, and I unceremoniously take a shot. The tequila is warm and smooth as it slides down my throat, immediately warming my belly. I take a big sip of my margarita to wash it down.

Cole's eyes go wide at my shot form. Hell, I drink with guys twice my size, and I've learned from the best. I've also only gotten drunk with those same guys. Guys I knew would keep me safe. I think I'm mostly confused by how I still feel safe with him in a short period of time and without the normal Decker vetting process. Safe but with a side of caution. I don't think I can keep his name in the friend zone. And I'm not sure I want to.

I watch his Adam's Apple bob as he drinks his beer. Why are men's throats so sexy? Damn. I'll need to check myself, or I'll make a fool of myself before the night ends.

"So tell me about yourself, Cole Davidson. Tell me about your family. One sister, right?"

Cole takes another drink of his beer. "Um, yeah. Darcy. She'll be a junior at the College of Charleston this year, majoring in interior design. She can decorate on a dime and rearrange stuff in the most interesting way."

"That's awesome. My decorating involves an abundance of throw pillows and fuzzy blankets. I could use her talents." I admire the way he lights up talking about her. He's proud of her, reminding me of my brothers' affection for me. I love that he's close with his sister. Another check in the yes column.

"I think she's super talented and has an eye for putting things together. She just has this amazing sense of style. Honestly, as long as she's happy, I don't care. I want her to have a career and life that allows her to shine. I'm her biggest fan. She checks all the boxes of what a perfect girl should be too. That's why I have to be the enforcer sometimes. She's too good for most guys."

At the mention of enforcer, I cringe. Is that how Xander and Jules see me? I guess there is another perspective to consider. But from where I sit, it's still suffocating.

"What exactly does being an enforcer entail?"

"Well, I'd like to think I'm not overbearing. I just want to make sure she's not taken advantage of. These perfect girls? They are kind. And trusting. Too trusting at times. I remind her that not everyone is as awesome as her big brother." He laughs at himself.

"Maybe she's smart enough to identify guys that aren't as awesome as her big brother on her own?" I'm not sure if we are talking about Darcy or me now.

"Oh, she's definitely smart. Smarter than her dumb jock brother, that's for sure. But guys can be tricky. It helps to have an inside track."

"I thought earlier you said the girls were the predators?" I challenge him with his own words. Bam! Maybe I should be a lawyer.

"Oh, there are predators in both camps. Remember, I said she was kind and trusting. I need her to trust less, that's all."

"Do you think that's the same advice my brothers would give me?" I muse to myself.

"I'm sure they just want to keep you from being hurt. Darcy's tears are my kryptonite. It's easier for me to prevent them. When she cries, it kills me." He finishes his beer and starts on his water. Our food arrives, and I order another margarita. We eat and continue our conversation.

"So why an all-girls college?"

The reason is dangerously close to my revealing my secret. During my first year in college at Wake Forest, I went on lots of first dates. If we could get to dessert without him asking for box seats to a Reapers game or asking me if I knew Tripp Stevenson, I considered it a successful date. It didn't mean I'd want a second one, though.

It's really sad if you think about it. Here I am, with a world of opportunities at my feet, and my social life consists of a deep and meaningful relationship with Netflix.

Even at Meredith, things didn't get much better. When Xander or Jules visit me, the gossip spreads like wildfire. It's like a sophisticated game of telephone, tracking us down at dinner or hanging out somewhere. Hey girls, they are ten years too old for you and way out of your league. Move on.

I dodge the question with a half-truth.

"I went to Wake Forest at first. It just wasn't a good fit. Too many, um, distractions. And Meredith has a great marketing and communications program. So I transferred after a semester."

"I bet you have lots of Janes at an all-girls school."

"Oh, there are plenty of Janes in the world, no matter where you go. So tell me, trouble, do you have a line of girls outside the stadium waiting for you after the games?"

I've finished my second margarita, and after that extra shot, my defenses are down. I'm feeling bold. Is Cole a ladies man? A player on and off the field?

"I don't really date."

"Oh." I guess that means he's more of a one-night stand guy. My heart sinks. I'm not wired that way. I want a relationship and feelings before things get physical.

"Yeah, not a lot of time for relationships when you play ball. That's always been my number one priority. Sure, girls are interested in an Instagram boyfriend, but I don't have a tolerance for the bullshit. So I'm usually running solo at the parties."

"I'm just surprised you don't have Janes lining up outside your door."

"Cleat chasers are always a thing. I won't allow them to be my Achilles heel, so it's best to avoid them. I dated a girl my freshman year, and she was a nightmare. Since then, I've gained a reputation as a monk." He's finished his food and steals one of my fries, popping it in his mouth.

"I thought you were going to be honest. A monk? Really?"

"Ask Matt. Girls don't even bother to try with us anymore."

"Matt too? Awwww, I'll keep my eyes open for a perfect girl for him." I love Matt. He's practically Captain America. When he settles down, that girl will be so lucky.

"What about me?"

"What about you?"

"You aren't going to play matchmaker for me?" He gives me one of his full smiles. His green eyes twinkle with a challenge. He runs his fingers through his curls and flips his ball cap backward. Oh, Cole, are you nervous?

"I don't need to play matchmaker for you, Davidson. You've already got your hands full with Jane." I laugh at the incredulous look on his face. He gives a half-hearted chuckle.

"Sweetheart, you've got to get that out of your head. I don't have time to waste on cleat chasers like her. She's nothing but a distraction."

"A distraction from what?" I barely whisper this thought. I'm the biggest distraction Cole could ever encounter. I can be the destroyer of his future, and my head says I need to pump the brakes. My heart, though?

"I want it all, Leigh." Cole takes my hand, sincerity wrapping around his words, his voice full of conviction. His eyes meet mine and speak deep into my soul. "I want a professional base-ball career. I want to take care of my family. I want the perfect girl to share my life with. I'm a greedy bastard because I want it all."

Wow. My heart swells thinking about Cole's future. I want that for him too. He's a good guy and deserves it all and then some.

"I want that for you, too," I say truthfully. "So let's skip the ghosts for tonight and get you home before curfew so you don't blow that future. The last thing I want is to be your downfall."

"You could never be my downfall." He takes my hand and helps me from my chair. His lips brush the back of my hand, a gentle kiss to my knuckles. I feel unsteady on my feet and I'm afraid it's not the tequila.

"Yeah, I wouldn't be so sure about that," I mumble.

CHAPTER
FIFTEEN

COLE

———

Playing for the Pajamas is always a pretty awesome summer. I play hard on the field and off. Coach Grant calls it flipping the switch. Focus on baseball. Scouts are watching, after all. It's why we are here. Then we flip the switch and perform for the crowd. We are allowed an out if we need it. Baseball always comes first. But most of us volunteer for performances, especially on our off-rotation games. It's scripted spontaneity. I love that we are allowed to make that call. We choose what's best for us and our game.

Tonight I'm on fire on the field. My bat is hot, I've kept everyone off my base, and we are entering the bottom of the sixth inning. I know several scouts are in the stands, but I'm not letting my nerves get the best of me. I know they are also looking at how we interact with the team. It's my time to shine.

It's been two weeks since our outing at The Turtle. Leigh and I have enjoyed a few lunches and our dinner at Spanky's. She even joined us for dinner at the Macs' house on Saturday. We've had a few moments of alone time, but we are usually around other people. She's become a solid part of our group.

I told her to be prepared for a surprise tonight. She's been busy behind her camera all evening, working her social media magic. I get her attention and give her a wink and a head nod. She smiles back and calls to her team on the walkie. It's time.

"George, Ringo, John, you ready?" I ask.

"Wait a minute," Brady shouts. "Does that mean you're Paul? Cause I thought I was Paul? I'm the cute one, after all."

Matt claps him on the back. "Keep telling yourself that, Brady. Maybe your fairy godmother will hear you and grant that wish." The entire dugout cracks up.

I grab the mics and my guitar while Drew gets the wigs. I nod to Chris to get ready with our big prop. I step into the first base coach's box, put my mic in a stand, and plop my Beatles wig over my hat. I look ridiculous, but that's part of the charm. I'm ready to perform.

The crowd goes wild, and phones start recording us from every direction. I'm sure they are expecting an encore performance of "Oh Darlin!" Leigh's TikTok went viral and became one of our most-liked videos this summer, with over a million views. While our *Bachelor* video did well, we don't need Alexander fucking Decker to go viral. Leigh knows what the people want, and it's the Pajamas.

Tonight, we have something different in store. On the down strum, I start with the first chords of "Yellow Submarine," and the place goes wild. The other three Beatles join in, singing loud and a little off-key. When we get to the chorus, the entire team comes out with a twelve-foot banner painted with a yellow submarine. It looks like a bunch of fourth graders made it, but I think that adds to the ridiculousness of the performance.

Trevor is on top of our dugout, doubled over laughing. I'm excited we pulled something off without his knowledge. I scan the stands until I find Leigh. She is laughing and enjoying the performance, making my heart swell knowing I made her smile.

As we come in for a big finale, I see Alexander fucking Decker walk up to Leigh and kiss her on her cheek. She stops watching us and gives him a big hug. I almost miss the last few notes of our song. What the fuck?

I'm stewing, trying to figure out what is going on between them. We haven't talked about him. He's a Pandora's box I don't want to open.

We finish the performance to a standing ovation. I try to flip the switch, but I can't. I strike out at my next two at-bats and almost bobble a catch at first, allowing a runner on my bag. Shit. Why do I care who she's into? Oh hell, who am I kidding? I want her to be mine. From the first time I saw her in the kayak, I knew. I've never had this reaction to a girl before, and it's fucking killing me. Now she's in my head and impacting my game.

"Got a problem, Davidson?" Coach Grant asks.

"No, sir." The last thing I want to do is admit I lost focus, especially over a girl. Coach will bench my ass in a heartbeat. We may be about fun, but baseball comes first.

"Seems you didn't flip the switch to me," he says casually as he leans against the dugout rail watching the game. I know it's anything but a casual comment.

"Consider the switch flipped," I respond. I just need to focus and get Leigh out of my mind. Easier said than done. I can't believe I'm letting a girl mess with my game. This is a first, and it needs to be my last. This tightness in my chest is an unfamiliar and unwelcome feeling.

Despite my poor showing at the end, we finish the game with a win and pretty impressive stats for the night. We've clinched our place in the playoffs as the summer draws to an end.

Everyone is meeting back at our house on Tybee for a bonfire. The team has the next day off, so I might even have a few beers tonight. I'm still pissed at myself and need a few minutes to work through everything to improve my mood. Matt catches a ride with Brady and Drew, leaving me alone in the locker room. I hear the door click and assume it's Kent, the equipment manager.

I look up from my chair to see Alexander Decker in the locker room. "If you want to get the call, Davidson, you have to stay consistent."

I glare at him. This is not the pep talk I need, and I most definitely don't want to see this bastard. He's quickly becoming the bane of my existence.

"Well aware," I mumble.

"Look, for her sake, I'm trying to be nice, but you make it difficult."

"What do you mean, 'for her sake'?" That statement rubs me wrong and raises my hackles. Why does he have to be nice to me for her?

"She asked me to give you a chance, and I'm trying. But here's the deal. I think you are a good ball player. Might even consider you a Reaper someday. But I need you to focus on baseball."

I arch an eyebrow at him. Consider me a Reaper? My childhood dream come true? The fact that this asshole controls that pisses me off.

"You don't think I'm focused on baseball?" I stand and take a step closer, putting us in a familiar stance, eye to eye.

He gives me a partial shrug. "I think a certain girl has you distracted. Stay away from her, and your future could be bright." His face is stone again. No expression.

"Afraid of a little competition?"

He laughs and puts his hand on my shoulder. I knock it off.

"Don't touch me, motherfucker."

He's still laughing. "Kid, I'm no competition for you. But I love that girl. I don't like how you look at her. And she's messing with your game. So trust me when I tell you, move on. It's in your best interest."

My heart stops. There is a lot to unpack in that statement. I step back and grab my keys and phone from my locker, hoping to put an end to this meeting.

"Thanks for the advice, Decker. But somehow, I don't think you have my best interest at heart."

I storm out of the locker room and head home to the party. Alexander fucking Decker has accomplished one thing tonight. Consider my switch flipped. Thanks, motherfucker.

———

I hear the party on the beach when I pull in, but I decide to go into the house for a minute before joining the team. Mrs. Mac greets me at the door.

"Hey, Cole," she says as she pulls me into her arms. She's a hugger, just like my mom. I didn't think I needed a hug, but now that I'm in it, I squeeze her tight.

"You okay, sweetie?" she asks.

I take a deep breath and shudder a little. "Yeah, just wasn't my best game."

"You looked pretty good from where I was sitting. You're a great ball player, Cole. Don't get rattled. You know the mental game can mess you up."

She's right. Even the greatest ball players get in their own heads and screw up. It's a mental game between the pitcher and the batter, communicating with body language and signals. Sometimes actual words are exchanged. That's always fun for me. But I've never had an off-field distraction. Not until now.

"I know you're right. I know what I need to do." I've decided. My mind made up. "You need anything before I head down to the beach?"

"Why don't you grab a few more bags of ice to throw around the keg? It's a warm night," she says.

"Yes, ma'am. I appreciate everything ya'll do for us. I'm grateful for you." I give her another quick hug before I head downstairs. I grab two bags of ice from the freezer and head to the dunes. I've got a party to attend.

———

It looks like the entire team and most of the front office staff are out here tonight. The music isn't too loud, and we try to be considerate of others, but most of the Macs' neighbors don't mind our bonfires. The fire is raging. Mrs. Mac has a food table with snacks and all the fixings. Several guys are roasting hot dogs and marshmallows. She takes such good care of us.

"There's my boy," Matt says, throwing his arm around my shoulders. From the smell of his breath, he's a few beers in at this point. Matt is a lightweight when it comes to drinking. He takes our training seriously year-round and doesn't drink often or much. So when he's a few in, he tends to get loose lips and loose hips. He's one beer short of being the most confident dancer in the place. While I'm all for watching drunk Matt dance, I've got a different objective for this party.

"Hey, don't hurt yourself dancing tonight," I laugh. "Remember last time you almost pulled your groin."

"Nah, I'm good, bro. You get out of your head yet?"

"Yeah, mostly. Had a little locker room visit from Decker. He helped me see things clearly."

Matt puts a hand on each shoulder, searching my face for something. He leans in and whispers, "You didn't hit him, did you, Cole? Cause that would be bad."

"No punches thrown." Not that I didn't want to. "Scouts honor."

"That's good. Real good." He claps a palm on my cheek a little too hard. "Hey, I think I'm gonna go roast a hot dog or dance or something. And she's over by the boardwalk on the right." He gives me a goofy smile. I love this guy. He's the best friend I don't deserve.

I arch my brow at him, acting like I don't know who he's talking about.

"Not sure I know what you mean, buddy, but why don't you go get that hot dog? I'm going to go ice the keg and grab a beer."

I pour two beers and wander away from the party.

———

"Hey there, do you see any damsels that need saving?" I hand her one of the beers as I sit beside her on the walkway. "Looks like your drink was a little low."

"Thanks, Mr. Knight. Always coming to the rescue. But I'll take this one." She raises her cup to me. She pours out her old cup and slips this cup under the new one. "Mine was warm. I'm not much of a beer drinker, but I will absolutely not drink a warm beer." She gives me a little smile.

"Why are you sitting here alone instead of enjoying the party?" I want to know. Matt hinted before that she wasn't a party girl. Was he right?

She takes a little sip of her beer and puts the cup beside her. She wraps her arms around her knees, looking out toward the ocean.

"Sometimes I get overwhelmed around groups of people. I'm used to being by myself or in small groups most of the time, so sometimes I need a moment to breathe."

The moon is almost full tonight, bathing her in the moonlight, making her even more beautiful, if that's possible. Her hair is in a messy top knot, but the loose hairs around her face blow with the sea breeze. I reach up to tuck a strand of hair behind her ear, leaving my hand on her cheek. She turns her head to look at me. Her eyes search my face, and she nibbles on her bottom lip. Our eyes lock, and I lean in, waiting for her to come to me. I need to make sure she wants this too. Because I want it more than anything. Apparently, more than the Carolina Reapers.

CHAPTER
SIXTEEN

COLE

————

The silence hangs between us. My warm palm cups her cooled face, and my calloused fingers slowly brush back and forth near her hairline. It feels nice, comfortable. I lean in, and our scent mixes with the salt water and bonfire to make my new favorite aroma.

I feel like she's spent so much energy this summer avoiding me, but now we're here.

I begin to lean in and stop. My eyes lock with hers.

"Leigh," I say in a whisper. "I want to kiss you so fucking bad."

"Then why don't you?" There's the consent I've been waiting for.

She leans in and closes the gap, our lips touching. Our kiss is gentle, sweet even. I feel a smile form on her lips, and I smile too. I interpret her smile as an invitation to deepen our kiss. My hand slides behind her head, pulling her tighter to me. My tongue parts her lips and explores her mouth like I'm Indiana

Jones looking for that lost Ark. She responds with a contented sigh, which sends every nerve ending I have on high alert. I've never experienced this sensation before, especially not after a kiss.

I've never had a kiss that made my body feel like it would spontaneously combust. I could kiss her forever, although I don't know if kissing will be enough. Other parts of my body are waking up, wanting more.

Her hands find the nape of my neck, her fingers stroking the curls that always peek from the bottom of my cap. I'm grateful I'm hatless tonight. Her fingers run through my hair, and it feels fucking fantastic.

I gently pull away, peppering her lips, cheeks, and forehead with little kisses. With my forehead against hers, I whisper, "Umm, bubble gum."

"What can I say? I'm just trying to make a good first impression and be memorable." Memorable. That's an understatement.

"I've wanted to kiss you since I saw you on that kayak."

"I thought you didn't see me on the kayak?" she teases. "That's why you dumped me in the water."

"Well, I may have seen you and was so dazzled by you that I forgot to slow down," I confess.

"I suspected as much. You create situations so you can swoop in and be the hero," she teases.

"You've figured me out, my damsel." I kiss her on the tip of her nose and stand up. I reach out to her and pull her up. "Come on, sweetheart, let's leave our shoes here and take a little stroll down the beach." If we don't move, I may not be able to stop what we started. My body is screaming at me that it wants more.

I take her hand in mine and lead her toward the shoreline. She leans in and pushes me with her shoulder. "Don't tell me you are the kind of guy that likes long walks on the beach and puppies. I just might swoon." She giggles as we walk away from the party. I got a giggle out of her, and it is the most beautiful sound I've ever heard. I'm on top of the world.

"Swoon away, sweetheart. I love puppies. Kittens too. And a long walk on the beach with a beautiful girl. But only when we stop and do this along with way."

I stop and pull her toward me, my arms wrap around her, holding her tight. My lips crash down on hers, making our first kiss seem like an easy warm-up. This kiss is heated and passionate, and her knees go weak. I hold her tight, keeping her upright. The effect I have on her spurs me on.

The waves rush up on the shore and wash over our feet, securing us to the spot. As the water rolls back to the ocean, I pull away and say, "Yeah, let's go for a long walk with lots of that." I flash her my charming smile, and she can't help herself. She smiles back. My chest tightens, and a warm feeling fills up my heart. I don't know what that smile did, but it somehow transformed me. It's like it activated a new feeling I've never had, and I'm craving more.

"Let's go," she says as we walk hand in hand down the beach. The summer may be winding down, but this is an unexpected but welcome turn.

We walk along the shoreline, talking and kissing, losing track of time. We must have played twenty questions three times. With every answer, I'm more convinced this girl is some kind of special and she's meant for me. Our conversation goes from fun and light-hearted to serious back to playful. Each round is sealed with a kiss that warms me from the inside out.

I don't know if I've ever gotten to know anyone so fast. I know her favorite foods, her worst childhood injury, and all about her best friend, Emma.

All tonight did was cement the fact that I'm falling for this girl. She's kind and caring. Loyal. Reserved. Guarded. Funny. Feisty. Passionate. Perfect. Leigh Rutledge. Mine.

My phone buzzes like a swarm of bees in my pocket, but I don't want the outside world to bust our special bubble.

"Answer it," she says. "Matt's probably about to call the Coast Guard if you don't."

I pull out my phone, and she's right. It's Matt, with nine text messages and three missed calls. I figured after his fourth beer, he might be sleeping it off somewhere. I glance at the texts. His drunk texts usually require some interpretation.

MATT:

you k

stay out of the water

you aren't in the water are u

dogs are low want me to save you one

she's sweet pretty too

are you mad at me

I like her too

Decker looking for u mad

I decide to text him back. Yeah, I know Matt likes Leigh too. Hell, all the guys like her. I can't ignore the pull, the way her touch soothes my soul. Decker had told me to stay away from her, or I could kiss my baseball future goodbye. I'll just work harder. I can still play ball somewhere else if I'm not a Reaper. There are other teams.

I should thank him for pushing me to go for what I want. What I need. This evening with Leigh is perfect.

I'm fine. Go to bed. I'll be home shortly. Decker can fuck off.

I notice Leigh is checking her phone too.

"I guess our absence is noticed?" I ask.

"Um, yeah. I probably need to get back." She tucks her phone into her back pocket and moves toward the direction of the party. We've walked so far that I can barely see the fire.

I reach for her hand, and she pulls away, crossing her arms over her chest.

I put my hand on her arm, stopping her from walking further.

"What's wrong?" I search her face for some clue. The happy smile she's worn for the past three hours is gone, replaced by a sad smile.

"Nothing," she says. She gently shakes her head. I know enough that 'nothing' and 'fine' are code words in the female vocabulary. Nothing usually means something, and more times than not, I'm the focus of the something. Living with my mom and sister has taught me a thing or two about the female language.

"It's not nothing. What is it?" I put my hand on her cheek, making her look at me. "Come on, Leigh, don't pull away. This. You. Me." I gesture between us. "It's a good thing, right?"

She sighs heavily. "Cole, I really like you. I do. More than I should. You are kind and funny and make my toes curl when you look at me. I won't tell you what happens when you kiss me, but…"

Is she breaking up with me before we get started? I want to ask that, beg her to give me a chance, but my mouth works faster than my brain.

"Is it Decker? He told me today that he loved you and I need to stay away. Is it him?" Please say it's not him. Please.

She takes a step back as if I slapped her. The distance feels cold and fills me with dread.

"What?!" She practically yells at me. "He tells you to stay away, and you seek me out? What are you thinking?"

"I'm thinking I like you. I want to see where this goes. I don't give a fuck about Alexander Decker." Then it hits me.

"Unless you do?" If she was with him, she wouldn't kiss me, would she? She's not the kind of girl to cheat, is she? No. But she's never said if she had a boyfriend. Always skirts around it.

Damn. But that's not Leigh. It can't be. She's too good of a person to be a cheater.

"But you want to play for the Reapers," she says quietly.

"Sure, the Reapers are my dream team, but I just want to play ball. And I want to get to know you better," I plead with her. "I want to be with you, Leigh. More than anything. Don't you want this?" I take a step closer. She takes a step back, my heart cracking.

"You don't understand, Cole. I can't." Her arms are wrapped around her torso like she's trying to hold herself together. I think I see a tear slip down her cheek, but she turns too fast for me to confirm. She starts to walk down the beach, moving at a quick pace. I'm stunned. I can't? What does that mean?

"Leigh, wait up," I call after her. I catch up, but it's clear she will not stop and have a conversation. "Leigh, stop. Please. Can we talk about this?"

I reach for her arm, and she jerks away from me.

"No, Cole, we can't," she says as she continues to speed walk down the beach.

I can't help myself. If I'm going to bleed, I want to bleed out. So I ask the question I don't want the answer to.

"Do you love him?"

CHAPTER
SEVENTEEN

ASHLEIGH

———

"Do you love him?"

That stops me in my tracks. He gets in front of me and reaches for my hands. He looks at my face and drops his hands to his side.

He thinks I'm with Alexander. I've never done anything to change that perception. This is my fault.

But he doesn't understand I can't be the one to mess up his future. Cole doesn't need a distraction. I noticed that his game changed tonight after he saw me with Xander. His coach saw it too.

I could clear up the entire misunderstanding, but then, he'll know I've been lying to him. And he'll know who I am. Will he think his draft call is because of me and my connections? Or worse yet, doesn't get drafted because of me?

I look at him and decide what is best for him, his future, and his dream. My heart breaks into pieces as I stand on the beach, looking at his gorgeous face. I vow to build the strongest wall around my heart to hold in the pieces. I'm shattered.

He wants honesty. Honesty is what he will get.

"Yes."

His mouth falls open. His eyes are pained, and he visibly flinches. This is what it looks like to destroy someone, and I have a front-row seat. I told him I would be his downfall.

I can't stand it. The look on his face is utter devastation.

I turn around and take off at a run, leaving Cole stunned on the beach. My hurt and pain fuel my body as I run at a full sprint back to the party. I reach where we left our shoes, grab them, pass the crowd, and head to my car.

As I approach, I see Alexander leaning against my car, his face illuminated by his phone screen. Tears fill my eyes at the sight of him, anger racking my body.

"Get the fuck out of my way, Alexander," I shout at him.

"Ash, what's wrong? What did he do?"

"Are you serious right now? What did HE do? He cared about me, Xan. It's what you did! Now MOVE!" I'm sure my yelling will get the attention of the neighbors.

"Ash," he pleads.

"I said move," I growl at him. I don't think I've ever been so angry in my entire life.

Alexander steps away from my car as I get in and speed away. I'm grateful my house isn't far because it's hard to drive with the tears clouding my vision. I get home, storm upstairs, and throw myself on the bed, sobbing.

How could this night have gone from one of the best nights of my life to one of the worst in the span of a few minutes? I allow myself a few hours of crying, then rise and make a plan.

I'm done mourning my reinvented life. Leigh Rutledge is dead.

———

I've already taken a shower and packed my bags before the sun is up. A quick text to Trevor, and it's done. He didn't ask any questions. I wonder if Xander already filled him in? It doesn't matter. Not really. I don't want to explain it to anyone anyway. I want to slink away and put it behind me.

The horrified look on Cole's face when I said yes will haunt me for the rest of my life.

It's what's best for him. I can't be the reason his dream is crushed. I can't be the one to make him find a plan B. I can't do that to him. We talked about his dreams, and he doesn't even have a plan B. He doesn't want to think about not making it to the Majors.

So here I am. My summer internship cut short. My summer of reinvention a failure. Well, a partial fail. I rocked the work and was good at it. I made friends. I met a guy who was something special. I fell in love. I think he liked me too.

Clearly, he doesn't know about my connections because I couldn't tell him. But he likes me for me. Or at least the version of me he got to know.

Or should I say liked. Definitely past tense after last night. I let him think Alexander and I are in a relationship. He promised me honesty, and I gave him lies. I can only imagine what he thinks of me now.

My heart is broken. I feel like I have pieces of glass floating around inside my body, creating tiny cuts everywhere. The tiny cuts are the worst, and I feel like I have a million of them.

I need to regroup. Finish school and graduate. Go to work for my dad. It's not what I want, but it's better than I deserve. I ruined Cole's life, but maybe, just maybe, if I cut deep enough, I can free him from my poisonous web. He'll be fine once he achieves his dream. He deserves it.

I tell Mrs. Jones I'm heading back to Charlotte for a few days before returning to Raleigh. I give her the short version.

It's for the best.

Season's winding down anyway. I met a guy, and I can't be a

distraction for him. Best if I leave and go back to being Ashleigh Decker. Leigh Rutledge doesn't exist anymore. She died on a beach last night. Washed out with the tide. A failed experiment.

I turn my phone on when I get in the car and see dozens of missed calls and texts from Xander. I can't deal with him right now.

Jules tries to FaceTime as I'm driving back to Charlotte. I answer his call.

"Ash, darlin', where are you?" I can hear the concern carry through my car speakers. It's coming in Dolby stereo. Loud and clear.

"On the road to Charlotte. Should be there in about four hours." I know my voice sounds flat. I barely recognize it.

"Are you okay driving?"

"Yep. I'm good. Fine." Focusing on driving keeps me from crying. I'm pulling out all the coping mechanisms.

There is an awkward silence, something we don't usually have.

"What did he tell you?"I ask.

"That he fucked up. That he was truly looking out for Cole because he knew you liked him and would want that for him. Your silence is killing him. Trevor said he drank all night until he passed out on the couch."

"Jules, Xander broke me." Tears start to form, but I will them away. I can't drive if I cry, and I need to get as far away from Savannah as possible.

"I know. He's sorry. I've never heard him like this. I told him you need time."

"Yeah, I guess I do." I sniffle a little.

"Well, I've got a plan. Don't go home. Head to the airport when you get to Charlotte. Let's have a girl's getaway. I've already talked to Emma, and she agrees."

"Jules, I can't. I just want to be in a dark room with Ben and Jerry."

"Yes, you can. Go to the airport. Check all the bags you have with you. The ticket will be there at the American counter. I'll see you shortly, darlin." He hangs up.

Girl time? That might be what I need. And he mentioned Emma? I definitely need her.

It's time to put on our rally caps and turn this around.

I drive faster and head to the airport.

CHAPTER
EIGHTEEN

ASHLEIGH

———

I get to the airport to find a first-class ticket waiting for me and realize my flight leaves in an hour. Jules didn't give me much time to back out. Good thing I always carry my passport and didn't hit traffic. I make my way through security and arrive at my gate as they begin boarding.

I stow my bag and settle into my seat. I'm doing my best to hold it together. I watch the ground crew load the bags through my window. When the flight attendant asks if I want a drink, I decide I'm at the drink away my sorrows part of the process, so why not. I'll take a double vodka and a splash of cranberry. It's afternoon, right? Or does that even matter when my heart is shredded? I'm day drinking now. Yep, totally winning.

Now that I'm sitting here, I'm just ready to go. I'm about to crawl out of my skin with anxiety. I'm falling apart.

My phone pings with a text.

JULES

You on the plane?

Yep. I'm not sure I'm packed appropriately.

JULES

If you need it, I'll buy it. See you soon. Be nice
to your seatmate. 😇

What does that mean? I pity the poor person who has the misfortune to sit beside me for several hours. I chug my drink, and as the vodka hits my empty stomach, I realize I haven't eaten. Oh well, one more and I'll forget about everything. At least for the duration of this flight. If Xander can do it, so can I.

I put my AirPods in, set my phone to airplane mode, and hit shuffle on my playlist. I close my eyes to shut out the world until I see Jules. My music starts, and the second song that plays is "One Call Away," and tears slip out and down my cheeks.

The memory of Cole singing this washes over me. I know I should skip to the next song, but I can't. My heart warms at the memory of him, making me believe it might still work. And then I picture his face last night, and my heart splinters into a million pieces. Another tear slides down my cheek.

I feel someone wipe my tear away, startling me from the unexpected touch and causing me to jump toward the window. I practically jump into his lap when I look up to see who is in the seat next to me.

"Chance!" I jump up and hug him tight. Another example of my brother's overprotectiveness. This time, I'll take the rescue. Jules has pulled out all the stops.

"Hey, gorgeous," he says as he hugs me back. I pop back in my seat, realizing people are looking at us. I'm jumping on Chance Fuller, NHL superstar, voted the hottest guy on the ice for the last five years. Hot as a player and hot as in OMG, panty-melter hot. Chance is Julian's best friend, and he sent him here for me. These guys. Just seeing him makes me sob again.

"No, no, no." He uses my cocktail napkin to dab at my face. "Dry those tears. This is an official tear-free zone. We have almost three hours to drink, laugh, bash guys, play games, and do anything but cry. I'm not equipped for that. You know I only have brothers." His voice is full of panic. His face looks like he might cry any minute too. "You can cry with Jules."

Chance looks painfully uncomfortable. As the other passengers pass by to get their seats, they look at him, trying to figure out how they know him. They probably wonder why this gorgeous guy is also talking to the hot mess beside him. I suspect that any minute, the flight attendant will offer to try and find him another seat to get him away from me.

He gives me a lopsided smile. He's teasing me, but he's not. I don't think Chance knows how to handle tears. I give him a weak smile. I need to pull it together for him. The last thing he needs is someone to take a picture and post it online.

I wrap my arm around his bicep and squeeze. "Thank you. Really. I have no idea what you were doing when you got Jules's 911 call, but thank you for answering."

"I was actually in Charlotte. Caught Tripp's game last night. And then, Jules called. Do you think I could pass up an all-expense paid trip to Cancun? You know we will make Jules pay." He says that with a chuckle and a twinkle in his eyes. I know he's not here for a free vacation. Chance is here for me, making me love him even more.

"You know, because you are there, it will just be a business expense." I laugh, and for the first time in twelve hours, I feel a little better. I take my first full breath, the recycled air filling my lungs.

"That bastard! You're probably right. We'll have to find another way to torture him then. We have a few hours to plot." He leans in, and we start thinking of ways to prank Jules.

I don't know if it's the bottomless drinks or Chance's company, but the flight is over in no time. He grabs my carry-on and his duffle in one hand and puts his arm around my shoulder as we walk through the airport, heading to baggage claim.

From the time he sat down, Chance kept a hand on me. He was always touching me, not in a romantic or possessive way, more like he was trying to hold me together. He had his hand on my knee, would hold my hand, or put his arm around my shoulders.

My breathing would get unsteady, and he'd add a little pressure to the touch. When my mind drifted to Cole, I'd stop breathing for a minute. Like holding my breath would stop time and fix this mess. I don't even think I realized I was doing it until Chance would squeeze my arm or bump my shoulder. Then I would take a breath again. He never said a word about it, but I know he was watching me closely. I think I scared him. After all, he's a hockey player, not a medical professional, and certainly not a mental health professional. I'm a hot mess.

I can only imagine what I look like. I've been crying for hours. I don't have any makeup on. No need to cover up my tears when I wasn't expecting anyone to see them. I'm dressed in a Savannah Pajamas baseball shirt and cut-off denim shorts. My old Tevas complete the unfashionable ensemble. My hair is loosely braided, and I have a Pajamas baseball hat on backward to cover up my messy hair.

We get to the baggage claim in Cancun, and Chance drops his arm from my shoulder. Are there paparazzi here or something? I bet he doesn't want to be photographed with me. I get it. I'm a mess and don't look like his typical flavor of the month. I look at him to see what happened and start apologizing when I'm scooped up and swung around in a boa-constrictor-tight hug.

Chance has delivered the package. His job complete. He was the surrogate brother I needed.

Jules has me now. I hug him back and don't let go. I'm all cried out for the moment, but between the alcohol, lack of sleep, and emotional upheaval, I'm exhausted and moving into the next stage of grief. Anger.

I'm mad at Xander. I'm mad at myself. I'm just mad at the world. It's a shitty situation that I probably could have handled better. But this is where I am. Holding on for dear life to my brother in a foreign country, hiding from it all.

Jules holds me tight and whispers in my ear that everything is going to be okay. I'm sure I'm a sight, and the vacationers are getting an eyeful. Sorry people.

After Chance gets my bags, we are whisked away in a limo, me sandwiched between the two guys. Jules has his arm around me, and Chance is holding my hand. Damn, these guys. They are the best balm for my wounded heart.

We pull up to a palatial gated estate. The driver enters a code, and we approach the front door. Somehow, with very short notice, Jules has arranged for a six-bedroom house on the water, complete with house staff that includes a chef, a bartender, and a housekeeper. It's amazing. I have no idea how he made all this happen with a few hour's notice. I'm not even sure how he beat us down here.

Chance puts my bags in a large suite with an amazing ocean view. I know he thought it would make me happy, but hearing the surf reminds me of last night on the beach with Cole. I quietly move my things to another room overlooking a lush garden in the center of the house. Jules notices but doesn't comment.

The alcohol is wearing off, and I'm tired. I want to crash and cry. Instead, the guys insist I join them by the pool.

"I can't believe you got this fantastic house on such short notice." My attempt to act excited falls flat.

"It's Tripp's," Jules says. "I was already here. Told him you needed it, and here we are."

"No shit," Chance says. He's on a giant flamingo float in the middle of the pool. His large, sculpted body against the pink float is comical. I pull out my phone and take a picture of a smiling Chance holding up a pink drink, complete with an umbrella. It's the kind of thing his social media following will love.

"You need to get me better contracts, you bastard." He takes a sip of his drink and splashes water toward Jules.

"Ten million a year wasn't enough?" Jules replies. "Buy a beach house if you want one."

"And the house staff?" I raise an eyebrow at Jules. The staff doesn't feel like Tripp at all. A full-time bartender on call? That's totally Jules.

"Maria, the housekeeper, lives on the grounds with her husband, Juan. He's the personal chef for us. He normally works at the Sandals Resort but will cook here when Tripp has guests. They take care of the house year round." The bartender brings me a fruity concoction, and Jules continues. "Manny, here, is Maria's nephew. When I was arranging other services, she offered him up."

"Thank you, Manny," I say. "I hope we aren't too much of a bother."

"Oh no, señorita. I am happy to be here. I want to work at a resort, so this is good practice."

"Well, you can practice drink-making for me as much as you want." I take a sip. I don't need another drink after our flight, but I can't say no. It's a wonder I'm not passed out somewhere. "This is delicious. Yummy." He smiles and disappears back into the house. I look at Jules. "What other services might that be?"

"Well, it's emergency girl time, so, you know, girl stuff." Jules just shrugs. Manny appears at the door. "Señorita, your man is here."

"My man?!" I look at Jules, shock and dread overwhelming me. "What the hell, Jules?" Chance laughs so hard that he falls off his float with a loud splash.

"Calm down, Ash. He's here for a massage. I thought you could use one." Jules is pulling out all the stops for this girl time. "Go relax. I've got you, darlin'. And Emma will be here tomorrow." He gives me a wink. "Go spend time with your man." He gets up from his chair and cannonballs into the water, spraying Chance.

I take a deep breath. It's going to be okay. It will. Right?

———

After my massage, I told myself I wouldn't cry anymore. At least not in front of anyone. Juan prepared a fantastic dinner last night, and we watched *Iron Man* on Netflix. Even though we tend to lean toward chick flicks on girl's nights, Jules let Chance pick the movie. Smart move to avoid romance right now. I didn't cry. At least not until I was alone. Then, I cried myself to sleep, letting my tears attempt to wash my sadness away.

I woke up with a bottle of water, multivitamins, Tylenol, and a cup of coffee on my nightstand with a note from Jules. *Hydrate and shower. Emma gets here at 1. Love you. J*

When did he sneak this in here? I look at the clock. It's eleven-thirty. Time to get it together.

"Ohmygod ohmygod, I missed you so much," I say, hugging Emma as she walks into the house. The driver brings her bags into the foyer and leaves. I can't let her go because she'll see the tears in my eyes.

"Missed you too, girl. So I didn't get many details about this detour, but I'm not mad about it. This place is sick!" Emma looks around.

"Come on. I'll show you around and introduce you to everyone."

Emma cocks an eyebrow at me. "Everyone?"

"Yeah, Jules went a little extra. We have a chef, a house-keeper, and a bartender."

"We have our own bartender?"

"Sure do," Chance says as he enters the foyer. "Hey, pixie girl. Glad you're here. I'll take your bags to your room." Chance scans me head to toe. "Slight improvement, Ash. You need more water. And maybe something for your eyes. They're all puffy."

He says it so matter of factly, with no concern for my feelings. Emma looks at him and then at me and shakes her head. I know, this is all surreal. "Emma, are you opposed to the ocean? I'll put your stuff in that room since Ashleigh didn't want it. That okay?"

"So, is Chance Fuller the houseboy?" she asks, laughing. "Julian left out that information."

"I'm at your service, ladies," he says as he carries her bags down the hall.

The main living area of the house is an open floor plan. The kitchen, dining room, and den are one large room decorated in tans, with brightly colored red, orange, and yellow tiles around the kitchen. It's cozy.

Emma grabs my hand and pulls me into the den and down onto the large sectional in the middle of the room. The sofa still has blankets strewn around from our movie time last night. Throw pillows are scattered on the floor, in the chairs, and one managed to make it on the hearth.

She pulls me into her lap, my back to her front, and she starts to braid my damp hair. "So start from the beginning. No detail is too small. Tell me how we got here."

Jules walks into the room, kisses Emma on top of the head, and keeps walking into the kitchen. "Hey, Ems. Glad you're here." He grabs a bottle of water from the fridge and gulps, watching us on the couch. "I see we moved quickly to the hair-braiding portion of girl time. I'll leave you to it. Facials and pedicures in two hours." He walks by us again, kisses my head this time, and says, "Chance and I will be in the gym. Music will be loud. Get it all out, girls. This is your only alone time. Then we teach Chance what Decker girl time is really like." He gives us a wink and leaves us to catch up.

We both laugh. How can we not? Julian is the best sibling a girl can ask for. So I start at the beginning. I tell her everything. I tell her about my work and the internship. I tell her about how fun it was to stay with her parents. I tell her about the local gossip on Tybee Island. I show her some of the videos I didn't post.

Then I tell her about Cole. About how I feel around him. About his talent on the ball field. About his singing. About his kisses. About his relationship with Matt. About how he pushes my buttons and his accusations of my gold-digging. I tell her how he thinks Alexander and I are a thing. How I fed that narrative. I tell her Xander's role in all of this and how he hurt me more than I thought possible. I hold it together, telling her everything.

"He wrote MINE on your tag before he even knew your name? Wow."

"Yeah. Wow. But I can't get involved with a ball player. I can't be a distraction or influence his chances at his dream. I just can't." Telling Emma didn't hurt as much as I thought. If anything, it reinforced my decision to walk away. It's what's best for Cole.

"But why did you leave? I mean, honestly, he sounds like a great guy. Why not tell him the truth? Why not try to make it work?"

There are so many answers to that question. Do I regret leaving him on that beach? Yes. Was it the right thing to do? Probably.

"Don't you see?" Emma looks at me and gently shakes her head no.

"Not really. Sounds like there was something there. It's not what you expected to happen, but he likes you for you. Isn't that what you wanted?"

"It is. I do. It's just..." It is what I want. He kissed the college intern with no connection to his baseball future. Will that change if he knows? Will he want to stay with me because of who I am? Will he be angry when he finds out I lied to him? Will he forgive me? Maybe he likes the chase? It's all so complicated.

"Just what?" Emma always knows how to push me and

make me face my truth. I can tell her because I know she'll stay by my side regardless.

"He wants to be a Reaper."

"And?"

"Don't you get it?" I hop up from the couch and pace. I need movement and space to explain. "If he doesn't get drafted, he'll blame me or Alexander. If he gets drafted, he'll think I had something to do with it. It's for the best that he carves his path without me muddling it all up."

"I mean, it could go that way. Or it could be a happily ever after, you know? But you didn't give it a chance."

Did I walk away without giving us a chance? Maybe. But it's for the best, for him at least. I can't be the one that destroys his life. I won't be the one that does that to him. No, he's better off without me. I'm protecting him. He's usually the one to rescue. Now it's my turn to rescue him.

Besides, I'm not sure he feels the same way I feel for him. I care about him in ways I've never felt before, which scares the hell out of me. Getting to know him this summer has been fun, exciting. I didn't make it easy for him, but he didn't give up, and I let down my guard and let him get wrapped around my heart. I think he has the potential to wreck me if I let this go further. Yes, this is for the best. Definitely for him. Maybe for me. He doesn't need my complications in his life.

"Did Alexander really tell him to stay away from you? I thought he promised to stay away this summer. I don't get it." Emma looks thoughtful.

"Well, he broke his promise."

"Something's missing. Alexander is protective, but he'd never, ever hurt you, Ash. Have you talked to him?"

"Nope. I don't want to talk to him. I'm so fucking angry with him, Em."

"You know you'll need to talk to him, right? I know he's worried about you. Trevor told me he was a mess."

What? Emma talked to Trevor? That's twice that information has caught me off guard.

"Just say you'll talk to him when we get back." Emma's right. I can't freeze out Xander. I think he was trying to make amends with Cole in his own way.

I sigh. "Xander and I will be fine. I just need some time."

"Thank fuck," Jules says as he and Chance enter the room. "Let's eat and then get this girl time in gear. We've got pampering to do."

"Are we really doing pedicures?" Chance asks.

"Oh yeah, pretty boy," Emma says. "I hope you are prepared for the ultimate pampering experience that is Decker girl time. You've no idea how lucky you are to be part of this. Welcome to the inner circle. It's a great place to be."

CHAPTER
NINETEEN

COLE

———

It's been three weeks since the night that changed me down to my very soul. I know Matt is worried about me, but I tell him I'm fine. Fine. Ha! Now I get the power of those words when women use them. It's a lie. I'm not fine, but there isn't anything to do about it, so fine it is.

When he asked me what happened, I told him she was with Decker, we argued about it, and she took off. I honestly didn't think she'd leave Savannah. This internship was everything to her. She told me it was the most important thing she's ever done. It must have been bad for her to give up her dream and possibly jeopardize her future by cutting her internship short. Internships are important for the resume, and I'm sure leaving one without notice won't help her future job prospects. I guess getting away from me was a higher priority, and that hurts.

I remember every detail of that night. The kisses. The laughs. The confessions. The connection. It wasn't fake. It was real. More real than anything I've ever felt. I was falling for her. Hell, I think

I already fell. Hard. Obviously, hitting my head along the way. I have a dull ache in my chest, and I wish it would get worse and kill me or go away, but instead, it's just a steady ache, reminding me of what I'm missing. Leigh.

Trevor told us she had a family situation she had to deal with and had to leave, but I know the truth. She left because of me. Or Alexander fucking Decker. That bastard.

It's time to return to school and try to put this summer behind me.

Stepping back on campus, I should have all these positive emotions. I should feel excited, hopeful, and even relieved. But I don't feel any of those things. I feel empty.

It's been three agonizing weeks. Three weeks since I had feelings and emotions I didn't know existed. And with one word, it all went away. Yes. She said she loved Alexander fucking Decker.

I never believed in fate before, but this girl. Damn. This girl has me all twisted, and I figured fate, the heavens, destiny, whatever it was, had us meet for a reason. But now, I can barely sleep, my mind repeating every encounter we had all summer. Her smile. Her laugh. The way she would stomp her foot when she was mad - usually directed at me.

I remember the first time we met. I was reckless and got too close to her on the jet ski. I was drawn to her, a moth to a flame. She was lost in her thoughts, and I just had to talk to her. My wake capsizing her kayak wasn't part of the plan, but maybe it was kismet. I smile when I think about the way she stomped back up to the house, soaked but fucking adorable. She turned to see if I was still watching and got caught. How could I look away?

I went to her host house the day after our fight to talk to her. I needed to see her. I found our first meeting spot and knocked on the front door. Literally, with hat in hand, I begged Mrs. Jones to let me see her. To talk to her. But she was gone. Leigh left her prized internship. Left her friends. Left me.

Now I'm back at school, reunited with my friends and team-mates, sharing summer stories and basking in the glory of my senior year. Everyone is laughing and joking, commenting on the viral videos Matt and I starred in, and I give hollow platitudes. Those videos make me think of her.

Yeah, it was fun. Savannah was hot. Baseball was great. Met cool guys. Scouts were impressed. This is our year. Glad to be back. We are the team to beat. College World Series this year. Blah, blah, blah.

Matt takes the lead and fills everyone in on our summer. The antics. The stats. The camaraderie. Listening to him makes me realize how magical the summer was. His description is straight out of a Hollywood movie. It was a great summer. I was grateful he left out the part about the girl. I couldn't take the ribbing from the guys about being brokenhearted. This summer? The best of my life. Until it wasn't.

Now it's time to focus. Put all that behind me. Priority number one? Baseball. I focus on conditioning, nutrition, and batting practice. I have to get the call this year. If I don't, what was all this for?

CHAPTER
TWENTY

ASHLEIGH

———

"I can't believe we're seniors. It's our last fall semester," Emma says as we get home from the bookstore.

"Did you just squeal?" I tease her. Her voice always goes up two octaves when she's excited. It's adorable and endearing, coming from her tiny five-foot-four frame. Emma is petite, a hundred pounds soaking wet. What she lacks in stature, she makes up for in energy. She may be small, but she's mighty.

"You know I did. Now stop picking on me, and let's have a fun girl's night before our first day of class." She lights scented candles, pulls a box out of the hall closet, and tosses it at me. It's beautifully wrapped with a big red bow.

"What's this?"

"Open it and see." She claps her hands together and bounces. "I was home when they were delivered. I got one too. I already opened mine. Go ahead."

I slide the ribbon off the box and open it. It's full of scented tissue paper and the most luxurious bathrobe I've ever seen. It's soft, fluffy, and the most fantastic fabric ever made. I put it on, and it feels like being snuggled by one hundred of the softest kittens. Something falls out onto the table. I pick it up to find a note in a familiar scrawl.

I know you're still mad at me. I'm sorry. Ash, I need you to be happy. Enjoy girl's night. I know that's a Jules thing with you, but I wanted you to know I'm here for you too. Love you.

X

It's been a month since I've talked to Xander. I miss him. Maybe it's time.

"Were these hand delivered?"

Emma gives me a solemn nod. "Yeah. You were in the shower, and I told him we had to get our books. He's in town for the night. Talk to him, Ash. I've never seen a guy look so sad."

I send a text to Xander asking him to come over, and he shows up thirty minutes later with food from my favorite Chinese restaurant and a bottle of wine. Emma goes to her room to FaceTime her family, giving us time to talk.

"You look like shit, Xan," I say as a greeting.

"Thanks, Ash. You don't look so good yourself. Are you eating? You look thin."

He comes in and puts the food on the kitchen island. He opens his arms for a hug. I look at him for a few awkward seconds and rush into his arms. He squeezes me until I can barely breathe.

"I'm sorry, Ash. I really am. I need you to be happy," he whispers. He kisses my temple.

I gather my courage, get my emotions in check and take a deep breath. I know it's time to talk. I've played this conversation over in my head several times. We need to fix this.

I pull away, take his hand, lead him to the couch, and tell him to sit. I sit next to him, crisscross applesauce, as Emma calls it, and face him. It's time to talk not just about Savannah but about everything.

"Look, I know it's hard for you," I start. "I know it's hard for you not to be in control. I may have been a kid, but I watched you when Mom was sick."

"Ash, don't," he begs.

"No. I need to say this, and you need to hear it. It wasn't your fault. She got sick. It was nothing any of us did and nothing we could do to fix it. You are so much like Dad, keeping it all boxed up inside. It's like you thought that by doing that it would hurt less. Maybe it did?" He looks away. His eyes fixated on the window across the room.

"It didn't."

"Yeah, I didn't think so. But, Xan, you can't control everything, and that includes me."

His head snaps to me. "Is that what you think? That I'm trying to control you?" His voice carries an angry edge.

"No. Maybe? You're always so smothering. Sometimes, I can't breathe."

He puts my hands in his, holding them tight.

"You know you look just like her?"

"I know." Dad tells me all the time that I look just like Mom. Sometimes, I can tell it's hard for him to look at me.

"It's not control. I'd never want that for you. But, Ash, I can't lose you. You mean so much to us. My god, do you know what it would do to Dad if something happened to you? Me? Jules? I can't even think about it. Did you know one of my last conversations with Mom was about you?"

"It was?" We've never talked about Mom's death. When she was diagnosed with cancer, we were all in shock. She seemed fine, tired a little more often, but wasn't sick, as far as ten-year-old me noticed. She was doing okay for several months until she wasn't. She became weak and was bedridden for the last two weeks of her life. Then she was just gone. We spent as much time as possible with her, but she insisted we live. She made me go to school, even though I was terrified she'd die while I was away. We all stayed close, but none of us really talked to each other. We just existed in the same house, spending shifts at Mom's bedside. I haven't thought about those days in years.

"Yeah. It was the day before she died. You were at school, and I was with her, trying to get her to eat. She told me how we three were her greatest joy. She told me how proud she was of me and how grateful she was to be able to watch me graduate college. Sad that she'd never meet who we'd marry." He chuckles. "Yeah, not sure if that will ever happen for me. Anyway, we looked through family albums, and when we got to pictures of them bringing you home from the hospital, she lit up. I almost thought she would pull through the way the light filled her eyes as she looked at those baby pictures. Then she asked me to watch after you. She was so worried about you. You were so young, and she understood how important a mother is to a young girl. She made me promise to keep you safe."

"She did?" A tear slips down my cheek. He reaches up and brushes it away.

"She did. Ash, I'm not trying to control you. I'm just trying to fulfill our mother's dying wish. To watch over you and keep you safe."

His eyes lock with mine and fill with tears. His eyes search my face for something.

I lean in and hug him, both of us holding on for dear life. It was painful to lose Mom, but at least she didn't make me promise anything. I never thought about the motivation behind his behavior. A deathbed promise. That was a lot to ask of a twenty-two-year-old.

I need to release him from this obligation and guilt for his sake as well as mine.

"I'm glad you told me. But keeping me safe means teaching me to look both ways before crossing the street. It doesn't mean to follow me to Savannah and be overbearing to someone who…."

"I know," he mumbles.

"I really liked him, Xan. But I can't be a complication for him. I know you know that. I just…"

"I know, Ash. That's why I told him to stay away. Not to be overprotective of you but to help him reach his goal. I want him to succeed because it's what you want. But I'm sorry it broke your heart. I want your happiness more than anything in the world."

"I know. And it's my fault anyway. I didn't tell him who I was. I let him think we were an item. That's on me."

"Well, I helped fuel the story too. It's on both of us. But you know you can fix it? You know where to find him."

"Would you want me to find him?"

"If it makes you happy, then yeah. I think you should. But…"

"But what?"

"But I think you need to be honest with him. If he loves you, it needs to be all of you, not just the parts you let him see. Like it or not, you are part of this family, and we will not let you out of it. I'm sorry it comes with some complications, but most families do. So if you want a relationship, it has to start there. He needs to know Ashleigh Decker." I can't believe he's okay with me going out with Cole.

"Yeah, you're right, but I can't. It's for the best. We both have to focus this year." He told me he didn't date because it was a distraction. He can't afford distractions this year, and I would be a big one.

"Well, let's hope for a good year then. For both of you."

"Hey, I didn't think you liked him?"

"Don't really know him, but you need to know this. No man, and I mean no man, will be good enough for you in my book. But that doesn't mean I'll keep the one away who has earned your love."

"Who would have thought my grumpy big brother would be rooting for a happily ever after?"

"I'm getting a beer." He stands up and heads to the kitchen. I know I pushed him beyond his comfort zone tonight. Might as well go for broke.

"So, you wanna join us for girl's night?"

"I was hoping you would ask," he says with a wink.

Who is this new Alexander Decker? Yep, it's going to be an interesting senior year.

CHAPTER
TWENTY-ONE

COLE

———

"Man, it's hard to believe this is our last semester," Matt says as we drive home after practice. The holidays are behind us, and our first game is less than a month away. "This is it. Time to shine. Our last hurrah."

It's a strange feeling knowing everything you've worked for and dreamed about will happen in the next few months. Or it won't. Everything hangs in the balance. Right now, it's still a possibility, and I'm hopeful.

"You and me, man. We are going to kick ass this season and keep this dream alive." And then what? We'll go our separate ways. But we'll be professional baseball players. That's what's important, right?

"I'm psyched about the hockey game tonight, aren't you? Seats against the glass and a meet and greet after the game. The whole team is stoked." Matt has been looking forward to this for weeks.

Julian Decker kept his promise to Matt, reaching out to Coach

Bailey and arranging for the entire team to attend tonight's home game of the Raleigh Renegades. Thinking about that promise reminds me of the dinner we all had last summer. Memories of her flood back, my chest tightening. I've been pretty good about keeping her locked away, but this reminds me of everything I loved about her. Leigh. Mine. Man, was I a cocky and misguided bastard. Definitely not mine.

"Yeah, it will be great. The guys all think you are a rockstar for this connection. They are all clamoring to carry your books to class and shit." I've been teasing Matt about his popularity and his Chance Fuller connection with the guys. His Decker connection.

I try to hide the impact last summer had on me, but I have no doubt Matt is aware of my deception. My teasing him about this connection isn't fooling him, but I appreciate his discretion. He lets me pretend I'm okay, and that's a kindness I'll never forget.

I've never attended a professional hockey game before, and I have to admit, it was exciting. Everything moved fast, and when Chance Fuller got checked into the glass right in front of us, the team went wild. I appreciate the fire and passion. Maybe I picked the wrong sport?

After the Renegades win, we go to the dressing room for group photos. If this is a pro locker room, sign me up. Each player has his own stall that is nicer than my closet at home. But what's with hockey that they have a dressing room? I mean in baseball, it's a clubhouse, but still. And their jerseys are called sweaters? Hockey has its own language.

Baseball jerseys and hockey sweaters are a strange combination, but it works. The PR people are eating it up. That makes me think of her too. Our social media intern is taking videos and clamoring for the perfect shot.

A cross-pollination of sports with guys playing at the highest level can inspire anyone who dreams of getting to the big league, regardless of the sport. Being at the top of your game, and getting the call, is what it's about.

The Renegades sign our jerseys and we chat with them. Most of our guys are fangirling over these hockey guys like they are fucking Harry Styles or something. I'm not going to bust their balls over it. I get it. We are in the presence of hockey royalty. Under other circumstances, I'd be just like them.

I feel pressure on my back, and whoever is signing my jersey has strength. "Davidson? Cole, is it? I've heard *a lot* about you." I turn my head at the deep voice to find Chance Fuller signing my jersey. Chance Fuller has heard about me? Heard a lot about me? What the fuck Twilight Zone episode am I living in right now?

"Um, yeah. It's nice to meet you. I'm afraid to ask how you've heard about me?" I give a nervous chuckle as I reach out to shake his hand.

His hand is enormous and swallows mine. I'm no tiny guy, but Chance, he's huge. I wouldn't want to take a punch from him. Thinking about taking a punch makes me chuckle a little.

"Let's just say we have mutual, um, friends. You were an interesting part of the Deckers' summer."

Of course. The Deckers. Chance is Julian's best friend. Julian, brother to Alexander fucking Decker. I sigh. "Yeah, last summer feels like another lifetime ago."

He gives me a look that I can't quite interpret. It's a combination of pity and intimidation. "Well, good luck this season. Stay away from the jersey chasers and focus on your game."

"Yeah, girls aren't on the radar, so that's not a problem," I say, without even thinking about it. I haven't even looked at a girl in the past six months. No one holds a candle to her.

Chance breaks out into a big smile and winks. "Good to know. Just know I'm rooting for you, Cole." He claps me on the shoulder and then walks off to chat with another teammate.

Chance Fuller is rooting for me. What does that even mean?

CHAPTER
TWENTY-TWO

ASHLEIGH

———

"Thanks for meeting me on such short notice, Ash. I'm excited about handing over my social media to you. I'm getting pressured to post more content by a few potential sponsors, and Julian said you needed a senior project, so I thought this would be a win-win," Chance says.

Chance texted me yesterday asking if I could meet to discuss a project, and like he said, it is a win-win. Since he's in the middle of the season, getting time to connect is hard for him, but today he had a rare day off. We decided to meet at a coffee shop near the arena, which is near the NC State campus. When I arrive, he is seated in a cozy booth with a dirty chai latte waiting for me. Chance always takes excellent care of me. One of the good guys.

"Chance, this is perfect. I'm so grateful you're giving me this opportunity. I know you're busy, so we can talk about your goals and the story you want to tell, and I can take it from there. Do you want final approval before posts?"

"Nah, you're in charge. Just do your magic. Whatever you need, I'm cool with it."

"Well, I use software that will help track your posts. I'll ensure that posts increase your following and tell a story. You trust me with your pictures? I'm not going to see anything, um, private, am I?" Just the thought has me blushing like a virgin on her wedding night.

He reaches out and puts his hand over mine. "Ash, I trust you completely. And no, I'm not dumb enough to take a picture of anything I don't want my mother to see. Or my best friend's little sister," he says with a megawatt smile and wink. Damn, this guy is sexy—and the wink? Full-on panty melting. That is, for others. For me, he's still a surrogate big brother.

He looks over my shoulder, smiles, and nods to someone approaching our table. Probably a fan or one of his teammates.

Chance looks up and smiles widely. He removes his hand from mine to reach out to shake his hand. "Hey, man, good to see you again."

"You too. I didn't mean to interrupt your date." I freeze at that voice. The voice from my dreams. The voice that says loving words while I sleep. The voice that sends chills down to my toes.

I look up, and our eyes meet. He's let his hair grow out a bit. It's longer around his face. He hasn't shaved in a few days, and his scruff gives him a rugged look. He's wearing an NC State Baseball hat, putting his eyes in shadow, but I can see them open fully when he sees me.

His look transitions from shock to softness, and a warm smile slowly spreads across his face. He says my name in a whisper. "Leigh."

I haven't heard that name in months, but when he says it, it's like bringing her back from the dead. That name on his lips is an AED to my heart.

I'm caught by surprise, and it takes a few seconds for me to realize this is real. I look over at Chance, who is grinning like the Cheshire Cat. And then his greeting hits me. Good to see you

AGAIN? Does he know Cole? The feeling that floods my body turns my blood cold as I glare at Chance. My focus on Chance doesn't go unnoticed by Cole.

His smile fades, and his expression turns to one of disgust.

"Well, Leigh, looks like you landed your prize jersey. I knew you'd succeed at getting anything you put your mind to. Guess those vision boards finally paid off, huh? Congratulations." His tone is harsh and venomous. He's found his voice, his statement loud and clear. He gives a short nod to Chance, turns on his heel, and bolts out of the coffee shop.

A tear slips down my cheek. Chance slides beside me in the booth and puts his arm around me. "What was that all about? I thought he'd be happy to see you."

"Yeah, well, not when he thinks I'm a gold-digging jersey chaser," I say. "Chance, email me your information, and I'll start working on it immediately. But I gotta go," I say as I push him away and follow in Cole's footsteps, rushing out of the coffee shop.

CHAPTER
TWENTY-THREE

COLE

———

"She was with Chance Fuller, Matt. Chance, he's my secret crush, Fuller!" I'm pacing around the living room, my pent-up anger seeking an outlet. I have so much energy that I can practically hear it sizzling and cracking around me. Matt approaches with his hands up like he's approaching a rabid animal.

"Maybe it wasn't what it looked like," Matt offers up.

"He was holding her hand when I walked up. Before I knew it was her." How could she? I know it's been six and a half months. But I haven't been able to get her out of my goddamn mind. I've tried. She invades my thoughts in class. I see a girl with braids and think it might be her. I hear a laugh with just the right pitch, and I scour the room thinking she might be there. I know we go to school in the same city. I've thought about running into her in public places. People probably think I'm crazy as I scan coffee shops and restaurants when I enter, looking for her. And I haven't found her until today. And when I find her, she's with Chance Fuller. Was the connection only one-sided? I shake my head trying to knock those thoughts out of my head. No. I can't believe that. But clearly, she's moved on.

"Besides, even if it wasn't what it appeared, I wasn't kind. I'm sure she'd never talk to me after that comment." I'm a fucking idiot. I reacted. I didn't assess the situation objectively.

"Maybe. But look, you said there was a moment. Don't forget that."

"I need to forget it. I need to move on. Maybe find some girl and cleanse my brain of her."

"I can tell you from experience that doesn't help. It only makes you feel like shit."

Aw man, now I've poked at Matt's old wound. I remember the aftermath of Penny. Matt may have gotten lots of action, but he was a miserable bastard.

"I know Penny ripped your heart out, Matt. But that was years ago."

Matt gives me a look that communicates that I need to shut the fuck up about Penny.

Penny and Matt were high school sweethearts for three years. They tried the long-distance thing freshman year. Matt surprised her one weekend and discovered her with someone else. He returned to school and was a complete man whore for a few months, constantly looking for a girl to fill that void in his chest. It was ugly, and he's absolutely right. It was hell to watch him self-destruct. Focusing on baseball was the only thing that saved him.

"Irrelevant," Matt says. "I'm telling you not to go there. Not yet. We've got our first game in two weeks. Flip the switch. Let's start strong." Matt's right. I can't let this mess with me. I'm already struggling. No need to add unnecessary complications.

"Yeah, you're right. " I sink down on the couch. "You're right. I wish I had her number. Or I could find her on social media." She never accepted my follow requests, and those accounts don't exist when I search for her now. It's like she disappeared. "I feel like I should apologize. I feel guilty for…" I sit down and pull at my hair. "I finally found her, and I was a total asshole. Fuck me."

Matt gives a half smile. He's got something to say. "What?" I ask sharply.

"Maybe find her through Chance? Drop him a DM?" Matt's suggestion is stupid. I highly doubt he reads his DMs. And why would he help me connect with her if he's dating her?

Although, there is some merit to his idea. Maybe I need to stalk Chance Fuller's social media to find her? I can figure out if they are together.

I can't help myself. It's like I'm the poster child for self-sabotage. I pull up Chance's Insta, and the latest post is of the meet and greet with the team a few weeks ago. I start scrolling. Most of his posts are of him after a game or in the gym, all sweaty and shirtless. Damn, this guy is shredded. I can tell I'm not his target audience. He posts pictures of his community outreach projects, mainly at an animal shelter. There's an occasional post of him and Julian hitting the town in New York. He's not as active on social media as I expected. I keep scrolling back and stop. There she is.

The picture is tagged in Cancun, days after she left Savannah. She's between Chance and a cute, petite, brunette girl about her same age. I wonder if that's her friend Emma? The girls aren't tagged, and they aren't identified in the comments.

They are doing shots and getting pedicures. She looks tired but smiling. Not a full-fledged smile, but the end of her lips are curled up. Definitely not heartbroken. The caption reads, *Who knew girl time could be so fun?*

Something seems off, though. The timeline doesn't make sense. She leaves Savannah after telling me she's in love with Alexander Decker, and a few days later, she's with Chance Fuller in Mexico. Could she jump to Chance that fast? And Chance is Julian's best friend. Would Julian be cool with her cheating on his brother with his best friend? Not likely. She can't be with

Chance. No way. At least, I hope not. I'm going to cling to that hope.

I fucked up again. Royally.

Maybe Matt's idea isn't so stupid after all. I mean, it's a shot, right?

I message Chance. It's not like things could get worse.

CHAPTER
TWENTY-FOUR

ASHLEIGH

———

"I still can't believe Cole was there," I tell Emma when I get home.

"And he really accused you of being a gold digger?"

"Basically. His tone was so mean. I've never heard him sound like that before. I was shocked." But his eyes. My heart beat for the first time since Savannah when I looked into his eyes. Tears threaten to fall, but I refuse to let them.

"Well, you know he was shocked too. Why was he so set off by Chance?" Great question. I think about Cole's jealousy and how upset he gets around Xander. But Chance? Then it hits me.

"Remember when I told you about that dinner on Tybee with Cole, Matt, Jules, Xander, and Trevor? I was teasing Jules and said Chance was my secret crush. Cole got a little mad over that because, of course, he thought I was already with Xan. Then he sees me with him." I bury my face in the throw pillows on the couch. "AHHHH" Screaming doesn't fix anything, but I do feel a little better.

"Look, he's not a hard guy to find. One google search for their home game schedule, and you find him. Go. Meet him after the game and confess it all. Just clear the air."

Emma has a point. Could it be that easy? But I can't confess who I am. I have to remember why I stayed away in the first place. It was so he could focus on baseball. So he didn't get caught in my tangled web of the Decker family. At least not any more than he already has. My mind is racing, playing out the scenarios.

"I'll think about it, Em. But for now, I will focus on Chance's social media presence and school. If I do well, it could launch my career and get Chance those endorsements he wants."

I open Chance's social media and begin an analysis. Lots of workout pics. Not many personal pics, but I understand. He doesn't want his life under a microscope. But people want to feel like they know him, feel connected to him.

I can help there. Chance is a great guy. I need to share that selectively. A few more family pictures. Shots with him and Julian. More team pictures. Increase the use of hashtags. Increase his followers from hockey fans and puck bunnies to a more diverse audience.

One of his last posts is a group picture of the Renegades and the NC State baseball team. Then it clicks. *Good to see you again.* They met at the game meet and greet. At least that makes sense. Oh well. It doesn't change anything. I need to focus on this project.

I open his DMs and see he has over two thousand unread messages. I scan them to see that most offer phone numbers or sexual favors. I start deleting them. I hate puck bunnies. I save a few asking him for community outreach and have to ask Chance how he wants me to address those. Once I've reached the top, he's already gotten seven new messages. I go to delete them when I see one is from 1stBaseDavidson. Could it be?

I cautiously open the message, like it will jump out of my computer and attack.

> Hey Chance. It's Cole Davidson. I want to apologize for my rude behavior today. It wasn't cool, and I feel horrible. I know this is a big ask, but do you have Leigh's number? I need to apologize to her most of all. I know this is unconventional, but I'm desperate. She's amazing and didn't deserve the treatment she got from me. Thanks.

Cole reached out to Chance for my number. Oh, this is awkward. My heart starts to beat again, faintly. I can't stop the smile that stretches across my face.

"What's got you smiling, girl?" Emma throws a pillow at me, and my smile grows.

"Just going through Chance's DMs."

"Ewww. I bet it's flooded with puck bunnies. Lots of nudes?"

"Yeah, I deleted those already. I hope he knows what he signed up for, allowing me total access. Lots of bunnies, but maybe one handsome baseball player too?" I smirk and wiggle my eyebrows at her.

"What?" She looks baffled. "Tripp Stevenson slipped into his DMs? Don't tell me he sent Chance a picture of his cat?"

I laugh. "No, not Tripp. Why would Tripp reach out through Insta?" Emma shrugs.

"So who is……nooooooo." It's like a lightbulb goes off. "Cole didn't reach out to Chance, did he?"

I nod, grinning like Tripp's cat on catnip. "What do I do?"

"What did he say?" She gets up and comes to look over my shoulder, reading the message on my laptop. "Oh. That's quite a conundrum, friend. What do you want to do?"

"Do you think Chance would mind if I respond as him?"

"He's given you carte blanche, right? Go for it. Besides, you know he wants you to be happy."

I start typing a reply. "How's this?" I let Emma read it before I hit send.

> I don't know if I feel comfortable giving you her
> number without her permission, but I'll pass the
> message along. It's the best I can do. And yes,
> you are correct. She didn't deserve it. But can I
> ask why the change of heart?

"Send it." Emma squeezes my shoulder. "I'm dying to see what he says."

It doesn't take long when Cole responds.

> IF Leigh is with you, then I don't need to tell you
> how fucking lucky you are. And IF she's with
> you, it's because you are a stand-up guy. Leigh
> wouldn't waste her time or her love on
> someone unworthy. She's not a jersey chaser.
> She's special. You know that. I know that. And I
> know I was an ass. I just need her to know I
> think better of her than that.

"Um, wow." Emma sits next to me and fans herself. "That boy has it bad for you. Now what are you going to say?"

I sit back on the couch and close my eyes. Count to ten. Maybe twenty. What am I going to say? I feel like I'm playing with fire, and we all know the potential to get burned is high. What if? What if we meet? What if we date? It's probably best for him to keep his distance. Is it selfish to want to see where this goes? Em says he's got it bad for me. Well, I've got it bad too. How can that be after this much time? We haven't communicated in six months, but that pull hasn't lessened. I think I've just learned to live with a shredded heart. But what if I don't have to live with it?

I need to think about my response.

"What do you think I should do, Em?" Tears threaten to spill just thinking about him.

"Honestly?" I nod my head. Yes, I want her to be honest. Cole promised me he'd be honest. That's one thing I haven't been with him. "Follow your heart, Ash. You need to see where this goes. I think you should see him. Give him a chance."

"But I'm not ready to tell him everything." I don't think I can give him my secrets. Not yet. My secrets are the only protection I have right now.

"Then don't. But be you. The real you. The you we all love. Your name is just a label. Let him keep getting to know you." She holds my hands tight. "Meet him. I can be around if you need a rescue. I'll have your posse on backup if you want. But meet him."

"I don't need a rescue." I smile at that thought. How many times did I tell him I wasn't a damsel in distress? "And I don't want the boys to know. Not yet, at least. Let's just see how this goes first."

"So, are you going to respond?"

"No, I don't think so." Emma looks at me like I'm crazy. I open a new tab and do a google search. "Want to go to a baseball game with me?"

CHAPTER
TWENTY-FIVE

COLE

————

Opening day weather can be unpredictable in Raleigh. Today, Mother Nature decided to be kind. Even though I play for the other school, I can't deny a beautiful Carolina blue sky when I see one. The sun is out, and the temperature is perfect for an early spring ball game.

It's our first home game, and the clubroom room pranks are plentiful. The pranks help everyone work the jitters out. My teammates know I'm not to be toyed with lately, so they have given me a wide berth today. My smiles have taken a vacation this year. I've been wound tight at practices. But I'm okay. Baseball is my focus.

Even though it's been ten days since I heard from Chance, I feel at peace. I have to assume he gave her my message. At least she knows I'm sorry. I've done what I can do.

I've become an expert at flipping the switch, and I'm all about baseball. All the time. I guess I don't switch it back anymore. The guys call me Mr. Baseball now. My pre-season stats are impressive. I'm batting a .395 and protecting my bag like it's the crown jewels. Coach told me I've gotten the attention of a few scouts, so I keep doing what I'm doing. Eat. Sleep. Baseball.

Matt and the others can still think I'm Mr. Baseball, but they forget who they are dealing with. Sometimes, deception is a strategy, and it currently works in my favor. The guys will never suspect I've got my prank locked and loaded. They won't see it coming, and I damn sure know they won't think I'm behind it.

We head out on the field for warm-ups as the stands start to fill up. I don't typically look in the stands, but I can feel the energy and hear the chatter.

Today is a Saturday afternoon game, and I expect the first day of warm spring weather will bring out a lot of fans. Everyone is ready to enjoy the sun after winter.

I love playing the game for the fans. Ever since little league, the cheering raises the enjoyability factor for me. I love the performance. Maybe that's why the Pajamas are such an easy fit. I play baseball for the love of the game. And the fans. And the future it could give me and my family. I'm not going to lie. The money and security would be nice. Getting to make a living doing something I love - that's just the cherry on top.

We take the field for the start of the game, and it's three up, three down. At this pace, we'll be able to get the early bird special for dinner. Matt leads off our batting order. The announcer calls his name, and his walk-up song plays. Only it doesn't. His usual song is switched out, and they play "Barbie Girl." The dugout loses it, as does the crowd. Matt laughs, and it takes him an extra swing before he steps into the box. The crowd loves it, and they keep singing it after the ten-second cut. He must like it too. He hits a line drive past the shortstop and gets a double out of it. Maybe he should keep the song?

Our next two batters also have new walk-up songs. Maybe "Baby Shark" was a bad idea for Roberts because it's still playing in my head when I'm on deck. But Roberts gets a double, and

Matt is brought home. He gives me a high-five after he crosses home plate.

Of course, my walk-up song is changed too. I mean, if I didn't, then they'd know it was me, right? I walk up to a little "Oh Darlin" as a homage to my viral video. At first, I thought it might make me sad, but I decided to acknowledge the joy it brought at the moment. I sing into my bat like it's a microphone, leaning into the song. The crowd goes wild. This pitcher is all over the place, but I desperately want a hit with my first at-bat. After several pitches, I find myself in a full-count situation and think about her question. *Full count, Cole. What do you do?* Go for it. Take the risk. With her in mind, I swing.

As a batter, you just know when you hit it out of the park. The connection feels different. The crack of the bat has a distinct sound, and this one has that feel. I flip the bat and take off for first and slow as I get to the bag. I watch the ball sail over the left outfield wall. Yep. Mission accomplished. Home run on my first at-bat today. Hell yeah, I'll take that!

After I round the bases and bring Roberts in with me, the rest of the team greets us at home plate. Matt gives me a big hug and a hard swat on the butt.

"You make a pretty good DJ, dude." He's cracking up. "Wish you would've included me, though. Now this week makes more sense. I thought we were past the weird emo shit and sad songs, and then I heard boy band music coming from your room. I'll admit, I was worried."

"What makes you think it was me?" Matt knows me too well, and I can't keep anything from him. So he caught me listing to unusual songs earlier in the week? Now the strange looks make sense. He earns a smile from me.

"Is that one of those elusive Cole Davidson smiles? I thought they were extinct," he teases.

"Nah, just making them limited editions and bringing them out for special occasions."

We go into the dugout, leaning against the rail, and watch the game. We are off to a great start.

Matt leans in and whispers. "So, was the smile for me or her?"

"What?" I look at Matt. "I have no idea what you're talking about."

"She's here, you know," he says, knocking into me and bumping shoulders.

Matt has lost me in this conversation. "Who's here?"

"Leigh. She's here. Sitting at my base." He nods his head in that direction. "Thought you might have seen her. I wondered if the homer was for her." He says it casually, but he's watching me closely. He knows I no longer look into the stands once the first pitch is thrown. After that incident with the Pajamas, the stands are off-limits.

I look now. I scan the stands over the visitor dugout on the third baseline. And there she is. Four rows up. Cheering for my team. Her smile fills her face, looking like a heavenly vision. She told me how much she loves baseball, and here she is, enjoying my game.

Her hair is in what I consider her signature loose braids, and she has a backward baseball hat on her head. She's wearing a raglan shirt for the Charleston Ghost Peppers, a minor league team for the Reapers. She's casual and so damn beautiful. She's not dressed like most other girls our age at the game. They are always made up with hair perfectly done and impeccable makeup. Total Janes. But that's because they are all trying to snag a player. Not Leigh. She's here for the game. And for me, I hope. Whether she knows it or not, she's already snagged this player. She's singing along and laughing as they play Tristan's walk-up song, "How Far I'll Go," from *Moana*.

It's as if she can sense that I'm looking at her, no, staring would be more accurate, and she shifts her gaze from the field to the dugout to me. We lock eyes, and I give her a little smile. She winks back and elbows a petite brunette beside her, the same one in Chance's picture. Oh shit. She really is here.

We need to pick it up. Leigh is here. My heart is beating so loud I'm sure Matt can hear it above the crowd noise. This better not be a bad opening game prank being pulled on me.

Matt knocks shoulders with me, breaking my stare down. "I think she likes me best. After all, she's at my base, not yours." Matt is attempting to throw shade. It's weak shade, and he's waiting for a reaction. To her or him, I'm not sure. I don't bite at his teasing. I can't. My heart is beating right for the first time in months. I'm ready to do backflips up the baseline, and it takes everything I have to stay in the dugout. I want to run through the stands until I can see her and make sure she's not some figment of my imagination. I'm trying not to make a fool of myself, but I need to do something, or I might explode.

I decide to maximize this energy and focus it on the team and our game. It's time to bring a little Pajamas to the Wolfpack. We've got a good crowd and a special guest. "Let's have a little Pajama party, Matt." I slug him in the arm.

"Easy man, that's my money maker," he says as he rubs his arm. The coaches watch our exchange, and they give me a nod.

Coach Bailey comes from behind us, puts his arm across our shoulders, and drops his head between us. "Good job with the songs. Cole, glad to see the spark back. Mr. Baseball is kicking ass, but he's not nearly as much fun. I've missed the loose ball player."

"What makes you think we did the songs?" I ask, with a massive smile on my face. I say we because Matt and I are always the collective we, for good or bad.

"Because he knows you, Cole. And I agree. Let's have some fun today," Matt says.

Matt and I start hyping up the guys, getting them to dance between innings. We up our chirping game, rattling their pitcher. And their relief pitcher too. The mental game is just as important as talent. When you lose the mental game, it's a bad day all around. I should know. I've experienced it.

I'm not capable of looking back in the stands, though. I know it will be too distracting. I know she's there. My body senses her presence, and I can breathe again. I think I can hear her cheering over the rest of the crowd when I'm on the field. She's quiet when I'm at bat, or else I'm still wholly focused on the pitch, I'm not sure. Mr. Baseball is still here to play. I imagine she's cheering for me. And hopefully, waiting for me after the game.

We have a great game and win twelve to zero. Not bad for a Saturday afternoon. I look up at her before we leave the field, and she nods. She's here for me.

When we enter the clubhouse, the party atmosphere permeates the air. Everyone is celebrating the big blowout. Teammates are talking about keeping their walk-up song for the next game. Someone suggests we make them have a theme, like Disney songs or something. They acknowledge that the crowd loved them. My smile isn't hard to pull out today.

I will miss this team, but hopefully, I'll get to keep playing ball and take the fun with me. Getting paid to play the game I love is the dream. And my girl by my side as I navigate the minors, icing on the cake.

In the commotion, I hear someone mention scouts in attendance. Even better. I had a great game, and scouts this early in the season is a good sign. I don't even care if it was Decker. Hell, I can't lie to myself. I do care if Decker was in the same proximity as Leigh.

I take the fastest shower ever and head out while everyone is still chatting it up. Not slowing down, I grab my phone and wallet from my locker and head to the door, picking up my pace to find my girl. As I slam the crash bar on the door, banging it open, Matt shouts, "Good luck!"

I glance over my shoulder to find everyone looking toward me, stunned into silence. The guys are curious and hold their collective breath, waiting for me to clue them in. I don't have time for them right now. This is one of those times when the individual needs to focus on their game and not worry about the team. I need to focus on finding my girl.

As I rush down the tunnel, I pass families, girlfriends, and cleat chasers. They all greet me and shout, "Good game" as I scan the crowd, but I don't see her. I slow down and take a breath. She's not waiting for me here.

I walk back into the stadium. Maybe she's still in the stands? Hope fills my heart, knowing that I'm about to see her, talk to her, and touch her. She's here. Mine.

CHAPTER
TWENTY-SIX

ASHLEIGH

———

"That was so much fun," Emma says as the fans leave.

"It really was. Opening day is always special." My nerves kick in, and I'm starting to reconsider my plan or, rather, my lack of a plan. Maybe I should leave? He knows I'm here. Perhaps that should be enough for the first step.

"Did I get a glimpse of the Pajamas today? Because that was the most fun I've had at a baseball game in forever."

I laugh at Emma's dramatic statement. "Yeah, that was a hint of the Pajamas. I can't believe you've never gone to a game before. They are tons of fun. It's like going to a circus, and a baseball game breaks out."

The vibe of Division One ball is often intense, but I saw some Pajamas in them today, which flooded me with happy memories. Their team was fired up, and I know Cole was part of that. The team's reaction to the switched-out walk-up songs was a huge hit. The crowd kept singing each song long after the sound byte stopped, me included. Each at-bat was different, so the guys had multiple songs. It was evident that most of the songs had jokes or inside stories, judging by the reaction in the dugout.

Like Cole's "Oh Darlin." That one got me. Sometimes I watch that video at night, allowing myself to cry over him.

I put my hand to my stomach, trying to quiet the butterflies that are having their own circus at the moment.

"Cole knows you came." It's a statement, not a question.

"Yup." I pop my p.

I know he saw me today. Matt saw me first and told Cole. I watched his eyes scan the stands, locking on me after his home run. I studied his face for a tell. He appeared to go through a myriad of emotions in the span of seconds. Then, he got that familiar goofy smile that is usually accompanied by Cole-like shenanigans, and he never looked into the stands or at me for the rest of the game.

Most players are like that. After the call to "play ball." they don't take their eyes off the field.

Cole started the summer game-focused, only doing Pajama activities at games he wasn't playing. As the summer went on, he loosened up.

If I wasn't on the field with the guys filming and catching antics, I'd be in the stands capturing fan moments. I could feel Cole's eyes track me during those games. I knew he was watching me, and I won't deny I liked it.

Then there was the game he saw me with Xander. It was his worst game of the season. It was the game I realized I was a distraction.

When we walked on the beach that night, he confessed that seeing me messed with his head and affected his gameplay. Knowing that I could impact his game like that, it was one of the things I leaned on when I needed the strength to walk away. Cole doesn't need a distraction.

I smile at the thought that I didn't impact his game today, especially with a few scouts in the stands, including Johnny Wilkes from the Reapers. I am tempted to talk to Johnny, but I need to stay out of this. Seeing Johnny here is encouraging. Alexander said he wouldn't write Cole off, and at least he's holding up his promise to me.

"Are you ready for this, Ash? You sure you want to see him?" Emma may have enjoyed the game, but I noticed her watching me too. When I'd hold my breath a little too long, I'd feel a nudge, or she'd ask me a question to make me talk. I appreciate that she allows me the option to bail. I slowly nod my head. I'm not sure if it's for her benefit or mine.

Nope. I need to do this.

"Yeah, I'm staying. But I think I'm going to sit here for a minute. It will take him some time to change, and his coach might need him. Do you mind waiting with me, and let's just see how it goes?" For all my bravado, I'm a nervous wreck, and Emma knows it.

"Girl, you know I'm here for you, no matter what. Ride or die. And I have the others on speed dial." She laughs as she holds up her phone, showing a group text with Jules and Chance.

"We decided to keep them out of this for now, remember?" The last thing I need is an overprotective big brother and a hulk of an NHL player swooping in.

"I know, but just in case." Emma's eyes grow wide as she looks behind me. She bites her bottom lip and smiles like a kid at Christmas. "Um, don't look now, but..."

"Hey." His deep, southern voice sends goosebumps down my spine. I inhale deeply and slowly turn around to find Cole standing behind me. His hair is still damp, and his clothes are spotted with water droplets. It reminds me of the first time I saw him in the water after he rescued me in the kayak.

I can smell the strong scent of his Old Spice body wash, so I know he showered, so definitely not sweat. I'm not sure he even dried off out of the shower. He looks like he got dressed on the run. He's still gorgeous in his disheveled state. He opted for speed over appearance. I'm exhilarated knowing he wanted to rush to see me.

He looks down at me, his face holding a tentative smile. His eyes don't leave mine. Is he trying to read my mind? I wonder what's running through his. Is he asking himself why I'm here or if I will run? He's practically holding his breath.

Emma gives me a nudge to respond. I absently rub my side. My ribcage is going to be sore after today.

"Hey." I'm practically catatonic, and it's the only word I can seem to muster. My brain is running fast, words and ideas rapidly firing, but nothing connecting to my mouth. I knew I'd see him today but thought I'd have a few more minutes.

Emma hops up and throws her hand out to Cole, effectively reaching across me.

"Hi, Cole. I'm Emma. You had a great game today." She's bouncing on her toes, her usual bundle of energy. She successfully breaks our stare down, and I'm grateful for her save. She can read a room like it's her superpower. It goes along with her ability to see human auras. I wonder what she senses about Cole? I'll have to ask her later.

Cole gives her his full smile and shakes her hand, and when he lets go, he drops his hand to my shoulder. His simple touch sends a shock through my body, like jumper cables to a dead battery, bringing me back to life.

I tried hard to forget my attraction to Cole. I've convinced myself that my memories were just exaggerations because they couldn't have been that intense. Obviously, I've been lying to myself.

Cole's manners must kick in because he responds to Emma. "It's nice to meet you, Emma. Thanks for taking care of our girl here."

That comment snaps me out of my haze. I cock my head to the side, giving him one of my "what the hell" looks he said I should trademark. Taking care of who? Oh yeah, I also remember how he pisses me off too.

His reaction is instant. "Not that she needs taking care of. I don't know if you are aware, but she is NOT a damsel in distress." He leans in and winks at Emma, and she giggles. What the hell, Em?

My courage is wavering. My head is telling me I need to leave. Now. This is a terrible idea. Unfortunately, my heart has a different agenda. Head or heart? When my heart tightens, I know who is going to win today.

I gather what little courage I have left and face him head-on. "Why don't you have a seat, trouble? I'm sure you're tired after all those bases you had to run around." I pat the seat next to me, and he sits. We both turn toward one another, our knees touching. His eyes lock with mine again.

"On that note, I'm going to bounce. You guys okay here?" She looks between me and Cole, pointing her phone at each of us. "I'm not going to have to call in the reinforcements, am I?" She turns her phone to me, reminding me who's on her speed dial.

I give her a weak smile. "No, we should be fine, but keep your phone close, just in case. We might need to implement our emergency plan." She leans in for a hug.

"I've got the shovel and tarp in the trunk just in case," Emma says loud enough for Cole to hear.

"Thanks, Em. I hope we don't have to do that again."

"Again?" Cole asks. He quirks an eyebrow, giving Emma a quizzical glance.

I shrug.

Emma laughs. "I think we figured out where we went wrong last time. Won't make that mistake again. Those true crime podcasts are paying off."

Cole's eyes widen, and he gives her a look of fear and a bit of respect.

She starts toward the exit, walking in front of me and Cole. She looks over her shoulder and says, "Nice meeting you, Cole. I hope to see you around." As an afterthought, she says, "Don't screw up."

"Thanks, Emma. Appreciate the support," Cole says with a slight chuckle.

He turns his attention back to me. Emma stops and turns behind him and gives me the double thumbs up. She mouths, "I like him," as she walks away. I laugh. Her approval means everything to me and gives me the confidence I need.

He turns around to see what he's missing, but Emma is almost at the top of the stairs as she heads home.

"Emma seems great," he starts.

"She is. The best friend a girl could have." I'm not sure what to say. But then, he was the one to request this meeting. "So, I understand you had something you wanted to say to me?"

He clears his throat, clearly nervous. This is a different side of Cole. He's usually so confident. This case of nerves is kind of endearing.

"Um, yeah. I guess Chance Fuller told you I reached out." I give a slight nod.

"That's a sentence I never thought I'd say," he continues, mumbling. "Anyway, I wanted." He shakes his head like he's trying to clear his thoughts. His hands twist together in his lap. "No, not want. I need to apologize. Look, what I said to you when I saw you a few days ago, that wasn't fair of me, and I wasn't nice. I hated myself as I said it." He grabs his hat, rakes his hand through his damp hair, and puts his hat back on backward. There's that familiar tell I'm used to. I let a small smile escape.

He takes a deep breath and continues. "I was shocked at seeing you and, honestly, jealous. I've looked for you all over Raleigh, and then to see you there, with him? No excuse, but I snapped." He looks down at his hands. "But you didn't deserve to be treated like that. You'd done nothing wrong." He takes another deep breath and continues. His head comes up, and his emerald green eyes bore into me. "If you are with Chance, then I respect that. I want you to be happy. But I was hoping we could still be friends." He finishes his speech and looks down at his hands, waiting for a response.

I immediately miss the intensity of his eyes. A cool breeze blows through the stands, reminding me it's still early spring. I cross my arms across my body and rub my hands up and down, bringing warmth back. Losing his gaze adds to the coldness I feel. I haven't felt warm since Savannah.

I think about what he said. He thought I was with Chance. When he said that in his DMs, he kept saying *if* as if he wasn't sure. But he's right. I didn't deserve his comment. Does he really think so little of me? That I'm a gold-digging cleat chaser?

"You're right. Your words were hurtful, and I didn't deserve them." His shoulders and head drop lower at my reprimand. I reach over and put my fingers below his chin, making him look at me for this part. "But let me clarify something. I'm not with Chance. We are friends. He's helping me with my senior project. That's it."

His eyes dart across my face like he's trying to decipher what I'm saying. A small smile starts to emerge. He swallows deeply and takes a deep breath. "And what about Decker? Do you still love him?"

I close my eyes for a second. I knew this was going to come up. I'm not ready to share that. I know I need to come clean, but I can't. Not yet. I can't impact his future like that. When I open my eyes and look at him, his smile is gone.

"It's complicated."

He looks crestfallen. My need to see his smile again is overwhelming. I need to fix this in the best way possible without divulging the truth. At least not yet.

"But he's not my boyfriend. I'm one hundred percent unattached." I give him a shy smile and a shrug.

His smile slowly creeps back, this time stopping at full force. No longer a hint of a smile but a full one that reaches his eyes. His dimple pops, breaking the last bit of protective wall I have around my heart. He cups my cheek, his thumb gently brushing against my bottom lip. My body reacts to his touch, goose bumps covering my arms again, but not because I'm cold this time.

It all comes rushing back. The memory of his touch. His lips. The memories I haven't allowed myself to think about during waking hours, at least.

"Leigh," he whispers. He says my name with sweet reverence. Even though it's not a name I'm used to and haven't heard in months, I still love to hear him say it. It's not foreign to my ears. It's who I am with him. Somehow, that makes it special. "I want to kiss you." His breath caresses my skin, raising my body temperature as he leans in, inches from my face. He waits for my response.

"I'd be disappointed if you didn't," I whisper.

CHAPTER
TWENTY-SEVEN

COLE

———

Third base is now officially my favorite spot on the field. I lean in to kiss Leigh, and it's more magnificent than I remember.

She breathes life into my soul. Her lips against mine are my reason for living. I've been a zombie from the walking dead until this moment when she brings me back. She's the cure. She is my missing piece. She completes me. Shit. I sound like a fucking rom-com or something. But I don't care because I feel fucking fantastic right now.

Our kiss is gentle, tender, and hesitant. When our lips connect, a welcome home feeling fills me. She tastes like bubble gum, and I can't help but think one thing. Mine.

I pull away, even though it's the hardest thing I've ever done. I want to consume her. But not this time. This time, I'm going to do it right. I think whatever made her run away on that beach still exists. It's complicated, she said.

So I'll take it slow. Woo her. Give her what she deserves. Let her see how good we are for each other. I can't spook her. She's run before, and I don't want her to do that again.

I've thought about this moment and played all the possible scenarios out in my head.

I lace our fingers together, and electric currents run up my arm. Her touch is my personal TENS device. At least she's letting me hold her hand. It means she's not running. For now.

I press my forehead against hers. "That was nice."

"Yeah. I wasn't sure if I'd remembered correctly. For the record, I did." She gives me a shy smile, her baby-blue eyes dancing with happiness. I want to stop time and keep us together, in this moment, forever. She can't leave. Not yet.

Next step. Don't let her go. Holding her hostage wouldn't be a good idea though.

"You hungry? Let me take you to dinner," I ask, practically begging. Anything to get more time with her.

"Um, sure. I guess you worked up an appetite after that game. Besides, Emma was my ride. So I'm kinda at your mercy."

"Well, in that case, sweetheart, let's go." I pull her up, and we head to the parking lot, hand in hand. I know I'm sporting a goofy smile, and I don't care who sees it. I'm swinging our arms and practically skipping to my car. Leigh is here. With me.

Matt and several other guys are coming out of the team entrance. They are pushing and shoving each other, horsing around, the high spirits of the afternoon still strong. I'm sure low-key party plans are being discussed. It's a Saturday, and we won our home opener with a shutout. A party is required.

Leigh drops my hand, and I stop in my tracks. Faster than I can react, she runs toward Matt. He sees her, and a fucking ear-to-ear smile appears on his face. He takes a few steps to meet her, picks her up, swings her around, and kisses her on the cheek. It doesn't bother me a bit. Nope. Not a bit. Well, not much. I'm missing our connection already. But it will take more than that to come down from this high of the kiss we just shared. I'll let them have their moment.

I'm positive she's put Matt in the very popular Leigh friend zone. That zone is a fucking list of who's who, and Matt is in good company with the likes of Chance Fuller and possibly Alexander Decker. That makes me laugh nervously. I mean, everyone that meets her loves her. And her list of friends? It's a little unnerving. But she kissed me. So I will cling to that like a cleat chaser to a spring training hotel room key.

As I walk up, I hear Matt introduce Leigh to the guys. When I reach the group, she puts her arm around my waist and hugs me. She fits perfectly against my body as she takes my hand and gives me a little smile.

Mine? Hell yeah, she is.

"I'm glad you caught the game, Leigh," Matt says. "You might just be our lucky charm. What's your schedule look like for the rest of the season?" He gives her a wink.

She laughs. "I don't know. That's quite the commitment. I'm not a cleat chaser. I do have other things to do." Ouch.

The other guys laugh and encourage her to come to the games. They tell her baseball players can be superstitious and lay it on thick. She lets them school her on baseball players, and she never tips her hand that she's well-versed in our world, extending them the kindness she shows others.

She reaches her free hand out to Matt. "But for you, my friend, I will see what I can do." Matt grins and gives her a slow nod.

"You guys coming to the party tonight?" Matt asks.

"Well, since it's at our house, I'm not sure I can avoid it. But we're grabbing dinner first." I look at Leigh to ensure she's still okay with that plan. I'm not assuming anything with her again. She nods in agreement, her smile rivaling mine. "Then we'll see what happens next."

"That's the plan," she says.

We say our goodbyes, and Matt leans in for another hug with Leigh. He whispers something in her ear, and she blushes my favorite shade of pink.

She takes my hand, and we head to my car. "Do I want to ask what Matt said?" My curiosity gets the best of me.

"You can ask, but it's between us." She has a flirty tone, and I decide not to push my luck. He'll probably tell me later. Maybe.

I shrug. "That's fine. I'm the one that gets you alone tonight, and I'm pretty damn happy about that."

When she says she doesn't have a preference for dinner, I take her to a trendy bistro not far from campus. Lucky for us, we are a little early for the Saturday night dinner crowd, so no waiting for a table.

We sit at a little table for two and get caught up on everything we've missed over the past six months. The conversation is easy and flows from one subject to the next. It's like no time has passed, even though we both know it has.

We talk about baseball, school, the holidays, and the end of the Pajamas season. We avoid her abrupt departure. I don't mention Cancun with Chance. We don't acknowledge the reason we've been apart for months.

We've talked for three hours, and the waiter is anxious to turn the table over. I tip him generously and ask Leigh if she's ready to leave.

"So, what's next?" I ask. "My place is overrun with baseball players and beer, but a guaranteed good time, nonetheless. But not quiet. Or do you want me to take you home and call it a night?"

She nibbles on her bottom lip like she's thinking about it. After a few seconds of consideration, she says, "Let's go back to my place. We'll Netflix and chill if you are up to it."

"Hell yeah, sounds good." I will be happy to hold her in my arms and pretend to watch a movie.

"Just so you know, Emma will probably be home. So don't get any ideas. Chill isn't code for anything."

"No expectations here. Well, not totally true. I hope I'm lucky enough to get your number before the night ends." And I mean it. I'm taking this slow. I will not screw it up.

Leigh gives me directions to a trendy neighborhood near the Meredith campus. While we haven't discussed families in depth, I assume her family has money, given the private school and this house. This is an expensive part of town and not the typical college housing most of us are used to. Her Mini Cooper is parked beside a shiny silver BMW SUV in the driveway.

Realizing that she lives less than four miles from me hits me hard. How have I not seen her at all in the past six months? It's not like I haven't been looking. I don't know if I can confess that. Every time I'm at the grocery store, I've been looking for her. Every time I'm off campus, I look for her. I haven't let her go.

I almost reached out to Trevor in October to ask for her number but convinced myself it wasn't a good idea. He didn't seem to appreciate the label I wrote on day one, and I didn't want to give off stalker vibes. I may have a google alert for her name, but that's normal, right? I scan social media daily for her profiles to see if she opened them back up, but it's like she doesn't exist. But I know she's real. She exists, and the world is better for it.

We get to the door, and it flies open before Leigh can find her keys. Emma greets us with a plate of freshly baked cookies in her hand.

"I was hoping to see you again," she says with a wink at me. "Everything OK?" She looks back and forth between us like she's watching a tennis match.

"Yep. All good," Leigh answers as she walks into the house. She drops her bag on a table in the entryway and kicks off her shoes.

"We thought we'd watch a movie or something. There's a big party at Cole's house, full of cleat chasers, and he decided to stick with this one." She points her thumb at her chest.

"Um, wow," I say as I follow her into the house. Damn. Another cleat chaser dig. She's not letting that go, and I guess I can't blame her. It insults a girl like Leigh, who wants to be taken seriously.

"You wound me, fair damsel." I put my hands against my heart, trying to stop the bleeding from the near-fatal wound. "I thought I was forgiven?" I give her my best charming smile and bat my eyes at her.

"Please," says Emma. "You may be forgiven, but it doesn't mean forgotten, buddy. That one's gonna haunt you for a long time." She laughs, and her giggle practically tinkles.

"Is she always this mean?" I ask Leigh. I hope she knows I'm kidding. No pissing off the best friend. That's like rule number one in the dating guidebook.

"She might be tiny, but she's mighty," Leigh stage whispers. "She's like a real-life Tinkerbell. She's adorable, but you have to watch out for her and absolutely don't cross her. She may be small, but she can be lethal. Don't ever underestimate her."

"Oh, definitely giving her all the respect. Are the cookies safe?" I eye the plate of chocolate chip cookies she put down on the kitchen table, still warm from the oven.

Emma takes a big bite of a cookie and laughs. "You decide. I'm heading to my room. You two kids behave. Speed dial, remember." She heads down a hallway, and when I hear her door click, I know we are alone, sort of.

"Speed dial? What's that code for? Is that the safe word?" These two are cute, and their banter reminds me of conversations between me and Matt, where there is so much backstory no one else can keep up. They have the kind of friendship like we do, an unbreakable bond. Nothing will come between them.

"She's threatening to call my, um, girl's night support group. I need to delete those numbers from her phone," she says, almost to herself.

"And that would stop her?"

Leigh laughs. "Probably not. That's why I don't bother."

Yeah, Emma is someone I need to befriend, and soon. Best friends are a vital part of the dynamic. Always good to get them in your corner early. It sounds like Emma knows the history, so I have some work to do. Despite what she's been told, I sense she's cheering for me. Come to think of it, Chance said the same thing. What's Leigh said about me? About us?

Leigh takes my hand and leads me into the den. Her house is more decorated than the baseball house and feels like a real home, not just someplace to hang out and sleep. There are framed pictures of her and Emma on the mantle, a half-opened book bag by the coffee table, and an abundance of throw pillows and blankets on the couch. Two oversized overstuffed chairs finish out the sitting area. Each of them has three throw pillows too. Leigh said pillows were her decorating style, and she wasn't kidding.

The built-in bookshelves are filled with games and books, and a plant is placed here and there. It feels homey and more like an adult home than a college house. I guess that's the difference between guys and girls when it comes to aesthetics. We hang a flag or poster on the wall and call it a day. Girls make us more civilized and make a house a home.

She motions to the couch and hands me the remote, telling me to pick a show. She comes back from the kitchen with two glasses of water and sets them on the table with the plate of cookies. She snuggles into my side and puts her head on my chest. My heart is beating fast and hard. It feels like I just finished two sessions of wind sprints. Can she hear my heart piecing itself back together?

I flip through Netflix and notice she's been watching *New Girl*. I hit play. I couldn't care less what we watch. I don't plan on watching it anyway. I'm just not ready to say goodnight.

CHAPTER
TWENTY-EIGHT

ASHLEIGH

————

I snuggle up with Cole, and we both pretend to watch TV for a few minutes. I think we are both taking time to get our bearings and enjoy this moment. But I'm also asking myself what the hell I was thinking, inviting him back here. I have pictures of my family in my bedroom, so that area is off-limits, no matter how much I think I'd like to invite him to spend the night. I scan the room we are in now, looking for anything that might out my secret identity. Well, my real identity. I guess I'm still under my secret one, aren't I?

Fortunately, it looks like Emma cleaned up a bit, and nothing is sitting out. The pictures on the mantle are of me and Emma, so that's safe. I see a Carolina Reapers duffle by the mudroom, but that's not necessarily incriminating. I exhale, thinking I'm safe for now.

Cole tightens his hold, probably assuming I'm just content. Well, I'm that too.

I'm curious why he picked this show. "Why did you pick *New Girl*? Are you a fan?"

"Never watched it. But it was in your continue watching queue. If you want something else, I'm not picky."

He puts his finger under my chin and turns my head to him. He leans down, his eyes silently asking permission before he kisses me. I give the faintest nod. His lips touch mine gently, another pure, almost chaste kiss. Our positioning on the couch is awkward. And as sweet as this kiss is, it's not enough for me.

I swing my leg and put myself onto his lap, straddling him. He's slightly startled by my sudden move but then takes this as the permission he seeks. The kiss becomes urgent. His tongue seeks entrance as he teases the seam of my lips. I sigh, and the invitation is granted. Our kiss is passionate, feelings flooding every part of my body. I can practically smell the ocean as memories rush back from our night on the beach.

Our mouths get reacquainted, his tongue dancing with mine. His mouth brings my body to life, waking up parts long dead. His hands gently brush up my sides, never venturing into anything considered first base. I start to giggle, and he pulls away.

"What's so funny, sweetheart?" How do I tell him nothing is funny? It's far from funny. And his growing erection is signaling he's not finding the humor in our situation, either.

"Nothing," I say, giving him a shy smile.

"Oh, it's not nothing. What's going through your wicked mind?" He leans in and nibbles on my earlobe.

"Well, I, um, well, I was thinking about you getting to first base, and I just got tickled."

He shifts me off his lap, trying to be inconspicuous as he adjusts himself. "Leigh," he says, a little growl in his voice. "I'm trying here. I want to be respectful and let you know it's not about sex for me. But damn, sweetheart, you are making it hard on me. Literally and figuratively."

I giggle again. I'm missing our contact, my body temperature dropping from the loss of his heat. The butterflies in my stomach are having a rave, no end in sight for them.

I thought I was falling for him, but now I'm pretty sure I fell months ago. I think I love this guy. I'm keeping that to myself for now unless I want him running for the door.

Why am I keeping him at arm's length, not taking him to my room, and letting him have his way with me? Oh, that's right, because my room will expose the secret I'm not ready to share. The one that could destroy his baseball future. The reason we probably shouldn't be doing this anyway.

"Sorry, you're right. Do you want to go?" Please say no. Please say no.

"No, sweetheart, I just want to hold you right here. I don't want to ever let you go again." He pulls me tight. "I've missed you so much," he whispers as he kisses my temple.

There is palpable sexual tension between us. We both want to take this further, but both are pumping the brakes, probably for different reasons.

He doesn't know the truth about me. I don't know what Xander will think when he hears about us. He's still watching him on the field. Would that change if I get involved? He said he wanted me to be happy and even told me to go for it if I wanted.

I lean over and give him a peck on the cheek. "Okay, let's watch the show. Jess's awkwardness will make us feel a little more normal."

His eyes close, and he takes a deep breath, probably calming himself. I snuggle up, happy to be in his arms and watch the show. His fingers gently play with my hair. The feeling is practically hypnotic.

After two episodes, his breathing slows. His eyes are closed, a hint of a smile gracing his face. I think he's asleep, even if his hold on me never loosened.

He looks content, totally at peace. I reach for his phone on the side table, use his face to unlock it, take a quick pic, and give him what he wants tonight.

CHAPTER
TWENTY-NINE

COLE

———

I'm having the best dream ever. Leigh and I are together, and it's a fairy tale life. I'm playing ball for the Reapers. She's a successful marketing executive. We have the house, the cars, the kids, everything. It's like my personal Hallmark movie, not that I'll ever admit I've watched one.

A tickle under my nose wakes me up, bringing my reality into focus. It's not quite the fairy tale, but it's not a bad start. My perfect dream girl is snuggled up against me, her head on my chest. She's asleep.

I'm not at the happily ever after in our story, but this feels fucking fantastic to know we got past the dark time, and it's going to be good from here on out. I'll make sure of that. I'll never let her go again.

I glance at my phone and see that it's almost midnight. I kiss Leigh on the head and gently wake her up.

"Hey, sweetheart, I need to head home, and you need to get to bed." She nods but holds me tight. She knows how to kill my resolve. I want to scoop her into my arms and find her bedroom.

I can't rush and scare her off. She ran once, and I won't allow that to happen again. We haven't talked about it, but I suspect whatever had her running scared still exists.

"Mmm, k," she mumbles as she wakes. She's so cute when she's in this half-asleep state. I know she's not a damsel that needs protecting, but at this moment, she looks so sweet and vulnerable. I want to protect her forever. *Mine.*

We get up, and she walks me to the door. With her arms wrapped around my waist, I give her a light peck on the lips and another on her forehead.

"I can't wait to see you again." I'm hoping she'll want to see me.

"Come back tomorrow?" she asks. "Bring Matt, and we'll have brunch?"

Not quite what I had in mind, but sure. She wants to see me again, so I take it as a win.

"I'll see if he's available." One more light kiss. If I stay another minute longer, I know I won't leave. "Get some rest, sweetheart. This is just the beginning of us." I can't believe I just said that. I must still be living in that Hallmark movie. But the funny thing? I mean it.

She hugs me tight, and I breathe her in, giving her one last kiss on the top of her head. "Lock the door when I leave," I tell her as I pull away and walk to my car. I turn around to see that the door is already closed. She's tired. I smile, thinking about her stumbling back to her room to go to bed. She's excited about this thing we started too, right?

The drive to my house takes less than ten minutes. Damn, the realization that she's that close hits me again. The anxiety of looking for her is lifted and I feel free. Happy. Excited. Nothing can bring me down from this high. Leigh. Mine.

Tonight's party at the house was the exception to the no parties during the season rule. We won. It's Saturday. It's a pseudo-holiday because it was the season opener. But because it's the exception, it won't be late, and as I pull up, the crowd is thinning out.

Matt is shutting it down and I get home just in time to help lock the doors. He's kicked almost everyone out, but there are teammates still crashed on the floor. He's throwing pillows and blankets at them from our crash closet by the front door. I count five bodies in the living room. That's almost a regular Tuesday. Our house is the central gathering place for the team, so it's not uncommon to have guys on the couches or floor on any given night. That's why we have a crash closet full of bedding supplies.

"Good time?" I ask. Matt rolls his eyes and throws a pillow at Kade, our starting catcher. Matt is the mother hen of the team, but tonight he seems more irritated than usual.

"Fucking lacrosse team challenged our freshmen to a chugging contest. I was out back and found out a little too late. Coach will be pissed if anyone throws up in the weight room tomorrow."

Fucking hell. Matt's right. Coach will not be happy. But even the thought of a pissed-off coach can't kill my buzz. "I'm going to kill Carter and those damn lax rats."

Unfortunately, the lacrosse team has a control issue. They tend to take things to the extreme. I'm not in the mood to deal with those assholes right now. I'll add it to my list of things to do Monday.

I clap him on the shoulder, giving him a reassuring squeeze. "We'll be fine. I'll make the freshies run to the gym in the morning. That'll teach them a lesson anyway. Coach won't have to worry about it."

Matt nods in agreement. He doesn't appreciate it when poor choices impact baseball, which we agree on. Yeah, these freshmen will pay at our hand in the morning. They can clean up the house while they think about their poor choices and then run the three miles to weight training.

"Thanks for holding it down." I make my way toward the stairs.

"Not so fast, Romeo," Matt says. "What's going on with Leigh? Are you two…"

I give him a half-shrug. "Maybe. Yeah." I rub my hand across my jaw, feeling the scruff, remembering what her lips felt like against mine.

"We had dinner and caught up. I took her back to her place, where I very stupidly fell asleep on her couch." That was after our make-out session that made me hard as a fucking rock. He doesn't need that level of detail, but just thinking about it makes my dick come to life.

My phone buzzes in my pocket. I pull it out to see a text from a contact listed as XOXO. Next to the contact is a picture of me, asleep, and Leigh kissing me on the cheek, winking at the camera. It's my new favorite picture of all time.

In my sleepy fog, I realize I forgot to get her number. A smile creeps across my face as I realize she gave me what I wanted tonight.

> XOXO
>
> Get home okay?

>> I did. Just doing a damage assessment with Matt. Glad you weren't here to see the carnage.

> XOXO
>
> Carnage? Really? Cleat chasers that dangerous?

>> Some more than others. 😉

> XOXO
>
> You calling me dangerous?

>> You should come with a warning label. But honestly, I'm more afraid of Emma.

XOXO

HAHA As you should be.

Brunch. 11 am. My place. Don't forget to bring Matt. He can help Emma with the digging.

> Wow. You are terrifying. But I won't be late. Sweet Dreams. See you in a few hours.

XOXO

Good night, trouble.

I laugh at the name. Trouble. Her label for me. I have that goofy grin again. Matt throws his arm around my shoulder.

"When are you seeing her again?"

"You and I are going to brunch at eleven. Don't make me late," I say. "I've got a girl to woo."

He laughs as we get to his room. "Woo, huh? This I can't wait to see."

"Hey, that reminds me, what did you say to her this afternoon?"

"Nothing you need to worry about." His tone is serious, signaling that I shouldn't ask again.

I get to my room and get ready for bed. I pull out my phone and look at the picture. My mind conjures other images. The look when she let herself get lost in our kiss, the desire in her eyes. Her smile when she thinks I'm not looking at her. Her peaceful look as she slept on my chest. My Leigh. Mine.

I drift off to sleep with images of Leigh and me running the bases, and they aren't on the diamond.

CHAPTER
THIRTY

COLE

———

"I've gotta say, that was the best breakfast I've ever had," Matt declares. "I'm gonna have to double my cardio time to work that off."

"Emma is magical," Leigh says, giving her a wink.

"And a little scary," I add. "All the respect, Emma."

"Thank you, boys. Just remember, we are complex creatures. Always be respectful and a bit wary." She takes a slight bow. "Thank you for coming to my Ted Talk." She giggles, making us laugh.

Matt and I insist on cleaning up the kitchen since they prepared a breakfast fit for kings. Since I supervised the hungover teammate's run this morning, I was extra hungry. The girls prepared an athlete's breakfast full of protein and sweet carbs for dessert. Matt was undoubtedly thrilled, his sweet tooth clearly satisfied.

"This was fun, but I'm study hall monitor this afternoon," Matt says.

"Study hall?" Emma asks.

"Yeah, we may be athletes, but we have to make the grades too. We have required study hall for the freshmen and anyone struggling with a class. The seniors rotate supervision. It's my turn," Matt explains.

"I wish I had that," Emma says. "I'm doing my student teaching this semester and taking my last math class because, well, math. Ugh. I'm struggling."

"I can help with math," Matt volunteers. "Physics major here."

Is Matt hitting on Emma? It will be the first time I've watched Matt show interest in a girl in a long time, and I'm fascinated.

"You are a baseball player majoring in physics?" Leigh asks. "How did I not know that about you? You are the whole package." She gives him a wink. I stand behind her and wrap my arms around her waist. The hem of her shirt rises as she leans into me, and my hand rests on her stomach. I let my thumb idly rub circles around her belly button.

"Pff. Like that's hard," I say. "I'm studying the human mind. That's twisted shit."

"Umm-hum." She laughs at my apparent jealousy. "I bet you think you have us all figured out in less than sixty seconds."

"Nope." I kiss her behind her ear. "It will take me years to figure you out." I whisper in her ear, "And I'm willing to put in the time." I feel the shiver go through her body. I don't know if it's my words or proximity, but I'll take it.

Matt watches us carefully. He clears his throat, getting us back on task. "Thanks again for brunch," he says to the girls.

"Are you serious about helping me with math? Can you have a guest at study hall?" Emma asks him.

"I'm in charge, so I can." He winks at her. "But you can't go distracting the freshies." He looks at her petite form in a tight t-shirt and bike shorts. I know what he's thinking. She's a tiny but definite distraction. "It's cold in the library. Why don't you change so you'll be comfortable and warm, grab your books, and I'll pay you back for brunch with some tutoring."

Emma bounces up and down. "Really? That would be so great! I don't have time for study groups with my student teaching." She looks at Leigh. "You okay if I go with Matt for the afternoon?"

Leigh leans back into me. "Yeah, I'll be fine. Go and soak up the math because you know I can't help you with it."

"K. BRB." Emma bounces down the hall to get ready.

"Thanks for helping," Leigh says to Matt. "She's struggling and needs this class to graduate. You sure she's okay to crash the baseball team study hall?"

Matt laughs. "Oh yeah, she's fine. I'm glad to help. And I think she's going to make my afternoon all kinds of entertaining. The guys are going to shit themselves over her."

"Matt," I say in a warning tone. "She is rule number one, remember?"

Leigh twists to look at me and gives me a skeptical look.

"Rule number one?" she asks.

Matt and I make eye contact. "Um, yeah. Rule number one. It's the best friend code. Gotta always make sure you are in the best friend's good graces."

She laughs, and I swear, my heart practically leaps at her joy-filled sound. "Well, in that case, help her get through this math class, and she'll be baking you cookies for life."

Emma joins us, and I laugh at Matt's expression. She's wearing more clothes, but I'm not sure it's any less distracting. She's in leggings instead of shorts, an oversized Tripp Stevenson jersey over her tight t-shirt, and a worn Reapers hat pulled low. She has her book bag slung over her shoulder, and it's almost as big as she is. Matt reaches over and takes the book bag from her.

"Come on," he says. "This will be fun."

Emma looks at us, confused. "What? Is this not okay?" Leigh and I just chuckle as Matt slightly shakes his head. "As—Leigh?" She's genuinely confused.

"No, you are adorable," Leigh says. "Just remember, don't feed the zoo animals. You'll be fine."

"Have fun, you two," I yell as they leave the house. Leigh and I wave from the doorway as they leave, like two parents sending their kiddos off for the first day of school. I can picture that as part of our future, and another piece of my heart clicks into place.

"Poor Matt," she says as we close the door. "He has no idea what he just volunteered for."

"Emma has no idea what she's walking into either," I say, and we laugh.

I pull Leigh into my arms. "So now, what will we do on this unsupervised afternoon?" I wiggle my eyebrows in her direction.

Leigh bites her bottom lip and blushes. "Well, I was, um, thinking..."

"Yes?" I growl as I skim my nose from her ear down her neck.

"Well, I thought I'd give you a tour of the rest of the house," she says shyly.

I'm kissing her collarbone and stop and look at her quizzically. House tour? Not exactly what I was thinking, but anything with my girl is fine with me.

We look at each other, trying to determine what each other is thinking. "I thought we could start with my bedroom," she says.

Oh. That kind of house tour. I give her a wicked grin. "I'd love to see the rest of the house," I respond. "Lead on, sweetheart."

She takes me by the hand and leads me down the hall toward the back of the house. She opens the first door on the left, sweeping her arm dramatically. "This is my room. What do you think?"

I step into the room and look around. If I saw this room on an HGTV show my mom loves so much, I'd immediately think of

Leigh. The walls are painted a pale blue, giving off a tranquil beach vibe. A Reapers hat hangs on the corner of her mirror. She has one of those girly bulletin boards full of ticket stubs and pictures tucked under ribbons. Leigh is everywhere in this room. It's obvious this room is her sanctuary.

Her bed has a white comforter with twenty or more pillows in various shades of blue scattered around. There is an enormous painting of the beach above the bed. I'm unsure if it's a sunrise or sunset, but it's captivating, the sky painted in pinks and purples. I don't know why, but I feel like it's the beach on Tybee, where I fell in love with the girl in front of me. She follows my line of sight to the painting.

"Yeah, it's our beach," she says.

"Our beach." The beach where I had the best and worst experience of my life. "It's beautiful. Do you know the artist?"

"Yeah, my mom," she whispers.

"She was very talented." Leigh told me about her mother's death when we walked on the beach. A young girl losing her mother must be devastating. A familiar feeling hits me in the gut. It's like a young boy losing his father. I'm not sure which would be worse, a parent dying or one leaving willingly like mine did. Either way, losing a parent sucks.

"She was. Anything else catch your eye?" I think she's being flirty, but I need to make sure this is what she wants.

"Well, that is an extreme amount of pillows."

"I like to cuddle." She reaches behind me and closes the door. The click of the lock is the signal I was waiting for. I pull her close, my arm around her waist, her hand firmly on my chest.

"Good to know, sweetheart." I kiss her along her jaw, toward her ear. "Is that what you want to do now? Cuddle?" I'm down with anything my girl is comfortable doing.

She looks up at me, her eyes unfocused as I pepper her with butterfly kisses. "I don't want to cuddle," she mumbles.

"Tell me what you want, sweetheart," I whisper in her ear. I can see the goosebumps on her arms. I love the way her body reacts to me.

"I want you, Cole. All of you."

CHAPTER
THIRTY-ONE

ASHLEIGH

————

I'm not sure if I stunned him, but he freezes for a second at my request. I want Cole, but I'm not very experienced when it comes to sex. Overprotective brothers, remember?

I lost my virginity to Owen Jeffries my freshman year at Wake Forest to get it over with. He never called me after, which was okay with me. Not one tear was shed. It was uneventful. I think that's most people's first experience. I wish I had waited now because I don't think Cole will be uneventful.

"Did I say something wrong?" I worry my bottom lip. Leave it to me to mess this up.

Cole looks at me, his eyes searching my eyes for something. "Are you sure?" I barely hear him.

I nod slowly. Yes, I'm sure.

His hands tenderly cradle my face. His touch is gentle, and I feel cherished. I know our connection is deeper than chemistry, but I'm ready to add that layer of intimacy.

A smile stretches across his face. "Leigh," he growls, kissing me with a fierceness and passion I've never experienced. He walks me gently back toward the bed, and when the back of my legs hit the side of the bed, he lays me down gently. His battle of gentleness and passion makes me feel desired and valued. Loved?

He whispers into my ear. "I'm going to take my time with you, sweetheart. I'm going to memorize every inch of you."

He stands between my legs, and I look up at him. I see the fire burning in his eyes, and my lips desperately miss his. I tug at the hem of my shirt, pulling it over my head and tossing it on the floor behind me. I'm wearing a purple lace demi bra, and given the way his eyes hood, I think he approves.

I reach up to him and try to pull him down to me. "Come here, trouble."

He pulls away from me, and I stop. Damn. I'm doing this wrong.

"Nope," he says. I start to sit up, feeling the heat flush across my cheeks. I'm embarrassed and realize this is going horribly wrong.

"Sorry, I thought," I start.

"Nope," he repeats, a smirk teasing his lips. "You want me? Then let me call the shots, sweetheart. I will worship this beautiful body in front of me and take my time. You okay with that, Leigh?"

Am I okay with that?

"I'm more than okay with that. Make me yours, Cole."

I reach up to pull him to me. I need his kiss. I need him. All of him.

He breaks our kiss, his eyes never leaving mine, and pulls my leggings down, leaving me in nothing but matching purple panties. As he lowers himself to my center, he says, "Mine" for the first of many times.

CHAPTER
THIRTY-TWO

COLE

———

I'm conflicted. I want to take her now and savor every inch of her. Fast or slow? Either? Both? I'm prepared to live the rest of my life in this room with my girl.

I breathe in her scent of citrus and Leigh. She pulls the hair tie from her ponytail, her long hair falling around her face and shoulders. She's so fucking sexy. I love running my fingers through her hair, the softness against my calloused fingers feels incredibly sensual.

I kiss down her jaw and whisper into her ear. "I'm going to take my time with you, sweetheart. I'm going to memorize every inch of you."

I stand between her legs, and the look in her eyes communicates desire. But most of all, trust. We haven't talked about it, but I get the feeling she's not very experienced, and her trust in me with this intimacy means more to me than she knows. This isn't just sex for me. This is more.

She takes her shirt off and tosses it on the floor. I can't take my eyes off her perfect tits in a purple bra. I'm the luckiest bastard in the world right now. She's perfection.

She reaches for me and says, "Come here, trouble." I fucking love it when she calls me that. It spurs me on to show her what trouble is really like.

"Nope." She starts to sit up, and her cheeks redden with her blush. Oh no, I think I've upset her. That is the last thing I ever want to do. This girl. Fuck. She's killing me.

"Sorry, I thought."

"Nope. You want me? Then let me call the shots, sweetheart. I will worship this beautiful body in front of me and take my time. You okay with that, Leigh?" I need her to be okay with it. I need her like I need air to breathe. Her pleasure is my reason for existing. Making her feel good is my entire reason for being. But also making her feel comfortable. Making her feel cherished. Making her feel, well, mine.

"I'm more than okay with that. Make me yours, Cole." Her words are the encouragement and consent I desire.

Her eyes meet mine, and I'm transformed into a man on a mission. Those blue eyes are full of yearning and heat. She pulls me down, my mouth to hers, and she wraps her tongue around mine. Her kiss is so damn hot I may embarrass myself and come in my pants like a fucking teenager.

I give her a wicked grin and watch her eyes sparkle. I kiss down her neck and focus my attention on removing her leggings. "Mine," I whisper.

"Fucking perfect." She is incredible. Her pussy is covered in purple lace panties that I can't wait to unwrap. I kiss up her long, toned legs, alternating, giving each the same attention. I nip at the back of her knee, and she lets out a low moan that sends all the blood in my body to my cock. She pulls her legs together, seeking pressure and relief, but I spread her open. I kiss the inside of her thighs and let my hands drift closer to her center. I've got this. I've got her.

Her scent is like ambrosia, and I have to taste her. I gently pull off her panties and am greeted by the most luscious lips. I lick her with the flat of my tongue and savor the sweet taste of her. "Umm, perfect." She's so wet already. Wet for me.

"Cole, please," she whispers. Her pleading makes me smile.

"Please, what, sweetheart?" I breathe against her warmth as I let my finger enter her, and my thumb works her clit.

Her hips move, fucking my hand. She's so tight, and I stretch her with two fingers while I suck on her bundle of nerves. Her walls begin to pulse, and I know she's almost there.

"Come for me, Leigh. Let go. I want to watch you come."

Her hand comes down, and her fingers tug on my hair, pulling me away, but I resist. I want to watch her come on my tongue. My fingers bend and find that spot that makes her lose control.

"Oh, Oh, Cole," she starts. Her eyes flutter, and her hand grips my hair tighter as her orgasm takes over. I pump her until she relaxes and is sated. Leigh is beautiful, but when she comes? A fucking work of art.

"That's one," I say as I kiss her stomach. My hands graze her body and brush against her erect nipples, rolling them between my thumb and finger until my lips find her breasts. Her buds are hard and pressing against the lace of her bra. I nip at the right one and free it from the confines of her bra.

"Cole, I need you."

"You have me, sweetheart." I look into her eyes, full of longing and lust that I'm sure mirrors mine. I've had sex before, but it's never felt like this, full of something else. Emotion. I don't want to fuck Leigh. She's more than a means to an end. I want to make love to her. To every inch of her. She's pleading for me, so I'll give her what she wants this time. We have all the time in the world to take it slow.

"You have entirely too many clothes on." She's pulling at my shirt, trying to get it over my head.

I chuckle at her frustration. I strip quickly, and as I stand at the side of the bed, looking down at her, I'm in awe. She is my everything.

Leigh's eyes widen when she looks at my body and reaches out to me. She stands and runs her hands over my abs, kissing my chest. My heart races, and my breathing is shallow. It feels like heaven to have her lips on my skin, her hands exploring my body.

I wrap my arms around her and kiss her with everything I have to give. Our kiss is hungry, urgent, and needy. Her fingers wrap around my cock, and she rolls my balls. I'm about to explode.

"Sweetheart, you need to stop, or I'm about to embarrass myself. When I come, I want to be inside you." It's her turn to give me a wicked smile.

My erection is so hard that I can hammer nails. I quickly reach into my wallet, pull out a condom, rip it open with my teeth, and sheath myself.

"I thought you'd never ask." She wants this as much as I do, and I'm encouraged by her commitment to us.

I gently lay her back on the bed, and I settle between her legs, my cock seeking her entrance. I give her an inch, let her adjust, and slowly push my way in. Her back arches until I'm buried to the hilt. We move together, letting our pleasure take over.

"Yes, more," she moans. "I feel so full." Her nails dig into my shoulders, and the pleasure and pain send me to a new height.

I feel her pussy spasm against my cock, and her eyes close as she comes again. The little sound she makes sends me into a new dimension. "That's two," I say. My voice practically growls. My grin is gone, and I'm determined to give her another one.

I put her leg over my shoulder to deepen our connection and rub her clit with my thumb. Another orgasm quickly follows. "That's three," I growl.

She's sated, her golden hair fanning around her like a halo. Watching her come is euphoric, and I know I've found my life's purpose. I never want to leave this bed. I was put on this earth to make this angel feel good.

I kiss her deeply, our kiss in sync with each thrust. Her pussy clenches my cock as she comes again. This time, I come with her.

"Home Run," she says with a giggle. She buries her face in my shoulder and exhales. I roll her over on top of me and kiss her until her giggles are gone.

This girl. Mine.

CHAPTER
THIRTY-THREE

ASHLEIGH

———

For the past three weeks, Cole has slept at my house almost every night, and we fall asleep cuddling after the incredible, mind-blowing sex. Between baseball, school, and sex, I'm afraid I'm wearing him out. He looks tired but happy. He insists I'm the best thing that's ever happened to him, and I inwardly cringe when he says that.

I'm in my graphic design class when a text pops up on my laptop.

TROUBLE

Hey sweetheart, I want to take you on a date.
Pick you up at two after your last class?

Sounds fun! What about practice?

TROUBLE

Coach is giving us the day off since we have an overnight away series this week.

> What should I wear?

TROUBLE

Nothing

> That's generally frowned upon in public.

TROUBLE

I never frown when you are naked

> You can't say things like that while I'm in class

TROUBLE

Did I make you blush, sweetheart?

> More than that.

TROUBLE

BRB. Gotta go take care of myself, I mean, something.

I laugh and almost get caught texting in class. My professor wraps up his lecture, and I'm excited to see Cole this afternoon. It's a treat to spend daylight hours with him. I know his schedule is packed with baseball. I want him to be drafted, and this is how it's done. Baseball is his priority. I'm not the typical girlfriend who is jealous of the game. I support him one hundred percent. I won't deny I'm excited about a little us time.

I'm done with classes until after lunch. I grab a wrap from a food truck on campus and relax with my Kindle until my next class. I text Cole to continue our conversation. He's in class, so I'm not sure he'll respond. But this is how our texts go throughout the day. We respond when we can.

> All better?

TROUBLE

Not until I'm with you. See you in a bit. Wear something comfortable. We are going indoor rock climbing. I can't wait to watch your fine ass climb that wall. Ah hell, BRB. Thinking about that has left me with another situation.

Stop. 😒 I'm not sure I should let you out in public with your situation.

Aren't you in class? That must be awkward.

TROUBLE

With you, I'm always at risk of being in a situation. But you are worth the risk.

You say that now.

TROUBLE

Always.

I still worry I'm not worth the risk, but I can't resist him. I'm addicted to trouble.

See you later, trouble.

A few nights ago, we were in bed, and he pulled out his phone and started making a list. I've noticed he often does that, especially when he learns something new about me. I'm curious to see his notes app. He said he takes learning about me seriously, and clearly he does. I peeked over his shoulder to find he's making a list of my favorite things since, apparently, I'm his favorite thing. His sappy side makes me melt.

The other night, he asked me about things I've never done but would like to do. If he hadn't done it either, then it made the *Leigh and Cole Adventure List*. I think he was a little disappointed I had been axe-throwing because he really wanted to do that one. Surprisingly, neither of us had been indoor rock climbing, so here we are.

After some instruction and practice walls, we worked our way to the competition wall, where you race to the top to ring a bell. I may not be a Division One athlete, but that doesn't mean I'm not competitive too. I'll push myself to beat my brothers any chance I get.

Climbing the wall was difficult and required concentration. It was even more difficult when Cole and I climbed together because he made me laugh so hard at his antics. I think my abs got a double workout.

I love that he makes me laugh. His adorable goofball side adds an interesting balance to his competitive, focused side. But his serious, focus all his attention on me side? It's a little intense.

I worked up a sweat, beating Cole to the top of the wall to ring the bell. But I won. Barely. Did I pretend to slip and make him stop to check on me? Maybe. But all's fair in competitive rock climbing.

"Let's go back to my place for a quick shower and check something else off our adventure list." Trying to get a reaction out of him should also be on my Favorite Things list.

"Well, shower sex wasn't on the list, but we can add it." His dimple and wink are irresistible.

"That's not what I meant, and you know it!" I slap his arm, pretending I'm offended while thinking about being adventurous with Cole. I can't stop smiling. "I've never done that, have you?"

I've told Cole about being sheltered and not very experienced with sex. He's been patient and a fantastic partner. He told me he hadn't dated much, but that didn't mean he wasn't hooking up on occasion. So as the more experienced one between us, he usually takes the lead in the bedroom. He always makes sure I'm comfortable and consent to anything we do. He also always makes sure I enjoy it and feel good. If I don't, we stop. So shower sex? Sure.

He winces a little. "Yeah. But not with you, so that makes it a new adventure. But only if you want."

I give him a shy smile. I'm still getting used to his boldness and sex talk.

We arrive at my house, and Emma is home, baking cookies that smell incredible.

"How was rock climbing?"

"I beat him," I comment as I snatch a cookie off the cooling rack.

"Of course you did. Probably because he couldn't take his eyes off you," Emma comments.

"That's partially true," Cole says. "But she's more careful and cautious. I took the more risky path. You know I'm willing to take the risk to get what I want." He kisses me, his tongue swiping the chocolate on my lips. "I'm going to hop in the shower."

"Take your time," I tell him. I'm deciding if I will join him or not. My confidence wanes when Emma looks at me as if she knows I'm ready to jump his bones.

"You tell him yet?" She asks.

I know what she's asking, and she knows why I can't. How will he react when he finds out I've been lying to him this whole time? When we signed the consent forms at the climbing center, I almost outed myself. I practically had a panic attack at the front desk. Cole thought I was scared of climbing. I let him believe that narrative, and he hugged me, telling me I'd be okay. Oh, the guilt. He promised to always be honest with me. I hate lying to him.

"I will. Soon. He was so excited after the coach talked about the Reapers watching him. I can't get in the way of that. And I don't want to get in his head. But I will."

"For the record, I don't think it will matter to him." Emma's brought this up several times. I know she's concerned.

"I hope not." I shrug as if I don't care. I care more than I can admit. I finish my cookie and moan as the warm cookie fills my mouth.

"That's disgusting. Go make those noises with your boyfriend," she teases.

"I think I will. I mean, water conservation is important, after all." I give her a smile and a little wave as I go to find Cole. My boyfriend.

Cole has his back to the shower door as he rinses the shampoo out of his hair. Water droplets fall from his curls, and I watch one slowly descend his body. I'm taken back to the first time I saw him, the water rolling down his torso. I wanted to lap up the droplets then. Now I can.

I strip down and open the door, and the steam hits me, welcoming me in. He turns to me, and a wicked smile fills his face.

His hands embrace my cheeks, and he kisses me in greeting. His tongue seeks entrance to my mouth, and I swallow his moan.

"Mmmm, you taste sweet and decadent."

"I do?"

His hands roam my body, stopping at my breasts and playing with my erect nipples. Just being around this man turns me on, and I find myself in a situation.

I feel his hard erection poking me in the belly. I reach between us and take him in my hand, and when I let my hand slide up and down, I feel him harden more to my touch. I blush, knowing this is his reaction to me.

"Seems you have a bit of a situation here."

He nips at my shoulder. "That happens when I'm around you."

I guess it's my turn to try something on my adventure list.

CHAPTER
THIRTY-FOUR

COLE

———

Leigh kisses down my torso, her tongue lapping at the water as it hits my abs. Her smile tells me she's enjoying it. That's what I want. I need my girl to feel good and use my body for her pleasure.

Her hand works my cock, and I let my head fall back against the tile because when she touches me, it's like an electric current fills my veins. Electricity and water are a dangerous combination, but I'm here for it. My body reacts to her, craving her touch. Her lips on my skin make me shiver despite the warm water.

She continues to move down until she's on her knees, her hands still working my cock. She's beautiful, and when she looks at me with those ocean-blue eyes, I lose all ability to think clearly.

"Sweetheart, you don't have to," I start. I know she's only had sex one time before me, and it wasn't a satisfactory experience. That guy was an idiot. Leigh is perfect. How he took from her but didn't give tells me everything I need to know about him. It also means everything we do is new for her. I want her to experiment and find what she likes, but it needs to be about her. And while I'm thrilled with her mouth on my cock, I want her to do this because she wants it, not because she thinks it's what I expect.

Her lips wrap around my tip, and her tongue runs around my ridge. My head falls back further, and I close my eyes. Fuck that feels good. She runs her tongue down my shaft and licks me base to tip. She's magical.

"I've never done this before, so you need to tell me if I'm doing it wrong." She's a little shy when we try something new, but she's an eager learner.

My fingers hold her head, massaging her scalp. "Sweetheart, you don't," I start when she takes me as far as she can and begins fucking her mouth with my dick. "That feels amazing, sweetheart. Watching your lips around my cock is so sexy. My god, you are so perfect."

She continues to work me, hitting her gag reflex a few times, but it doesn't deter her. She keeps at it until I'm about to come. I pull her away.

"Sweetheart, I need you to stop." She looks up at me, crestfallen.

"Did I do something wrong? Don't you like it?" Her blue eyes are wide with worry.

"Leigh, I'm telling you that you did everything right, but I want to be deep inside you when I come. Nothing is better than watching you come on my cock." I pull her up and kiss her, assuring her she did everything more than right.

I turn her toward the wall. I take her hands, put them above her head, and finger her slit. I kiss her up her neck and breathe into her ear. "You are so wet for me. Did that turn you on?"

She nods. "I think I like shower sex."

"I think I like shower sex, too." I enter her from behind and feel her pussy clench around me. I reach around and rub her clit, and she comes hard. So do I.

I wash her body, and her citrusy body wash scent fills the shower. I love this stuff. I need to get some for my shower, too.

My hands skim over her skin, and I'm hard again. I can't get enough of my girl. I'm grateful for the endless hot water, and we go for round two. When she collapses in my arms, I laugh with satisfaction. I wore my girl out in the best way.

We step out of the shower, and I wrap her in an extra-large towel. She has the nicest stuff at her house. She's used to luxury.

She puts her hands around my neck, her fingers playing with my curls. I love it when she touches me like that.

"Can we add that to the list?" She asks.

"And which list would that be?"

"My Favorite Things list."

"Consider it done." I kiss her again. "Sweetheart, we are just getting started on that list."

CHAPTER
THIRTY-FIVE

ASHLEIGH

———

After the best shower of my life, we took a power nap. I thought we'd just hang out for the rest of the evening, but Cole was having no part in that.

"Sweetheart, I promised you a date and a date you will get. I want to take advantage of our time together, and besides, I want to show you off. So get dressed in something that makes you feel good. I love it when you have that extra shine in your eyes. It brings out your sass." He kisses me and hops out of bed.

I have no idea what he's talking about. I'm not sassy. "Whatever. Give me a clue where we are going so I know what to wear."

"Dinner and music. So comfortable and casual." He wanders into my messy closet. I hear him mumbling to himself, hangers sliding on the bar. He comes out and drops a few items on the bed. Most seem to be casual dresses in various shades of blue. "You are beautiful in anything you wear, but I love you in blue. So one of these? But your choice. And flats or tennis shoes. I don't want your feet to hurt. It's function over fashion, as Darcy would say." He kisses me on the cheek and goes to leave the room. "I'll be back in thirty minutes. Is that enough time?"

I'm staring at the pile of clothes he selected. I'm shocked at his choices as they are some of my favorite dresses. How did he know? He doesn't see me wearing dresses often because I usually opt for comfort. I realize I haven't made much effort to dress up and impress him. Maybe I should dress up more? Is Leigh a girly girl?

I'm a little nervous about going out with him. What if we run into someone who knows me as Ashleigh Decker? We spend most of our time at home or around his teammates. I'm safe there. But what if?

I give him a tentative smile. He's so happy, and I don't want to say no to him. I'll show him I can take risks, too, even if he doesn't know. "I'll be ready. I'll be the one in blue."

"Only if you want to, sweetheart. Be back soon."

I don't have time to curl my hair, so I opt for a sleek high pony and tie a yellow scarf around it, adding a touch of whimsy. I wear a little more makeup than my usual mascara and pick my favorite dress from his selection. I pair my dress with flats covered in tiny yellow bows to finish my feminine style tonight. The dress is twirly, flirty, and has pockets, all things I like in a dress. I hope he likes girly me.

One quick swipe of red lipstick, and I'm ready for date night. "Wow, you look nice," Emma says. "Cole looked pretty happy when he left." She smiles at me, and I blush, thinking about our shower. I hope the walls are thick and the water covers our exuberance for one another. I make a mental note to get her some quality noise-canceling headphones. "What's next?"

"Dinner and music, apparently. He's trying to make up for all the time he can't give me because of baseball. He doesn't have to do this, but I appreciate the effort. I don't need the dating stuff. I just want him."

"You know he'd do anything to make you happy. Today is important to him. Because, girl, he's all in. Enjoy it. But tell him."

I bite my bottom lip and catch myself. I'll need to reapply my lipstick if I keep doing that. "I will, I promise."

There's a knock at the door, and I look at my watch. He was gone exactly twenty-eight minutes. I can't help but smile as I open the door and watch his eyes drink me in from head to toe.

"You are so beautiful," he says as he leans in for a kiss. "Fuck. I'm addicted to you."

I giggle like a teenage girl. This adorable guy always says the right things to make me fall a little harder every day. I don't want this feeling to end.

"I'm addicted to you too, trouble."

"You ready?" I nod and grab my crossbody bag from the entryway table, almost knocking over the vase of flowers from Cole.

"You kids have fun," Emma says from the living area. She's behaving suspiciously. Did I see her wink at Cole? "Enjoy dinner."

"See you later, Emma," Cole says over his shoulder. He puts his hand on the small of my back and directs me to the door. He helps me in his Jeep and reaches over to buckle me in. I think it's just so he can reach in and kiss me, and I'm not mad about it.

"Where are we going?" My curiosity gnaws at me.

"You'll see." He winks and gives me a grin that makes my stomach flutter. Those butterflies are back.

We arrive at my favorite restaurant. "How did you know?" I run through our conversation the other night, and I don't remember mentioning this.

"You told me." He says it confidently. "I remember every-thing you've ever told me, sweetheart."

Wow. I don't recall telling him this. Do I have early stages of memory loss? "When did I tell you?"

"The day of our first date in Savannah. You were working on Pajamas' stuff, and I was, well, working on us."

My stomach drops. He's been working on us for so long. I recall that day and smile. He was peppering me with questions while I tried to work. He wanted to know all my favorite things. Favorite bands, flowers, movies, books, actors, candy, and restaurants. I shake my head and sigh. I can't believe he remembered. That was the day I decided to give in to trouble.

"I can't believe you remembered all that," I whisper.

"Sweetheart, there's nothing about you I could ever forget. Come on, let's enjoy dinner and make more memories. I've never been here before, so I want to try all your favorite things."

We enjoyed a great dinner, and our conversation never lagged. That's the thing about Cole. He's easy to be with. Our conversations flow easily. I don't have to worry about saying the wrong thing or be afraid I'll hurt his ego. I can relax and be me. Well, Leigh. And when we are together, he's not on his phone or distracted. Like Emma said, he's all in.

"I've watched Chance's followers grow. You're making a big difference on his social media," Cole says. One thing we still skirt around is Alexander and Chance. He doesn't bring it up, and I avoid it at all costs.

"Um, yeah, it's going well. My professor is pleased." He's never asked me about my project, and I panic, hoping he doesn't find out I was the one who read his DMs to Chance. Another thing I'm keeping from him. My joy starts to fade. Cole notices my change in demeanor.

He reaches across and takes my hand. "If you don't want to talk about it, we don't have to. I want you to know I support you. You have a talent for storytelling through social media. That's all. If something is important to you, it's important to me." His smile is sincere. Why is he so understanding? It makes me feel more guilty.

"No, no. I appreciate you asking. It's been a lot of fun working to move him from a thirst trap to a team and community leader and build his fan base. He's very hands-off and lets me run with it. Makes it easy."

"Happy to hear it. Especially the hands-off part." He winks and signals he's teasing. I know he has questions. Maybe I should tell him.

I start to say it when he breaks eye contact to look at his phone as it buzzes. He looks at it, and another smile crosses his face. "You ready for the next part of our date?"

The abrupt change of topic catches me off guard. "Sure."

We leave the restaurant and head to our next destination.

We park in front of a local music hall that often features local bands. It's an old theater with an open dance area, cheap drinks, and a sticky floor. The shoe choice makes sense now. The Marquis lists tonight's bands.

"Pineapple Sunset?" I practically squeal. It's one of my favorite local bands. They are a poppy boy band from New York, and when they come to town, Emma and I try to catch all their shows. I'm not sure they will be the next One Direction, but I have them on all my playlists. They do a lot of covers but also have some original songs. I've been so busy with Cole and going to baseball games I totally missed they had a show tonight.

"You said you liked them, even though you adamantly claim Emma is the one who likes boy bands. Don't deny it, sweetheart. You like boy bands too." He's having a good time surprising me with his date planning.

"You got me." I laugh as he pulls me into his embrace. Unfortunately, half of Meredith College likes them too. I pray I don't run into anyone I know.

"There you are," Emma says, pulling me away from Cole. "How was dinner?"

"What? Did you know about this?" I see Matt standing behind her, and he winks at me.

"I told you he was all in," she whispers. "Cole knew it was a you and me thing, so he invited me along."

"And Matt?"

"Figured you two might need extra security," Matt adds. "I heard you can get a little out of hand. Especially this one." He tilts his head toward Emma and flinches, waiting for some reaction. She playfully punches him in the stomach, and Matt laughs. I'm glad they get along. I'm not sure it's a love connection, but they seem to enjoy each other's company.

I take Cole by the hand and pull him toward the door. "Come on, trouble. And I apologize in advance."

CHAPTER
THIRTY-SIX

ASHLEIGH

———

Cole has an away game and is gone for the next two nights. We FaceTimed last night, but it's not the same thing. I've become addicted to Cole Davidson, and I need my fix. I've become so used to resting my head on his hard, muscular chest that I can't remember a before, and I can barely sleep without his arms around me. He has spoiled me and practically cured me of my pillow obsession.

My head on his chest is also on the Favorite Things list. We added a few more things this week, including attending concerts together. When Emma and I weren't dancing like fools, he held me tightly to his body, his hands wrapped around my waist from behind. I liked it, especially when he would sing the lyrics in my ear.

I'm about to login in to watch his game when there is a loud knock at the door. Usually, the Door Dasher rings the doorbell, but this person is practically beating down the door.

I fling the door open, ready to give whomever it is a piece of my mind when I'm scooped up and spun around before I can even react. Jules has me in a bear hug and keeps spinning me until he tosses me over the back of the sofa, depositing me on the soft cushions. I squeal and laugh until I snort.

I look up from my position on the couch to see Jules and Chance looking over me.

"Did you just snort?" Chance asks. "I didn't know you were a snorter!" He shakes his head at me. He has his arms full of bags and starts toward the kitchen.

I get my bearings and get up to greet them. "What are you guys doing here?" I wasn't expecting either of them tonight.

Jules closes the front door and yells into the house, "Emma girl, I'm gonna need some cookies to go with your favorite wine for girl's night!"

"Girl's night? I don't remember us scheduling a girl's night." I know I've been busy, but I usually keep up when my brothers are visiting.

Emma comes bouncing into the den and jumps into Julian's arms. "There's my pixie girl," he says as he kisses both her cheeks. "Chance is in the kitchen. We brought dinner, but I need some of your cookies for dessert."

"The dough is already chilling," she replies as she enters the kitchen. Emma isn't surprised to see the guys.

"Em, did you know about girls' night?" I'm happy to see them but confused about this visit.

"Yep. It was a perfect date with Chance's night off and Cole's away game. Ohhhh, Pad Thai, my favorite," she says to Chance. Chance hugs her and returns to making himself at home in our kitchen, pulling plates and glasses from the cupboard.

"So when did you three start talking without me?" I flop down in my comfy reading chair and hug the pillow to my chest. I feel a little left out and wary of what this is about.

"Did you just smell that pillow?" Jules asks as he begins lighting scented candles on the mantle.

"Um, no," I say indignantly. I scoff. Yeah, I totally did because it smells like Cole.

"She does that a lot," Emma says. She enters the den, sits on the floor pillow, and digs into her Pad Thai with her chopsticks. "Cause she's in luuuuvvvv." She makes kissy sounds in my direction.

I throw the pillow at her, and she ducks. "Traitor," I mumble. Everyone seems to be in on this girl's night, and I feel slightly uneasy and maybe a little betrayed.

Chance hands me a plate with coconut shrimp and a spring roll. Am I that predictable, or does he just know me that well? "Thanks," I say under my breath.

Chance and Jules sit on the couch and start to dig in. We all eat in silence for a few minutes. Jules finally puts his plate down and takes a long pull on his beer.

He looks at me and grins. "So, Ash, you want to tell us what's new with you?" He has a shit-eating grin on his face that makes him adorable. Jules's eyes sparkle with mischief.

I shrug. "You know, school stuff. By the way, Chance, have you seen your IG numbers? You've gotten almost fifty thousand new followers in the past few weeks. What are the sponsors saying?"

Jules answers for him. "Yeah, you are doing great work. Chance just landed a new contract for a body wash. But that's not all you've been doing with your time, Ash?" I feel all eyes on me.

"I might be going to a few baseball games now and then." I try to sound casual, but I know the lovesick smile I give them gives away my true feelings.

Chance looks at Jules and then at me. He looks me straight in the eyes with no indication of joking or even a hint of a smile. "He's treating you like you deserve?" I will always be grateful for Chance.

He saw me at my worst, so I understand his concern. He held me together until I was reunited with Jules while my heart broke into a million pieces. I shudder thinking about that pain. The joy I have now makes it feel like a distant memory. Chance was there for me. He's a gem of a guy, and there's some lucky girl out there for him.

I nod. "Yeah, things are good. Great."

"And he knows everything?" Jules asks, giving me the evil eye.

"Um, like what? I mean, we are dating and getting to know each other, so I wouldn't say he knows everything," I hedge.

"Ash......" Jules says.

Emma pipes in. "I told you. You need to tell him. It's not going to matter to him. He loves you for you, Ash. It's what you wanted. To be loved for you, not for your connections. You've got that now." Emma and I have this conversation almost daily now. I suspect this session is her attempt to call in backup. Realizing that this is an intervention with wine, Thai takeout, and cookies does not escape me.

"You think he loves me?" I ask. He hasn't told me that.

"Girl, one thousand percent. He's all in," she says.

Jules still looks at me like he's trying to figure me out. "Do you love him?"

Do I love him? Yes, I think so. I've never been in love before, but I think this is what love feels like. I need him to breathe fully. He's always on my mind. I crave his touch. I haven't told him all of that. Why? Because I still have a secret I haven't shared. I'm not sure what I'm waiting on anymore. I feel like I've gone past the point of no return. I should have told him weeks ago. Every day that goes by makes it worse. I know it. I'm scared.

I'm still worried about the draft and how he'll feel about my part in the outcome, good or bad. If he goes to the Reapers, will he think it's because of me? If he doesn't get drafted, will he think it's because of me?

I take a bite of my spring roll and shrug. What am I supposed to say? I don't think I should tell them before I tell him anyway.

Jules still seems uneasy. He stands up and comes to kneel

beside me. He takes my hands in his and looks at me with genuine concern. "Are you happy?"

I nod. "Very." That I can say with all confidence.

He squeezes my hand as he stands. "Good. That's the important stuff. Anyone want another beer?" He heads into the kitchen to grab another beer. "But you need to tell him."

"I know. I will. Soon."

"Who's picking the movie tonight?" Chance asks.

Well, I guess the hard part of girl's night is over.

"How about that new rom-com with Ryan Reynolds?" Emma says.

"No can do, Emma girl," Chance says. "Our boy here went out with the actress in that one, and I think the scorch marks are still a little fresh."

"Really?" Emma loves a good Jules story and add a dash of Hollywood? This will be the topic for the rest of the evening. Emma will be like a shark with blood in the water. Poor Jules. I'm just grateful the attention isn't on me.

CHAPTER
THIRTY-SEVEN

COLE

Leigh has stayed true to her promise and has attended all our home games for the past month. She says it's to support Matt, and that's why she sits at his base, but I think it's so she can watch me the entire game. She won't admit it, but I know it's true.

We are together as much as possible. My schedule is busy with practice and games, and there isn't much extra time during the week, especially in season. I apologize all the time for it. As a result, we both consider our limited time together sacred.

We hang out with Matt and Emma, and sometimes she hangs out with me and the team at my house. Whether playing board games with friends, doing school work, or exploring each other's bodies, I can't get enough of Leigh. I understand now when people talk about finding the one.

She's the perfect baseball girlfriend too. She doesn't complain about the time constraints. She understands. She really does. I can't help but think I want Leigh with me, even if baseball weren't a thing.

Last week was the first real date we've been able to have due to our busy schedule, and it was so much fun. I look forward to more of that, but not sure it will happen until the off-season. Which will be when? After graduation? After I get drafted? What does the future look like? I try to focus on the present. For now.

We just wrapped up another win tonight. My bat was hot, and I have no doubt she is my lucky charm. I'm rushing to leave the locker room when Coach asks to see me. I knock at his office door, anxious to get to Leigh but curious about what Coach has to say.

"Enter," he calls out.

"Yeah, Coach, you wanted to see me?"

"Come on in, Davidson. Close the door and have a seat."

Coach is scanning the stats from the game, making a few notes in the margins. He looks up and smiles.

"You're playing sharp, Cole."

"Thanks, Coach." My leg is bouncing, ready to move on with this conversation.

"I had an interesting conversation with a representative from the Reapers today."

He pauses, like I know where he's going. I don't.

"And?"

"Your on-field performance is strong. He was more interested in your off-field performance. I told him you are the all-star ball player every coach dreams of. This is your year, Cole. I just wanted you to know. Keep it up, kid. The call is coming."

"Thanks, Coach. I appreciate your support. Really. Thanks." The Reapers. My dream team. Everything I've ever wanted is within my grasp. I nod my head to my silent yes.

"Now get out of here, Davidson."

I leave Coach's office with a smile and grab my wallet and phone from my locker. I can't wait to see my girl and tell her the exciting news.

I see I have a missed call from Leigh and a text.

XOXO

Great game!

Going to have to cancel our plans tonight.
Sorry. Family thing. Matt needs some Cole time
anyway. You guys celebrate. We'll chat
tomorrow. 🤍

Disappointment washes over me. Not getting to see my girl tonight hurts, but she's right. Matt and I haven't had much non-baseball time lately. Our clock is ticking, coming to an end of an era.

"Hey, Matt, looks like it's you and me tonight, buddy."

Matt looks at me like I've lost my mind. "What's wrong?"

"Nothing. Leigh had something come up. Let's have a bonfire tonight." Yells go up around the locker room, and the guys high-five one another.

I'm going to miss this team. Spending a night with them is a blessing. "Baseball players ONLY," I say. I emphasize only to the guys. I'll try to keep it small tonight. We are still in season, after all. I want a smaller gathering, a meaningful night with the guys.

Thanks for coming today. We're hosting a
bonfire if your evening frees up. Call me later to
say goodnight. I'll have my phone on.

XOXO

K. Have fun. Beware of the cleat chasers. 🐾

That's the last thing you need to worry about.
I'm taken, Sweetheart.

XOXO

After picking up three family packs of chicken from Bojangles, I get home and put them in the kitchen. The preparations are in full gear for our gathering, with all the roommates completing our assigned tasks.

Matt and I live in a house with three other teammates. They are juniors and will invite two teammates to fill our spots soon. As we close this chapter, I'm grateful for the evening with my teammates.

Matt is in charge of ice and beer. He's filling coolers strategically placed in the kitchen, den, and backyard.

Blake and Jack are battening down the hatches. That involves putting our shit away that isn't for public consumption, including laptops, books, and food. The final step will be padlocking the bedrooms. We learned the hard way when Matt found a teammate and two girls in his bed last year. That isn't happening in our house again if we can help it.

Even though this should be a smaller gathering of trusted teammates, you never know what might happen after a few beers. Even though we said no girls, keeping them out is hard. Where several teammates gather, cleat chasers follow.

Tyler is outside putting the finishing touches on the fire pit. I walk out on the deck and survey the yard. I feel like a king inspecting my kingdom. A king that is about to say goodbye to the safety of college and enter the real world in a few short weeks.

"T, ya need some help?" I yell at Tyler.

"Yeah, that'd be great. I pulled the chairs out. Want to set them up?" I walk into the yard, head toward the pile of random folding chairs, and start putting them out around the fire pit.

"I'm glad you can make time for us tonight, Davidson," Tyler says, adding wood and paper to the pit. "Leigh coming later?"

"Nah, she's got something else going on tonight." I will miss her, but spending time with the team is important too. Coach said scouts are asking about team camaraderie. The scouts want to know if there is a bond besides baseball because they asked about my off-the-field performance. As a team, we need to be there for one another. One off player can upset the entire team dynamic.

I acknowledge I've pulled away some since Leigh and I got together. It's not that I don't care anymore. It's just a matter of time constraints and priorities. I ensure that I'm one hundred percent when I'm with the guys. When I'm with Leigh . . . well, it's more than one hundred percent, and that freaks me out a little. That girl. Damn. I'm all in.

I'm trying not to smother her, but I want to forget this party and see her. Her being in the stands wasn't enough today. I need to kiss her. Feel her arms around me. I need to look into those baby blues and see my future.

A football hits me in the chest, shaking me out of my thoughts. "Dude, you've got it bad for her, don't you?" Tyler has a smirk on his face as he looks at me.

"What?" He's caught me off guard.

"I've been talking to you, and you are somewhere else. I never thought I'd see the day when Cole Davidson was in love with something other than baseball."

Tyler lights a match and throws it in the fire pit. He has built quite the pyre with paper, lighter fluid, and wood, as flames shoot up several feet in the air.

"And that's how it's done!" he announces as he walks away.

Is that what this is? Do I love her?

Matt throws his arm around my shoulders, alerting me that I zoned out again.

"Yeah, man, you do."

I look at him, bewildered at his comment.

"You asked if you loved her." He cocks his eyebrow at me like I need to get with the program.

"I didn't ask anything." Did I? At least, I don't think I did.

"You were mumbling, do I love her, over and over. I thought I'd answer the question to get you to stop asking. It's obvious to everyone but you, I guess." He pops me on the shoulder and then begins setting up the chairs I abandoned.

Matt's right. I love her. I. LOVE. LEIGH. I can't wait to tell her. I wish more than anything I could see her right now, but we have forever, so for tonight, I will wait.

"You know, I'm happy for you. She's a great girl. I like how she gives you shit. Deep down, I know she likes me best, but she feels sorry for you." I process what he says and look at Matt, grinning at me.

I lean down and pick up the football at my feet. I throw it at his head. His quick reflexes grab the ball before any damage is done.

"Oh, sore spot, Davidson?" He laughs as he tosses the ball back at me.

We casually toss the ball back and forth. "Nah, I'm the winner in this one." I feel confident in what I've got with Leigh. It's just the cherry on top that she and Matt are friends.

"You know, I'm glad you have her. At least I know you won't be alone when you hit the road in the minors."

"What are you talking about?"

"Well, chances of us both getting the call and going on the same team are slim to none. You know that. I know that. I'm glad you'll have her by your side. You guys have talked about that, right?"

"What?!? No. No, we haven't talked about anything after graduation. I mean, I talk about the draft but nothing about what that really means. I'm not sure she understands the life of a professional ballplayer. And I can't imagine she'd follow me through the minors." I also can't imagine her not being with me.

To be honest, I haven't thought about the details after graduation. I've been so focused on the now. I've lost her once. I don't want to lose her again. But is that what's ahead? We talk about a vague future. Is it time to talk about what's ahead for us?

She is supposed to work for her family business in Charlotte but doesn't want to do that. I don't know what my future holds until the draft. The future is just something we avoid talking about. I guess staying in our bubble is naive, but it's safe for both of us.

I can't think about that right now. But there's another part to his statement I don't want to think about either.

Matt drops the football, grabs two beers from the cooler, and sits in the last chair I set up. I sit as he hands me a beer.

"It's gonna be okay, you know?" He clinks his long neck on mine.

I take a long draw of the beer, feeling the cool liquid slide down my throat. I can hear noise coming from inside the house. Other guys must have arrived and discovered the chicken in the kitchen. I guess I'll order a pizza later.

I take my hat off, run my hand through my hair, and put it on backward. Damn. It's all coming to an end. College. Me and Matt as teammates. Me and Leigh? I let out a big sigh.

"You know it's not an end?" Matt smirks at me.

"Yeah, it is. I don't even remember playing ball without you. It will be hard not having you around all the time."

"Yep. I know, man. I want to hit the pause button. We've got a lot in front of us. But no matter what, you'll always be my best friend. Nothing can come between us. I'm only one call away," he starts to sing. We both crack up. I remember when I sang that for Leigh last summer. I meant those words then, and they stay true now. But for now, it's one thing at a time. I'm living in the moment with my best friend.

"Here's to living in the moment," I say. We both clink bottles and slam the rest of our beer. "Let's grab dinner and have a good time tonight. Make this the best moment we can."

CHAPTER
THIRTY-EIGHT

COLE

———

I had a great time last night at the party. It was laid back and chill with just the guys. A few cleat chasers showed up, but they left when the party didn't take off into our typical rager. I guess as far as parties go, it was lame, but as far as guys hanging out, laughing, telling stories, and bonding, it was pretty great. I even pulled out the guitar and played for a bit.

When I went to get my guitar, I tried to call Leigh, but she didn't answer. I tried again when I went to bed and sent her a text. No response.

I missed her yesterday. I had a hard time falling asleep without our nightly good night conversation, and now, I'm tired and grouchy. No response isn't typical for my girl, but she said something came up. I trust her, but I won't deny I'm worried. The conversation with Matt left me unsettled. We can't keep living in the moment. It's time to talk about the future.

I need to see her. I want to tell her I love her. I'm ready to tell her. I need to tell her.

Leigh's not a morning person, so I stop by her favorite coffee shop and get her a Dirty Chai to make up for my early morning visit. I'll make up for the lack of a good night with a good morning.

I knock on her front door, bouncing on the balls of my feet, waiting for Emma to open the door. She's the early bird. I won't be surprised if Leigh's still asleep, but I bet she'll still be glad to see me.

When the door opens, it's not Emma. It's Alexander fucking Decker, in grey sweats, no shirt, and obvious bedhead. I'm paralyzed. My eyes must be playing tricks on me. He speaks, and I realize this is no trick.

"Hey, Davidson, I didn't expect to see you here this morning." His tone is nonchalant like he belongs here. He's almost cordial. Almost.

I'm frozen in shock. Alexander Decker is answering Leigh's door after spending the night. He's what kept us apart last night? She chose him over me? What. The. Everlasting. Fuck.

"Where is she?" I can barely form the words.

"She's still in bed," he replies, way too casually for my liking.

"Bed?" I can't process what he's saying.

"Yeah. I kept her up way past her bedtime last night." His grin pushes me over the edge. This smug bastard. She's mine. MINE.

My vision turns red. His cocky face is more than I can handle. I drop her latte, the hot liquid splashing my feet and her porch. I swing at him, my fist connecting with his jaw. He staggers back and bumps against the entryway table, knocking a vase of flowers and papers to the floor.

Leigh and Emma appear at the end of the hall coming from the bedrooms, their looks filled with confusion. Leigh rushes to Decker's side, putting herself between us. I want to take another swing, but I can't risk hitting her.

"Stop, Cole, just stop," she shouts, putting her hand on my

chest. Normally, her touch is a salve to my soul, but now, it burns me. I step back from her. She's choosing him. Correction, she chose him.

Decker puts his arm around her waist and pulls her to him. "Step back, Ash. I won't let him hurt you."

"I'd never hurt her," I spit. The blood is rushing in my ears, dulling my hearing. "Get your hands off of her," I yell.

Decker's smug grin is gone, and he's replaced it with a menacing glare. "Ash, I'm doing my best to keep my promises, but I'm not sure I can deal with him on my team. I'm not sure it's going to work out."

"Leigh, what the hell is he talking about?" I'm lost. What promise?

"Cole, I'm sorry," she says, tears sliding down her cheeks. "Please, just listen." She tries to come to me, and he pulls her tighter into him. He's keeping her from me.

"Ash, let them sort this out," Emma tells her. She pulls her to the side, leaving me and Decker face to face.

Once he lets her go, I exhale. I can't handle his hands on her. There's nothing between us now. I'm clenching my fists at my side.

Decker works his jaw and smiles at me. I'm ready to knock that smile off again. Now that she's not in my line of vision, my brain is able to catch up.

"Ash?" I cock my head to the side. Decker doesn't move.

I look at Leigh, and she flinches. That wasn't a reaction I was expecting. I'm looking at her for clues, anything, to help me piece together this shitshow I'm witnessing. She's wearing my NC State baseball shirt and pajama shorts. Probably not an outfit Decker appreciates, but I do. She's crying, tears rolling down her cheeks and spotting the front of her shirt. Emma is holding her like she's going to fall apart.

I want to reach out and make it all better, but then Decker speaks, drawing my attention back to him. "She told me you two were together. I'm still not convinced it's the best thing for her, but I made her promises. One was that I wouldn't interfere. See Ash. This is me, not interfering." He takes a few steps back and walks into the kitchen. "That other promise, though? Not sure I can keep that one, honey."

I'm still stunned. "Promises? What am I missing?" He calls her honey?

Leigh slumps against the back of the couch, her head in her hands. Every instinct I have says go to her, comfort her. Instead, I stay frozen in place.

"Leigh, what promise?" My tone is more insistent. I feel like this promise is the key to unlocking the mystery of what in the hell is going on.

When she doesn't respond to me, Alexander speaks up. "I promised her to keep you on my prospects list." With that, he turns and heads down the hall to the bedrooms.

Emma whispers to her, "I thought you told him?" Leigh shakes her head no. "Oh Ash," she says. She puts her arm around her shoulders to try to comfort her. Leigh puts her face in her hands and cries, her breath hitching as she fights back a sob.

"Tell me what?" I ask. My harsh tone startles her. "Leigh. TELL. ME. WHAT?" I yell at her.

Alexander reappears at the top of the hall. I'm sure he doesn't appreciate my tone, either. He's ready to interfere, promises be damned.

I look around, still trying to figure out what is going on.

She looks up at me, her blue eyes flooded with tears. I'm heartbroken seeing her like this. I want to go to her, comfort her, make her better. But I'm also angry. And still confused.

"I'm sorry, Cole. I'm so, so sorry," she says with a little hiccup. Her voice is barely above a whisper. She stands up, runs past Decker down the hall, and a door slams.

I take a step inside, ready to chase after her.

Emma looks at me, her eyes full of pity. "I think you should go. Give her time. She'll call you," she says quietly.

"What the fuck is happening right now?" I mumble to myself.

I look down at the mess around my feet. The tea, the broken vase, and the mail scattered everywhere. The envelope on the floor catches my eye. It's addressed to Ashleigh R. Decker.

Well, shit. I didn't see that coming.

CHAPTER
THIRTY-NINE

ASHLEIGH

———

"Come on, Ash, we've gotta go," Em says as she knocks on my bedroom door.

I look at my reflection in the bathroom mirror. My white dress contrasts sharply with the dark circles under my eyes. I tried to cover them up, but you can only use so much concealer. My hair is down in loose curls for the first time in weeks. I don't care what I look like, but my family will go into overtime protection mode if they suspect I'm not okay. Frankly, graduation is just a formality I could live without. I tried to skip it, but Emma and my dad were not having it. Something about a rite of passage and celebrating accomplishments. I don't feel like celebrating these days.

It's been three weeks since happiness stopped existing for me. Now, I'm all about going through the motions.

"I'm ready." I gather my maroon gown and graduation cap from my bed and open the door. When I reach the living room, I come to a stop. I'm greeted by a room full of handsome men, all lined up in a receiving line. Alexander, Julian, Chance, Trevor, and my dad greet me with smiles. Various "congratulations" are said as I look at them. With all this love and support, I still feel empty.

"Hey, princess," my dad says, getting my attention. "I thought we'd escort you girls to graduation in style."

"Um, okay," I say. Even as I go through the motions, having them all here, including Chance and Trevor, is touching. My family loves me. All of them. I'm the luckiest girl in the world. I know that. But I'm undeserving. I don't deserve love, luck, or even kindness after what I did to Cole. I lied to him and destroyed his future.

These past few weeks, I have been able to take exams and get through classes, but I feel hollow. Empty. Today will be harder to coast through. I will have to attempt to show up and pretend it's all fine so they don't worry. When they worry, they hover and close ranks. I can not deal with that right now. It's my misery. My mistake. My cross to bear. I ruined someone's future hopes and dreams. It's not something I take lightly. I punish myself for my sins. It's the least I can do as retribution for my deception. I don't deserve happiness.

"Hey, guys," Emma says, "why don't you all escort me to that fancy limo outside? Let's give them a minute."

"Yeah, I got you, Em," Trevor says. He puts his arm out, and Emma takes his elbow. Chance takes her other arm, and they leave me alone with my family.

Jules looks at me with sadness in his eyes, his normal twinkle dimmed with concern. He walks toward me and kisses me on the top of the head. "I love you and am so damn proud of you. You and me tonight. Just us." He hugs me and heads out to join the others.

Xander gives me a weak smile. He gives me a quick hug and kisses me on the cheek. "I'm sorry. Please don't be mad at me. It's all going to be okay, I promise." Does Xander think I'm mad at him? I don't blame him at all. This is all on me.

"I'm not mad at you. I love you," I whisper.

When he leaves, it's just me and my dad in the quiet house. He opens his arms, and I run to him, allowing him to wrap me in his warm embrace. I might be twenty-two, but I'll always be my daddy's princess.

I told myself I wasn't going to cry. Just another lie. That's all I do is lie to everyone, including myself.

"Now, now, princess, I got you," Dad says as he rubs my back. "This is a big day. You are graduating from college, and I'm so proud of the wonderful woman you are. Your mom would be too." At the mention of my mom, I sniffle.

Dad leads me to the sofa and pulls me down to sit beside him. He hands me the box of tissues on the end table and pulls me to his side.

"I'm sorry, Dad. I'm trying."

"I know. Alexander told me. I know it's been hard being raised by three men who are overbearing and protective. I know we weren't easy. But you know I want you to be happy. That's all I want, princess. And I'll move heaven and earth to make that happen for you." He kisses me on my temple. I let myself find comfort in the warmth of my father. I close my eyes as I breathe in his familiar cologne with its woodsy scent. Right now, I'm safe in my dad's arms. It's a luxury I don't deserve.

"I love you, Dad. And Xander and Jules are the best brothers a girl could ever have. I'm so blessed."

"But you still miss Mom," he says. I nod. "I know, baby. I miss her too. So much. Every damn day."

"How do you go on after you lose the love of your life?"

Dad and I never really talked about their relationship. Their love. I know they were happy together. They were always laughing and hugging. Dad adored my mom. As a child, I never really thought about it much. It was how I thought all parents were. As an adult, I've come to realize their relationship was unique. They were soulmates.

Dad pulls me in tighter.

"How did you do it, Dad? How did you keep going when she was gone?" When my mom died, my dad changed too. He was quieter. More introverted. He kept going, ensuring I had everything I needed, even though he lost a piece of himself.

I feel him take a deep breath. "I had you, princess. I had you. You are just like her in so many ways. She left me a part of herself right here." He taps me on my heart. "But I wasn't perfect. I worked too much after she passed. I know that. I wasn't there for you like I should have been. I'm grateful to Julian and Alexander for stepping in when I couldn't. Because honestly, sometimes, it's just hard to lose someone you love so much. But you have to keep going. Lean into the love you were fortunate enough to experience and keep going."

I'm gripped by the pain my father experienced. "I love you. You were always there when I needed you. You are the best dad a girl could ever want." We sit silently for a minute, lost in our memories of Mom and our family. Dad gently runs his hand up and down my arm.

"Come on, Ashleigh," he says as he stands up. He holds his hand to me, pulling me up from the sofa. "Let's get you and Emma to graduation. We have some celebrating to do. We can't let this accomplishment slip by. Then I'll get you back to Charlotte to start your job with the Reapers. I'll be happy to have you home again."

"Yeah, that will be nice." My chest tightens as I think about this future. It's not what I want for my future, but I don't deserve a dream. I killed Cole's dream, so why should I get one? No, I get what I deserve. I ruined my future with a lie. Happiness isn't something I get anymore. I'm the person who ruins lives.

———

After graduation, Emma's family joins us for a fun evening at a new restaurant in the historic district of Raleigh. Chance's friend recently opened this trendy place, giving us VIP treatment. We are in the private dining room, where drinks and laughs flow freely around me. Emma and I sit across from each other at the center of the table, surrounded by family and friends. Toasts are said, laughs are had, and promises are made. She gives me a kick under the table and an encouraging smile. I guess my acting skills need a little work. I give her a brighter, albeit fake, smile.

I know it will be a new chapter for Emma and me, but watching Xander, Trevor, Jules, and Chance, I know we'll be friends forever. Those college friendships survived and even thrived after they started their careers. Emma will stick with me, even if I don't deserve her.

She and I plan on packing over the next few days and leaving Raleigh behind us. For Emma, that means moving home with her parents while she finds an apartment in Savannah. Her job teaching Spanish at a local high school starts in August. She has six weeks of preparation, house hunting, and relaxing until her new chapter begins. I overhear Trevor inviting her to a Pajamas game this summer, and she sounds excited to attend. I'm happy she will experience the fun of the Pajamas, but thinking about last summer makes my stomach uneasy.

My new beginning is a little more uncertain. Dad is anxious for me to come back home to Charlotte and start working for him and the Reapers. I haven't committed. Something about it doesn't feel right. I told him I needed some time, a vacation of sorts, before stepping into a full-time job. I will pack up the house, but I don't have a plan of where to go. Maybe I'll ask Tripp if I can use his Mexico house again.

With the unease sweeping over me, I excuse myself to find the restroom and gather myself. Chance leans in as I start to get up. "I'm okay," I whisper to his unspoken question.

The restroom is on the other side of a beautiful bar area. People stand shoulder to shoulder, mingling over cocktails while waiting for a table. The bar is the place to be and be seen. I think about making a post for Chance to help promote his friend's business, but it doesn't appear he needs that boost. This place is packed tonight.

The smell of whisky assaults me and makes me want a stiff drink. I resist, deciding I'll drink when I'm alone tonight before I cry myself to sleep. That's become my routine.

I enter the lavish restroom and appreciate its design. They put a small settee and a sitting area near the entrance. The designer knew that sometimes women need a minute. Since this is a popular bar, I'm sure plenty of first dates and meet-ups are happening here. This area is exactly what I need right now. I need a minute.

After I wash my hands, I lean on the counter and look at myself. I'm a mess. No wonder they are all hovering. If I'm going to break free, I'm going to have to put on a better show than this. I reach in my bag for lip gloss and get a wistful smile when I pull out the bubblegum-flavored gloss I started wearing for Cole. My first kiss with Cole seems like a lifetime ago.

Two women enter the restroom. The older one makes eye contact and gives me a kind smile. I smile back and take a deep breath.

"I don't know, Mom, he's just not the same," the younger one says.

"Well, honey, love changes people. Sometimes for the better. Sometimes not," the older woman says.

I start to leave the restroom when I hear the younger one say, "I'm not sure love is worth the risk."

"All great things are worth the risk," the mother says. As I walk out, I can practically hear the eye-rolling from the younger one. The mother-daughter dynamic makes me long for those conversations I missed with my mom.

As I step into the bar, Chance is waiting for me. He brushes a strand of hair away from my face. "Just checking on you," he says. His touch is sweet and protective. His eyes scan me, looking for signs of a breakdown.

I reach up and grab his bicep. "I'm fine, really. I just needed a minute."

As the crowd jostles to allow a waitress carrying a tray full of drinks to pass, someone bumps into Chance. "Oh, sorry," a familiar voice says from behind Chance.

I freeze. I want to run and hide from the world. From him.

Chance notices my change and slowly turns to find Cole standing behind him. Chance looks at me for some sort of signal. He doesn't know what to do, and I genuinely smile. He's a big hockey player used to pucks flying at him at a hundred miles an hour and getting hit from all angles, but right now, he looks terrified. I can't tell if he wants to throw me over his shoulder, run, or puff up his chest and fight someone. It's practically endearing.

"I'll meet you back at the table in a minute," I say. I smile slightly and nod, assuring him I'm okay.

Chance turns and puts his hand on Cole's shoulder. "Great season, Davidson. Good luck in the Series." He glances back again, and I give him a slight nod. I'm okay.

The encounter catches him off guard. "Thanks," Cole mumbles to Chance.

When Chance leaves, we both stand there, face to face, an awkward silence between us.

The two women exit the restroom and approach Cole. The younger one wraps her arm around Cole's bicep, putting her head on his shoulder. Her natural beauty and her sweet smile are stunning. Her long, straight, lush brown hair looks like something straight out of a shampoo commercial. Full lashes surround her bright hazel eyes. She has the perfect pulled-together, trendy look. She appears content and comfortable on Cole's arm, like she belongs there.

I know he has every right to move on, but it still hurts. I close my eyes for a second to gather my courage to say something. Even if it's goodbye.

"Honey, are you going to introduce us to your friend?" the older woman asks.

I open my eyes to see Cole staring at me. His eyes are searching my face. I'm not sure what he's seeking, but it's not me. He probably realizes I look like shit, and he is better off with this new girl.

"Um, yeah, right," he starts. "Mom, Darcy, this is, um, I don't even know what to call you," he says. Ouch. That hurts. And it's true. He doesn't know me. I've been a lie to him.

I plaster on a smile. Time to pull out those acting skills again. Mom. Darcy. This is Cole's family. Okay, I can do this. I use every ounce of energy I can summon and hold out my hand to his mom.

"Hi, Mrs. Davidson. I'm Ashleigh Decker. It's so nice to meet you. You have an amazing son."

She shakes my hand, and I hear Darcy gasp. I look at Darcy to find her eyes wide with excitement. It's evident she knows the story. Or at least part of it.

I shift my attention to the gorgeous girl I thought was Cole's date. The irony isn't lost on me. Assumptions and siblings are our Achilles heel. "Darcy, it's nice to meet you, too. I've heard so many great things about you." I say that with genuine sincerity. I heard so much from Cole and Matt I knew we would be fast friends once we met. I mourn that lost relationship between me and Darcy. We never had a chance. Another thing I ruined.

Cole is still staring at me, speechless. Darcy pushes against him with her shoulder to get him to react. He blinks at me slowly. I miss those hazel eyes.

"Well, I better get back to my party," I say. "It was nice—"

"Party?" Cole asks. His face is blank, unreadable. "You aren't here with Chance?"

Not that again? "Um, yeah, Emma and I graduated today. We're having a small party with my family and hers. Chance and Trevor are here too. Do you want to say hi?"

"Trevor is here?" Cole is still piecing it all together. He cocks his head to the side, still looking at me with uncertainty.

"Yep," I say, popping my p. "Trevor is Alexander's best friend and a surrogate big brother. Chance is Julian's best friend. Again, another bonus brother." I give him a shrug to let him know that's just how it is. "You see, I grew up with an army of overprotective big brothers and a father who owns the Reapers."

I break eye contact with Cole and look at Darcy and her mom, who are watching us with rapt attention. I'm not sure what Cole told them, but they know about me. I address them when I say, "Alexander and Julian are my two older brothers. They can be a bit smothering. Makes a girl do extreme things sometimes." I give them both a half smile.

Cole's mom speaks up. "Congratulations on your graduation. I know they are all very proud of you."

"Thank you." I look back at Cole. He's still staring at me, his look full of confusion. I take that as my cue.

I direct my attention to his mother and Darcy again. "It was nice meeting you two." I allow myself to look at him one last time. "Cole, it was good seeing you again. I —"

I hesitate. What do I want to say? I'm sorry? I miss you? I love you? It's all true. But given his blank expression, I say what is probably best for this situation.

"I wish you the best." As an aside, I whisper, "Always." I give him a slight smile and make my way through the bar and back to the private dining room.

When I enter, the room goes silent, all eyes trained on me. I'm sure Chance has reported back regarding my delay, and I've been the topic of conversation for the past few minutes. I'm shocked they haven't sent a search and rescue team. Maybe they were drawing straws to see who it would be. I'll bet that Julian made them stay. He's wanted me to talk to Cole since he found out what happened. He's practically bouncing in his seat.

I thought about contacting Cole, but I couldn't face him. I'm a coward. I've taken his future and ruined it because I was careless, selfish, and dishonest. Why would he want to be with me? I'm not worthy of him.

I take my seat between Jules and Chance. Everyone is still staring at me. I grab Julian's hand under the table and slightly squeeze. That's all he's going to get. That's all any of them are getting.

The story of Cole and Ashleigh having a happily ever after isn't going to happen. Our story is a tragedy, and I'm the villain.

Alexander confirmed last week that he wouldn't be drafting Cole. I understand and I can't be mad at him. It's what I was afraid of - negatively impacting Cole's future. It was just another reason I couldn't reach out. What would I say? Sorry, I ruined your lifelong dream. Let's act like it didn't happen. Yeah. That wasn't going to work.

I meant what I said to him. I wish him nothing but the best, especially since I've ruined his dream of playing for the Reapers. I only hope his alternative future can allow him happiness.

Time to write the next chapter of my life. My reckless and deceitful actions come with consequences. Those consequences involve stepping forward on my own.

I put on a fake smile and think happy thoughts. "So what's for dessert?" I ask.

CHAPTER
FORTY

COLE

———

"Well, here we go," Matt says. "Fingers crossed for early rounds so we can kick back and enjoy the rest of the night."

Our families are gathered at his parent's house as the draft begins. Even the McIntyres are here for us. Matt's mom has put out enough food to feed two entire baseball teams, and Mrs. Mac is enjoying her time in the kitchen with our moms.

Coach Hartman is buzzing with excitement, but I can tell he's trying to act calm and collected. His son should be getting drafted today. As a father and coach, Mr. Hartman is doubly proud.

Is my father aware of my baseball career? He officially walked out of our lives when I was eight. The exact time Coach Hartman took me in as a surrogate son and brother to Matt. Family bonds aren't always formed with blood. Sometimes the ones we choose are even stronger. Like the bonds of the Deckers and their friends?

Mom and Darcy are here too. Everyone is optimistic about

my draft chances, but I'm not so sure. Punching the General Manager of an MLB team probably counts for more than three strikes when it comes to a draft call. It's a pretty tight community. People talk.

The MLB draft is long and spans the course of two days. There are thirty teams with twenty picks each, spanning college and high school levels. It's a big pool to pull from, and only the lucky and elite get the call. It's a very long, nerve-racking process if you are waiting for the phone to ring.

We made it to the playoffs for the College World Series this year. Although we didn't take it all the way, it felt great to be in the running for it all. That raised our visibility too, so I feel good about Matt going early.

Matt's phone rings and everyone holds their breath. "It's Coach Bailey." He stands up and leaves the room. We are just entering the third round, so it's still very early. The fact that our coach is calling Matt is a positive sign for him. He's about to get a life-changing call. I just know it.

I'm genuinely happy for Matt. I want him to have it all. My best friend is All-Star material. He deserves it all.

He comes back into the room with a massive grin on his face. His dad is holding his breath.

Matt joins me back on the couch. He leans over, puts his elbows on his knees, and lets out a huge sigh.

"Well?" I ask. "What did he have to say?"

He rubs his hands across his face. "Might be this round," he says.

"What?!?!?! Matt, that's awesome!" I start shaking him on the shoulder. Why isn't he more excited? I'm about to explode for him. "Who?" Any team that gets Matt is lucky.

Matt laces his fingers behind his neck. "Reapers, I think." He practically whispers it.

Holy shit! Matt is going to the Reapers. Our dream team. His dream team.

I jump up from the couch, punching the air. "Fuck yeah! Matt, you did it!"

He gives me a weak grin. "Yeah, I did. It's just bittersweet."

"What do you mean bittersweet? Man, this is everything! I couldn't be happier for you." I mean that with everything in me. I'm so happy for my friend. He doesn't have to say the rest. I already know. Bittersweet.

"I'm sorry, man." Matt looks up at me. We debated about spending these draft days together or separately. We knew it was going to be tough. But I couldn't be anywhere other than by my friend's side. I'm his number-one fan.

I grab him by the shoulders, shake him, and force him to look me in the eye. "Don't be sorry. Not for a fucking second. This is about you, Matt. I'm always going to be cheering for you. And I'll expect season tickets, too."

"Nah, you won't be in the stands. That doesn't feel right."

Matt's phone rings, and he puts it on speaker. His parents stand beside him, his dad with his arm around his son's shoulders.

"Hi Matt, this is Alexander Decker with the Carolina Reapers. We want to offer you a spot in our organization." I hear that voice, and I'm flooded with emotion. Not about baseball, but about her. Leigh.

"I'm excited to hear from you," Matt says. "The Reapers have always been our dream team." I don't miss his use of the word our. I give him a huge thumbs up and walk out on the back deck to let Matt have his moment.

I lean against the rail and look out into the backyard. I grew up in this yard playing catch with Matt and his dad. This yard witnessed the birth of friendship and family, where Matt's career was launched. Nostalgia washes over me, and I smile at the happy memories.

I hear the patio door open, and my mom joins me at the rail. We both look out over the yard.

"You okay?" Concern fills her voice.

"Yeah, I'm fine. I'm happy for Matt. Just thinking this was where it all started."

"The Hartmans are family and will always be a part of your life. I know it's hard, you and Matt going separate ways. But you'll always be best friends. Nothing can ever come between you two."

I shake my head in acknowledgment. She's absolutely right. "I know." I'll miss Matt. He's always been by my side. We knew this moment would happen. The chances of us being on the same team were almost nil. Even with all the preparation, it's still hard. But that's not really what has me feeling empty. Not if I'm being honest with myself.

I was able to focus on baseball and not think about her these past few weeks. But now baseball season is over. Hearing Alexander's voice fills me with feelings I locked away.

My mom senses where my thoughts have drifted off to. "Have you talked to her?"

"What? Who?"

"Cole Davidson, do not act like you don't know what I'm talking about," Mom scolds. "You are still in love with that girl, and I want to know what you are going to do about it."

"Nothing, Mom. I'm not going to do anything about it. You met her. She doesn't feel the same way about me. And her ties to baseball? It's complicated. That's her brother on the phone with Matt." I can't tell my mother I punched him. Alexander fucking Decker. The guy offering Matt his dream career right now. Leigh's brother. Mom would be appalled at my behavior.

"I saw a beautiful girl who hadn't slept in weeks and was doing everything she could to hold herself together. Unless she always has dark circles under her eyes and has a look of sadness all the time. But I doubt that's the kind of girl you would fall in love with, now is it?"

I scowl at her description of Leigh. Or is it Ashleigh? Or Ash? Damnit. She's always going to be Leigh to me. When we saw her three weeks ago at the restaurant, I only saw the most beautiful woman I've ever seen. Did she look sad? Maybe. Her blue eyes didn't have their usual shine, but they were still my favorite color. I don't know. I saw a piece of my heart in front of me, walking away. The girl I lo—

My phone buzzes in my pocket, interrupting my thoughts of her, and I see it's a number from New York. I look at my mom. What could this be?

"Answer it!"

"Hello?"

"Hi, is this Cole Davidson?"

"It is."

"Hi Cole, this is Patrick McCoy, and I'm a sports agent. I was reaching out to offer my services."

"What is this about? Why would I need your services?"

My mom grips my bicep, and a look of excitement fills her face.

There seems to be a scuffle in the background and a mumbled conversation I can't understand. If this is someone's idea of a joke, it's not funny.

"Hello? Who is this?" I know my voice has a slight edge.

"Sorry about that," a different voice comes through the phone.

"I'm hanging up."

I go to move the phone from my ear to disconnect when I hear a loud, "NO! NO! Don't do that."

"Who is this?" My curiosity is gone, as is my patience. I need to work on getting myself together to congratulate my best friend on his dream coming true. I don't have time for this call.

"Sorry, Cole. This is Julian Decker. Ashleigh's brother. We met once last summer."

"I remember," I grumble. I mean, how the fuck could I forget? I thought Julian was just another one of Leigh's suitors. Little did I know he was her brother. If I had known, everything would have been so much easier. I keep coming back to that question. Why didn't she tell me?

Just the thought of her stabs me in the chest. I turn from my mom and take a few steps away. I feel tears forming in my eyes, and I don't want Mom or anyone to see them. They will think they are about baseball, and they aren't. Not if I'm being truthful.

"Yeah, I guess you do." He sounds flustered. He was confident and jovial in our one and only meeting, so this version of Julian isn't lining up. "Listen, we don't have much time. But I need to ask you one thing."

"Yeah, what's that?"

"Do you still love her?"

"I don't really feel like discussing this with you." Do I still love her? How could I ever stop loving her? I fell in love with her the first moment I saw her in that kayak. I fell deeper in love with her whenever she laughed or showed kindness to others. Whenever she heckled batters or beat Matt in Scattergories, I knew I wanted her to be in my life forever.

"Cole, I like you. And my sister loves you. I want you to be taken care of because when you two figure your shit out, what happens to you will impact her, which in turn impacts me. Get it? So we need to have this conversation, whether you are prepared for it or not."

"That's a lot to take in."

"Yeah, I figure giving it to you straight might be a new approach from a Decker." He laughs at his own joke. I'm silent, processing everything he said.

I look over at my mom, who is waiting with bated breath. I can tell she's dying to hear the other side of this conversation. I give her a slight no nod. I watch her shoulders relax.

"What, too soon?" Julian says in response to my silence.

"Maybe. How is she?" At that comment, my mom grabs my hand. Her eyebrows go up, and she holds her breath expectantly. I'm sure that is not part of a phone conversation she thought she'd hear today. Honestly, I didn't think I would either. But she looks excited, like this conversation trumps baseball. Maybe it does.

"Yeah, she loves you, Cole. And she's miserable. She'd kill me if she knew we were even having this conversation. So let me ask you, do you love her?"

I do. I love her with every part of my being. And I never told her. That is probably my biggest regret.

"Listen, Julian. I don't know if I feel comfortable answering that." After the words come out, I realize I gave him an answer anyway.

"Okay, Cole, fair enough. Listen, I need to grab this other call. Draft day is always busy. But can you save my number and call me back in a bit? When you have time to think about your day? Please think about what will make you happy, like deep in your soul happy. Because, Cole, I have an idea that could make this the best day of your life."

"I don't know what you're talking about?"

"Let's just say I'm a sap and love a happily ever after. Oh, and hey, tell Matt congratulations. Give him my number. I love nothing better than representing a Reaper and making Xander pay dearly." He laughs at his own comment and disconnects our call.

What makes me happy? She loves me? I don't know what's happening. This certainly isn't the draft day I expected.

CHAPTER
FORTY-ONE

ASHLEIGH

———

"Hey, Ash, I'm home!"

"Jules, you don't have to announce your entrance. I can hear the elevator when it opens in the foyer." He announces himself every time he comes and goes. I think he's giving me time to make an effort to be presentable. I don't have it in me today, though.

"Whatever. Darlin', have you even showered today?" I'm on his couch, wrapped in blankets and surrounded by every pillow in Julian's penthouse. The pillows are a protective armor against the outside world. Or maybe they are holding me together. Either way, they serve a noble purpose.

When Emma and I packed, she moved out as planned. She went home to Savannah, ready to start her new chapter of adulthood.

I had everything packed, but I couldn't leave. I couldn't even leave my bed after Emma left. I didn't have to pretend anymore.

I was alone. I wrapped myself in a cocoon and let the hurt and heartbreak consume me.

Eventually, my phone died. I packed my charger somewhere and didn't have the energy or will to find it. The last thing I wanted was to talk to anyone anyway. Or worse? Know he didn't want to talk to me. My phone never rang from my contact named Trouble. Not that I deserved a call from him. He wasn't the one who lied. He wasn't the one who messed up.

After three days off the grid, Jules appeared on my doorstep. He found me in my bed, surrounded by boxes, hugging my favorite throw pillow that still smelled like Cole.

After a half-hearted lecture with a side of absolute pity, he forced me into the shower, rummaged through boxes until he could pack a bag, and brought me to New York.

He's let me wallow in my sadness for the past few weeks, but I can tell he's almost at his breaking point with me. I'm sure I'm cramping his bachelor lifestyle. I need to leave. I need a plan. I need to figure out my life.

"These are fresh pajamas, if you must know." I stick out my tongue at him. "I've read a book and even talked to Dad today. He wants to know when I'm starting as Marketing Director for the Reapers."

Jules comes into the sunken den and drops down on the sofa. He swats some of the pillows away and pulls me into his side. He kisses me on the top of my head and musses my messy top knot.

"What did you tell him?"

"I told him I couldn't. I mean, I just can't. I don't think I can be around baseball. Especially the Reapers."

"Have you kept up with it at all?"

I shake my head no. I know what he's asking. He's asking if I know what happened with Cole. The short answer? No. The weight of his future is too heavy. I know Xander didn't draft him because he told me. His dream of being a Reaper was shattered because of me.

"Hmph. I get it. So what are you going to do?"

That is the million-dollar question. Living on this sofa isn't an option.

I've thought about going to Savannah with Emma, but I don't want to be in her way. I can't go home to Charlotte, where I'll be reminded of his disappointment. I've thought about going to work at the Honduran orphanage Emma loves so much, but it's not realistic, especially since I don't speak the language. I don't know where to go or what to do.

What am I going to do? I give him my standard answer. I shrug and burrow further into the blankets and pillows.

"Well, I met with my team today and have a job offer for you." Julian hops up, knocking another pillow to the floor. He starts pacing in front of the fireplace.

"Jules, I don't want to work for you out of pity."

"No, no, just listen. I know you don't want to work somewhere and be treated like the boss's daughter. Or boss's sister even. You want to do it on your own. I get it. But, Ash, you are damn good at social media management. Look what you did for Chance. He landed several very lucrative contracts because of his increased social media following." He stops pacing and looks at me. "By the way, that bastard owes you something for that. Think expensive and sparkly or maybe something with four wheels."

"He doesn't owe me anything. It was a school project." Did he really get contracts because of my work? I enjoyed it so much that I still do it for him.

"He does owe you, and I need you to keep doing it. As a matter of fact, I have several clients that could use your services. Don't you see, Ash, you could start your own consulting company? You would be your own boss. I can send some clients your way, but once word gets out, you'll get clients from referrals. And you can be selective about who you represent. Social media is a lucrative business. It takes someone with the know-how to make it happen. Trevor can't stop talking about the impact you made with the Pajamas. I can help you set up your business model. And the best part? You can do it remotely. From New York, or Charlotte, or Savannah, or even Nashville. Anywhere, really. If it gets too much, hire an assistant or two. What do you think?"

I hadn't thought about doing this independently. Most corporations hire social media people these days, and my professors pushed me in that direction. But what if I could help individuals instead of organizations?

"Nashville is random." I've never mentioned wanting to live in Nashville. I don't even know anyone there.

"You know, new beginnings?" He bites his thumbnail, revealing one of his nervous tells. I can't think why he'd be nervous, so I focus on what he's proposed.

"Yeah, not sure about Nashville. But could I do that? Are there people that would trust me with their online image? Chance did, but that's different. He already trusts me."

If Chance did get big paychecks because of my social media influence, it could be enticing for others to want those services. I start to warm to the idea of being my own boss.

"Hell yeah, you can! It's brilliant, right?"

I give him my shrug again. I feel a tiny spark of hope light within me, but it's hard for me to get excited about anything. I feel so empty. This idea is the first thing that feels normal in weeks.

"I'll think about it." I can tell my less-than-enthusiastic response is not what Jules is looking for.

"Well, I have a few new clients to the agency that are up-and-coming stars. They need to start on the right foot when it comes to brand. Would you consider meeting with my agents and discussing it?"

I shrug again.

Jules sighs heavily and drops into the leather armchair. He puts his elbows on his knees and rubs his face. "Look, Ash, it would help me out too. I can't support these agents if their clients aren't at the top of their game, both on the field and off."

"Low blow, playing that card, and you know it." The last thing I want to do is hurt my family's business. "I'll meet with them."

His face lights up. "Fantastic! I have a meeting scheduled for tomorrow at three. And, uh, maybe I'll schedule a salon appointment for you in the morning to get you back to presentable." He waves his hand up and down at me and scrunches his nose. He pulls out his phone and starts typing. "We'll make Ashleigh college graduate into a sophisticated entrepreneur, and tomorrow will be her debut. I feel it will be the start of something wonderful for you."

Yay. I can't wait.

CHAPTER
FORTY-TWO

COLE

———

After my call from Julian, everything is a blur.

As I lay in my childhood bed, l let it all seep in. It was a day of happiness and dreams come true, but all I want is to connect with the girl I love. I turn my phone in my hand, composing texts in my head. I need to say the right words, and when they don't come, I opt to say nothing. I'm a coward, and I know it.

I haven't heard from her since our run-in at the restaurant. I was caught off guard, and honestly, I know I was pretty rude to her. Not my first time in that respect. Mom and Darcy cornered me the next day and asked me why I was not chasing after her. Not having a good answer for them, I shouted, "ENOUGH!" and didn't talk to anyone for two days after that encounter.

They left it alone after that, but I know they still talk about it. It's obvious when they stop talking when I enter a room, and I'm always getting pitiful glances from them both. I don't wear heartbreak well.

I hadn't planned to tell Matt about seeing her because I

needed someone on my side, even under false pretenses. Despite my attempts at controlling the narrative, Darcy told him about our chance meeting at the restaurant. I ripped his head off when he asked me why I didn't tell him, and we didn't talk for almost a week. I've firmly established that Leigh is my taboo topic, and they all abide by it.

However, I'm presented with the ultimate question from an unlikely person, Julian Decker. What is going to make me happy? The answer is easy. It's just complicated.

After quick and tear-filled goodbyes, Matt and I fly from Charleston to Charlotte to take the first step on our separate paths.

Here we are at the Charlotte airport, where I'll catch a connecting flight to New York to meet Julian because he insisted on a face-to-face meeting.

It's time for our goodbye.

"So this is it," Matt says as he looks at his feet. This is incredibly hard for both of us. He's already wearing his Reapers hat. I'm wearing my Pajamas hat, the feeling of nostalgia filling me. I know I need to focus on the future, but I can't seem to let go of the past. What will make me happy? That's the answer Julian is looking for. It didn't take me any time to decide, but finding the courage to admit it is taking a little more effort.

"Go get 'em, Matt. I'm a little jealous you are starting on their triple-A team in Charleston. Being home after these last four years will be awesome."

"Yeah, I'm looking forward to it. I've missed home." An awkward pause surrounds us as people pass by, catching their next flight. A life-changing moment is happening, and everyone around us is oblivious. I'm sure there is a metaphor in there somewhere. Matt clears his throat. "You let me know how it goes?"

"I will." I shuffle my feet, kicking at an imaginary rock.

"Hey, good luck today. With everything." Everything. There's so much to unpack there.

"Yeah, you too." I can't take this tension any longer. I grab Matt and pull him into a bone-crushing hug. He hugs me back, patting my back with hard love taps. I can't let go until I can pull the tears back. I'm sure our goodbye rivals any rom-com airport scene.

"I love you, brother. Take care of everyone at home for me." I take comfort in knowing Matt will be at home with our families. Knowing Matt will be around for Mom and Darcy makes this trip easier for me.

We both step out of our embrace. "You know I will. I guess I better run. Don't want to keep Alexander Decker waiting."

"I still can't believe.....never mind." I shake my head, trying to clear the image. "It'll take some time for me to hear his name without getting pissed."

Matt laughs. "I know, it'll take everything I have not to call him Alexander fucking Decker since that's your pet name for him. And I've only heard it a million times. If I let that slip, you are paying out my contract after I get fired."

I cringe a little at the Decker name and the idea that my past could impact Matt's future. We both chuckle at the thought. "Hey, one more thing." I reach into my bag and pull out one of my most prized possessions. "See if you can get this signed for me?" I hand Matt a Tripp Stevenson rookie card.

Matt's eyes widen at the gesture. "I'll see what I can do. Now, get to your gate. You can't be late. It's a big day for Cole Davidson. Let me know how it goes." We give each other a quick hug and part ways.

The solitary walk to my gate is the most alone I've ever been. I'm caught between my past and my future and am nervous as hell.

———

It's my first time in the Big Apple, and this airport is busy with people moving at New York speeds. With my bag in hand, I head outside, where there is a long row of black cars. Drivers hold signs with names, and I scan the row for mine. The one driver that stands out is an attractive woman in a tight, black skirt and low-cut, white blouse. She's holding an iPad with my name on it. I introduce myself, and she escorts me to a black Range Rover with dark-tinted windows. I throw my bag in the back, and she holds the door open.

"Get in, Davidson. We've got work to do."

I slide into the back seat next to Julian Decker.

"I thought we could use this time to bond. Let's start with a little story time." Julian gives me a devious smile and a wink. I'm officially in the big leagues.

As we sit in stop-and-go traffic, I watch the people going about life on the sidewalks of New York City. I pull out my phone and snap a few pictures to send to Darcy. She would love the vibe of the city. I'm sure her artist's eye would enjoy so many unique sites.

Leigh would love it too. I've done an excellent job of compartmentalizing my feelings, but I think my switch may be faulty. When Julian asked me if I loved her two days ago, it was like he opened that box and threw away the key. Yes, I love her. I can't stop loving her. I know I need to resolve my feelings for her.

In the car, he tells me stories about her. Her childhood. Their girl's nights. The trip to Mexico after she left the Pajamas. I knew most of the stories because she had told me a similar version. But this time, through Julian's filter, the stories have an added layer of context. He talks about her desire to be loved for who she is, not who she's related to. The desire to be independent. How her army of brothers smothers her out of love.

He didn't have to say it. I understand. It was the reason behind her deception. Her summer of reinvention. Hadn't she said that to me? I just didn't know the why or the specifics.

Listening to his stories, I realize she never lied to me, at least not about who she truly is. I may not have known a few details, like her family connections or name, but the girl I fell in love with told me the truth and shared her soul with me.

I want to ask Julian about her. Ask where she is. Ask if she's okay. But I don't. I'm not sure I'm ready. She walked away so easily the last time I saw her. I can't survive if she walks away again.

CHAPTER
FORTY-THREE

ASHLEIGH

―――――

Julian sent his assistant, Mary Kate, to the apartment this morning to escort me to the salon. She said something about him having an important client meeting, and he wanted to ensure I had everything I needed for my corporate launch.

I've known Mary Kate for years but never spent much one-on-one time with her. I know Mary Kate made the arrangements for us to have brunch and a salon day, and every detail has been delightful.

Today is a treat for Mary Kate as well as me. Julian takes care of his people. I think that's part of his success, but it's also who Jules is. He's got a heart full of love for the people in his inner circle. I asked him once if he had dated Mary Kate, and he scoffed. He said he doesn't mix business with pleasure.

We ate at a charming cafe where she regaled funny stories about Julian and some of his dating disasters. Since she fields his calls, she has plenty of stories to share. When I asked her if she would ever date Jules, she said she would never cross that line, and their working relationship is better for it.

At the salon, we both had head-to-toe treatments. Hair, nails, and makeup. The works.

"Tada! Damn, girl, you are gorgeous! You are going to knock his socks off!" my stylist announces.

"No one in socks, I'm afraid," I mumble.

She spins the chair around until I face the mirror. I see a person I barely recognize. I said I wanted a change. New beginnings and all that. Wow. This is quite the change.

My hair is much shorter, with loose beach waves surrounding my face. The days of braids and baseball caps are over. The makeup artist gave me a soft, natural look that makes my blue eyes pop. The change is dramatic.

"Wow," Mary Kate exclaims. "New beginnings always require a new outfit, don't you think?" She holds a garment bag from my favorite New York designer and hands it to me.

I slowly shake my head at the ridiculousness of Julian's extravagance. I open the bag to find a designer dress with a full, pleated A-line skirt. The light blue and white floral pattern is soft and romantic. The slight v-neck and cap sleeves give it a vintage, almost timeless look. It even has pockets. It's like something you would see in an episode of *Mad Men*. A pair of strappy kitten heels and a coordinated clutch are included in the bag to finish the look. Julian, or should I say, Mary Kate, thought of everything.

I admit that today has made me feel like a new person. I absolutely look like a new person. I don't think I was this girly for prom. It's not my typical sporty look, but it's time to grow up and become an adult. I question the appropriateness of this look for a business meeting, but I love it nonetheless. I can't thank Jules enough.

Here's to day one of the new beginnings.

When I leave the changing room, Mary Kate gasps and puts her hands over her heart. "Oh, Ashleigh, you look amazing."

"Thanks." I run my hands down the smooth silk of the pleated skirt. The dress is tight in all the right places and shows off all my curves. I take a deep breath and attempt to release my anxiety. "I feel better than I have in weeks. You might be right. New beginnings require a fresh new look. Thank you. I know this may be from Julian, but you made it happen."

Her smile lets me know she's pleased with her work today. "Other than booking the appointment, he insisted on taking care of this. It's all him."

"Oh. Wow. That's a surprise." When did he have time to shop and make this happen?

"You know, when it comes to you, he does most of his own planning. I may mail those girl's night boxes, but he curates everything. I love watching him select items for the mood or occasion. He's very particular." I've always known Julian had layers, but this one is surprising, even for me.

"Oh, one more thing." She reaches into her bag and hands me a Tiffany blue box with a white ribbon.

"What's this?" Julian has officially crossed a line. He's gone over the top.

"Julian said it's from Chance." She blushes at the mention of his name. I find most women blush when thinking about Chance. After running his IG, I discovered many, many women blush at the thought of him. And some have no blush mechanism and go straight to bold and spicy.

I open the box to find a delicate sapphire necklace and matching earrings. They complement the dress perfectly. These guys. They are too much.

The gemstones sparkle in the salon lighting, the surrounding diamonds making the deep blue stones appear to sit in a bed of glitter. It's all so sparkly.

The jewelry almost matches my eye color, making them appear a deeper shade of blue. I can hear Cole in my head. Gah, he loved my eyes. *Look at me, Leigh. I want to see your baby blues. They shine when you are happy.* I give a wistful smile as I remember the caress of his hands on my face as he would kiss me tenderly. My chest tightens, thinking about him. On reflex, I put my fist to my heart to lessen the pain.

Mary Kate notes my change in demeanor. "Only love can make you have that far-away look in your eyes. Chance?"

Her comment brings me back to reality. "What?! No! Chance is like a brother." He's seen me at my lowest. I've ugly cried on him on an airplane. If that's not a friend zone, I don't know what is.

"Yeah, a gorgeous, un-blood-related brother who gives you amazing jewelry. No one would blame you," she encourages.

"No. Not Chance." Never.

"You may have said there was no one to knock those socks off, but I don't think that's entirely true." I'm honestly surprised Jules hasn't shared my misery with her. It's evident that Mary Kate is the keeper of Julian's secrets, and I always assumed she knew everything about him. I suppose I'm not his story to tell. I appreciate him even more for his protection of my pain.

I start to tear up. I thought that with time, the pain would lessen. It hasn't been that long, I guess. I just need more time. If I'm going to move forward, I have to own it. Saying it out loud makes it real.

"I ruined his future, and I can't imagine he'd ever forgive me. Hell, I can't forgive myself. So, it's over. Tragically over." I take a deep breath and let the realization of the truth wash over me. I straighten my shoulders and put on a brave face. "All part of my new beginnings, I guess."

"Oh, girl, I'm a sucker for true love. Fate will have a way of making it work out. Now let's not mess up this spectacular makeup. Come on, let's get you to the office for your new beginning."

Mary Kate is sweet, but I never thought of her as naive. After all, she works for Julian, and I'm sure she's seen the realities of dating a Decker. Love isn't in the cards for us Deckers.

I take another long look in the mirror and barely recognize

myself. This grown-up, non-sporty woman looking back at me is a complete stranger. I guess that's what new beginnings look like.

I take a quick selfie and send texts to Jules and Chance with lots of hearts. I thank Chance, wondering if he even knows what I'm thanking him for. It doesn't take long for my phone to start buzzing. Chance sends a gif of fire and a cartoon skunk with his heart-eyes beating in and out. He says he owes me more than a few baubles, but that will do for now. I guess he did know. He closes with a good luck message and a wink emoji. I wonder what Jules has shared with him.

My phone starts buzzing again.

JULES

Woah. Your hair!

You don't like it?

JULES

No, I love it. You look like Mom in her engagement pictures. It's uncanny. Absolutely stunning.

Thank you. You are too much. Here's to new beginnings!

JULES

Ask MK to bring you back here when you finish up. I'll be with a client but you can wait in my office.

To new beginnings. See u soon.

Mary Kate and I make our way back to Julian's office. She's texting someone the entire drive back, which gives me time to think. New beginnings. I want to ask Cole for forgiveness but don't know how to start. It doesn't feel right to say sorry over text. I vow that I'll call him tomorrow. To move forward, I need to end that chapter. I owe him a proper apology.

Mary Kate takes me into Julian's office and hugs me.

"Good luck, Ashleigh. It's going to be fine. Love always wins." She gives me a wink and closes the door as she leaves.

What? I'm here to discuss social media.

I toss my clutch on the coffee table and make myself comfortable on his red tufted couch. I pull out my phone and look at Chance's latest pictures. What has he been up to? It's been a week since I've posted for him. He's done a few himself, but they consist of shirtless workout pictures. Again. Always a winner with the ladies, but he needs that broader audience.

I find pictures of him and the most adorable pit bull at the animal rescue. Chance loves animals and desperately wants a dog. Due to his schedule, it's impractical, so he volunteers at a shelter to satisfy his dog fix. Maybe I should move back to Raleigh and be Chance's dog sitter?

I do a quick post for him with #secondchance and chuckle at my pun. I always include how to volunteer and adopt in the post. This is the kind of post to go viral with the cuteness overload.

I hear the door open, and jokingly, without looking up, I say, "You kept me waiting long enough."

The footsteps stop at the door. I wait for Jules to respond, but I'm greeted with silence.

I look up and am stunned. Have I finally lost my mind, and I'm hallucinating? This can't be real. Standing in the doorway is the most gorgeous man I've ever seen. The dark charcoal suit accentuates his broad shoulders. The crisp white shirt and open collar show off his tan. His curls are tamed with product, and I've never seen him more polished. Professional. "Cole," I whisper to myself.

He looks shocked. It's the same expression he had the last time I saw him. His face is unreadable. It appears neither of us was expecting this reunion today. But he's here. In New York. In Julian's office.

I'm speechless.

CHAPTER
FORTY-FOUR

COLE

———

I finally worked up the nerve to ask Julian about Leigh, and he said she was staying with him in New York. However, he failed to mention she was waiting in his office, looking like a fucking vision from heaven. She's sitting on his couch and is frozen in place.

Her beautiful hair is shorter, more shoulder length now, but my fingers crave to run through the waves surrounding her face. She's wearing a blue and white floral dress that hugs her curves, and I want to hold her close and never let her go. But it's her eyes. The most captivating shade of blue looks at me with utter surprise.

"I guess Julian didn't tell you I was here, either?" My voice cracks as the words get stuck in my throat.

She barely shakes her head. Tears fill her eyes, and she bites her luscious bottom lip. She stands slowly, and we stare at each other, neither moving from our spots.

I take her all in. The sparkle in her eyes. The slope of her collarbone. The shape of her calves in those heels. The uncertainty in her faint smile. My Leigh is here.

My head is swimming with all the things I need to say. I don't know where to start.

I take a few tentative steps toward her, and she matches my slow steps until we close the gap. A tear escapes, trailing down her cheek, and I brush it away with my thumb. I don't remove my hand from her face. I can't. I need to touch her to ground me in reality. At least she doesn't flinch at my touch.

"You look beautiful. I like your hair. It's shorter." I'm using every ounce of restraint not to run my fingers through her hair, no matter the length.

"You too. Look good, I mean. I don't think I've ever seen you in a suit. You're all cleaned up like Matt gave you lessons or something." This banter is strained, but it's still our thing. The push and pull.

"What did he do to get you here?" I ask.

"I was supposed to be meeting with some of his clients that need social media help." Her voice is tight, her words practically robotic.

"So I take it you aren't working in the family business?" Once the truth surfaced, it all made sense. She wanted to stand on her own merits, not get a job because of her name and relationship to the Carolina Reapers. Her summer of reinvention? It was about finding herself out from under the shadow of her family. I get it. I really do. I wish she had told me, but I understand why she didn't. It was complicated. Hell, it still is. But I don't care about the complications anymore.

"No. I'm going to try to do this on my own." I'm so proud of her for taking the risk, the harder road.

"I've missed you," I whisper.

"I'm sorry I've ruined everything for you." Her bottom lip is trembling. I can tell she's forcing herself to be brave.

"Sweetheart, you didn't ruin anything."

"I did. I'm not good for you. I come with baggage. Complications."

"We all have baggage. Yours just happens to be designer." I smile at her. I can't stand the pain in her eyes. She thinks she's crushed my dream, but she hasn't. Does she even know what my dream is now?

"I'm sorry, Cole. I've made such a mess of everything. You promised me honesty, and I wasn't honest with you. I'm sorry. So sorry." She tries to pull away. I'm not letting her go this time.

"I don't need you to be sorry. I'm not." I say that with firm conviction. I hold her face between my palms, searching her eyes for my answer. "Your brother asked what would make me happy. You know what I realized makes me really, truly happy?"

She gently shakes her head, but her hopeful look makes me smile.

"You. You make me happy. Ashleigh Rutledge Decker, you are my happiness. You are my future."

She tries to step back. Nope. That's not going to happen. I'll never let her go again.

"But I ruined your future. I know you aren't a Reaper. Alexander told me before I saw you at the restaurant. It's all my fault." Another tear escapes her magnificent blue eyes. I lean in and kiss it away.

"No, sweetheart, I'm not a Reaper. And I have you to thank for that." I give her a wink.

Her lip starts to tremble, and she tries to pull away again. I drop one arm around her waist and pull her tight to me. She lets out a small gasp.

I realize I'm taking a leap here. I don't know her plans. She hasn't told me she loves me. This is a full count, two outs, bases-loaded situation. What do I do? Swing. Always swing.

"No, don't you see? You gave me a future that's better than I could imagine." She furrows her brow, and it occurs to me that she doesn't know. "Sweetheart, I'm a New York Liberty. That's why I'm here in New York. My baseball career is going to be amazing. I'm heading to Nashville in a few days to join my new triple-A team. Nashville. Music City. Leigh, it's a dream come true. Baseball and music. But you know what's going to make me extremely happy? That's having you by my side. That is if you want to be with me."

"What? New York drafted you?" She's shocked.

"Yeah, third round. They are excited about signing me, and Julian hooked me up with one of his agents, Patrick. He's working out a fantastic contract. That's why I'm here. Devlin Millbanks, the owner of the Liberties, walked me out to first base in Liberty Stadium today, and all I could imagine was you sitting at third base watching me play. It's all happening, sweetheart. It's better than I could have ever imagined. But I need you. To be really happy, to be complete, I need you. Do you want me?" My thumb caresses her cheek, and I stare into her beautiful blue eyes.

"Cole, oh my god, Cole, are you serious?"

"Serious? Absolutely. About all of it. You. Baseball. All of it. Leigh, I love you. I love you so damn much." If I don't kiss her, I'm going to explode.

My desire for her lips overwhelms me, and I can't wait a second longer. I have to kiss her, to taste her. My lips crash with hers. I hold my breath, waiting to see if she returns my kiss. And she does. Oh, she does.

This kiss is full of passion and longing. This kiss is needy. It communicates all the heartbreak and hope and desire I have for her. Her lips mold to mine, welcoming me. My hand slides to the back of her head, my fingers find their way through her hair, and pull her closer, tighter.

My girl heightens all of my senses. I inhale the light floral scent of her perfume. I taste her sweet tongue and bubblegum lip gloss. I can't close my eyes because her beauty is captivating. Her skin against my fingers sends electricity through my body. Everything about this kiss is perfect. It's full of promise. Love. A future.

We slowly pull apart, and I look into her eyes, still searching for the answer to my heart's question.

"But your dream of being a Reaper? I ruined that for you." She tries to step back again.

"Sweetheart, you didn't ruin anything. Don't you see? I've got it all. I mean, being a Reaper might have been nice, but baby, a New York Liberty? That's everyone's Plan A if they are brave enough to say it out loud. Baseball is solid. I'm good. My dream is better than I could have even imagined. But what's not okay? Doing it alone. Tell me this isn't one-sided. Tell me you love me just a fraction of what I feel for you, and I can die a happy man."

The edges of her lips turn into the most seductive smile I've ever seen. "Cole Davidson, I love you. With my whole heart." She leans in and gives me a sweet, gentle kiss. She pulls away, and I resist allowing the distance between us.

She giggles and swats at my arm. I already feel the loss of her touch as she walks back toward the sofa and reaches into her purse. She puts something in her hand and walks the few steps back to me.

"I have something for you," she says. Her smile is mischievous and playful. She puts a worn Post-it note above my heart. I look down to see familiar handwriting.

It says *MINE.*

EPILOGUE

ASHLEIGH

———

The life of a minor league ball player is busy and demanding, filled with practices, workouts, games, and travel. We fall back into a familiar routine, except we are living together this time. In a hotel, but no more his place and my place. It's been six weeks since we moved to Nashville, and nothing has ever felt more right. Or cramped.

Cole is on a six-day road trip, and I have a surprise for him.

I bought a house and plan to have it ready when he returns on Sunday. No more hotels. I want to give him a home. Our first home together. I asked Darcy and Emma to spend the week with me to help pull off this surprise. We painted, decorated, and bought way too many throw pillows. It's finished, it's Saturday night, and I'm ready to celebrate.

Darcy has been an absolute godsend, pulling together a home that will make Cole comfortable and let me have something that doesn't feel like a frat house. Her design skills are exceptional. And just like I thought, we have become fast friends.

We even created a home office for me to work on my social media consulting company. Jules was right. This job is perfect for me. I can work from anywhere and be my own boss. It's a win-win. Cole and Matt are two of my first clients. I'm still running Chance's accounts and helping the Pajamas occasionally. Tripp Stevenson and I are working on his social media accounts to focus on pitching tips and advice for young players. I love the variety and positive ways to use social media. Several of Chance's friends have reached out too. My client base is taking off.

My favorite room in the house is the combo music room and library Darcy designed. There is an entire wall of shelves filled with my books and an overstuffed chair to curl up and read when I need an escape. She set up a space for Cole's guitar and a giant whiteboard for him to write down lyrics and music as he writes songs when he's feeling inspired. I can imagine coming in here and pretending to read so I can watch him play his guitar and get lost in the music.

His music is just one of a million things that I love about Cole. He's multifaceted and brilliant. His music is beautiful, and when he sings to me, I feel his love surround me in the notes and words. Sometimes I wish he'd share his talent with the world, but he says it's just a hobby he enjoys sharing with me.

Darcy, Emma, and I are stretched out on the outdoor sectional that surrounds a large backyard fire pit. The fire isn't necessary since it's still warm on this August evening, but I like the ambiance.

It's been a busy week, and we are all exhausted. We are discussing dinner options when I hear a commotion in the house.

"Tequila and tacos?" Jules asks as he carries a tray loaded with margaritas into the backyard. Chance is beside him with a tray stacked with tacos. It smells delicious.

"Yes, please," Darcy says as she grabs a drink.

"You are speaking my love language," Emma giggles.

"What are you doing here?" I ask.

"We heard there was a girl's night, and we decided to join in," Chance says. Jules gives me a wink.

Darcy looks at them both with wide eyes. "OMG, Ashleigh, you hired strippers for girl's night? This is incredible!"

Jules laughs so hard that he almost drops the tray of drinks. I take the tray from him, setting it on the ottoman.

Chance winks at Darcy. "That can be arranged, beautiful," he says seductively, giving her a hip thrust.

Emma hops up, punches Chance in the arm, and relieves him of the taco tray. "Down, boy," she mumbles. She sets the tray next to the drinks and selects her first taco. Emma's love language has always been tacos.

"Darcy," I say, "let me introduce you to my brother, Julian, and Chance Fuller."

Darcy turns a brilliant shade of red. She throws her face down on the cushion and buries her head in a throw pillow. We all laugh.

"It's a fair assumption," Chance says. He pulls the throw pillow out of her hands and reads the message. *Where's my cabana boy?* He quirks an eyebrow at me. I give him a half-shrug. What can I say? It was a perfect color for the brightly colored cushions.

"It's nice to meet you, Darcy," Julian says. His shoulders are still shaking from silently laughing.

Emma is eating her second, or is it third, taco.

"Pixie girl, where do you put all that?" Chance asks. He sits next to Emma and takes a taco, consuming it in one bite.

"It's okay, Darcy. Our evening just got a lot more interesting. Try one of these," I say, gesturing to my margarita.

Darcy sits up and takes a margarita, and gulps it down. Jules grabs the pitcher and refills her glass.

"I like the place," Jules says as he looks around. "How's Cole going to react when he sees it? Will he be upset you didn't get his input?"

I thought about that. I worry my bottom lip. Cole isn't used to extravagant gifts and surprises. We've promised to be honest and not have secrets, ever. I hope this doesn't fall into that taboo category.

"Oh, he'll love it," Emma says confidently. "He's so in love with this girl, she can do no wrong." The four of us give her a skeptical look. Yes, he loves me. But they've all lived through me doing Cole wrong. And I'm sure no one wants that again.

"I hope so," I say. "I just want him to have a place to relax and escape when the pressures of the game get too much. And I want him to have a place to invite the guys to hang since most still live the bachelor lifestyle."

"He's a lucky guy," Chance says.

"No, I'm the lucky one," I say. "So lucky."

We settle around the fire and enjoy the tacos and drinks for hours. Darcy meshes with our girl's night group quickly. Chance and Jules tease her, making a game of who can make her blush the most.

Darcy shares stories of growing up with Cole and some of his antics with Matt. I enjoy the insight into Cole's childhood. Chance comments on how much he admires Cole and wants to get to know him better. I think it's his way of showing support, and I'm glad they will be friends.

"So, what's the deal with you and Matt?" Emma asks Darcy.

"What? Nothing, what do you mean?" Darcy stutters.

"I think the lady doth protest too much," Jules says.

Darcy blushes. "No, he's Cole's best friend. We're just friends."

Emma narrows her eyes at Darcy. I don't know if she's examining her or seeing double. I lost count of the margaritas. "Matt and I are friends too, you know. I couldn't have gotten through my last semester without him."

"What? I didn't know you guys were close," Darcy says.

Emma's smile slowly spreads across her face. I've seen this one before. She's going in for the kill. Small but terrifying.

"Oh, we are *very* close. We spent hours alone together any chance we could get. One plus one equals two and all. And all that time at the ball field sitting on the third base line...." Emma says, giving her best goo-goo eyes.

"Oh, I didn't know," Darcy says with a tinge of sadness.

"Emma, stop," I scold her. "Be nice."

I take Darcy's hands. "Matt tutored her because she couldn't do math. Total friend zone, even though I think he's just the best guy. You need to know that girl's nights are sacred. Anything shared stays in the girl's night trust."

"That's too bad," Darcy says. "Because I wanted to tell Cole that Chance has a huge crush on him."

The comment catches Chance off guard, and Margarita shoots out his nose. "You'd better not tell him," Chance chokes out. Jules slaps him on the back. "Don't worry, Ash. I won't steal him away."

"Good luck with that, big guy. Like I'd ever let him go again."

We all laugh and enjoy the evening.

Fingers crossed, Cole likes the surprise.

COLE

———

"That game was incredible," Darcy says. "That was my first hockey game, but it won't be my last."

Leigh and I are having a housewarming party this weekend, even though we've been here for almost two months. This is our first opportunity to get all our friends and family together in our new home in Nashville. When Leigh surprised me with our house, I was blown away. Because who gives a house as a gift except for the daughter of a billionaire? The house was a hell of a gift, but it was more than that. She gave us a home. It's our place of respite and togetherness. And this weekend, we are squeezing in all the family, friends, love, and celebration we can.

We kicked off the weekend watching Chance play against Nashville and invited everyone back tonight for a late dinner and get-together. Chance and Julian will drop by after the press and other media obligations.

We want to celebrate our home and new beginnings with loved ones. Now that baseball is over, we can slow down for a few months and enjoy the life we are building together. Chance's season is just starting, but this weekend aligned perfectly to include him.

"Hey, I thought you were a baseball girl," Matt says, pretending to pout.

Darcy looks around the fire pit at the baseball guys, screws up her mouth, and shrugs.

"Baseball players are far superior to hockey players, and you know it. I mean, hockey players are brutes with tempers and dental issues," Matt retorts.

I crack up. These two will argue for hours now. Darcy knows how to wind Matt up.

Alexander and I spent time bonding this morning in the batting cages. While we talked, it was a great way to focus on something physical, letting the tension go productively. I assured him that I'm committed when it comes to his sister. All in. It's been almost four months of living together, just the beginning of our forever. While I appreciate his role as a big, protective brother, I've got her from here. He agreed to back his protection down but assured me that if I ever hurt her, he and Emma would know how to take care of things. We may have started off rocky, but I think we'll be fine.

"First of all," Darcy starts, "I'm not a baseball girl. I'm a sports fan. I appreciate the game." She stands over Matt with her hands on her hips, attempting to intimidate him. I don't think her posture is working.

"Yeah, right," Matt says, taking a long pull on his beer. "You can't deny you like the baseball uniform and baseball butt. I've heard you gossiping about it over the years."

Darcy reaches over to the side table, pulls a marshmallow out of the bag, and throws it in Matt's face.

"Oh, party foul, Darcy," Trevor chimes in. "Don't waste a good marshmallow on the likes of Matt Hartman." Trevor kicks back and watches the drama unfold. It's one of his favorite pastimes.

"You might want to stand back, Trevor," Emma chimes in. "Darcy can hold her own."

"Says the pixie girl," Trevor teases, giving her a wink.

I walk up beside Leigh and drape my arm around her shoulders. I kiss her temple, and she leans into my embrace.

"Is this what you pictured, sweetheart? Bickering and fighting all weekend?" I ask with a slight chuckle.

"Is that what you see?" she muses.

I give her a half-shrug.

She gazes lovingly at the crew assembled in front of us. "I don't see fighting. I see love. Family. A future."

"At least no one is taking a swing at anyone," I say. "That's progress."

"Give it time," Julian says as he and Chance walk into the

backyard. He clasps my shoulder as a greeting and kisses Leigh on the forehead.

"What are they fighting about?" Chance asks, motioning toward Darcy and Matt as he kisses Leigh on the top of her head. My momentary jealousy settles as I remind myself they love her too, but not like I do.

"The merits of a baseball player over a hockey player, I think," I reply.

"Well, I need to settle that," Chance says and heads straight to Darcy. He picks her up and throws her over his shoulder. I flinch, watching my sister get manhandled by Chance, but Leigh puts her hand on my arm, signaling me to let it go. Darcy giggles and swats Chance's back. Matt jumps out of his seat.

"Hockey players have endurance and skill and do it all while balancing on knives. Baseball players stand around for a hell of a lot of time, waiting for something to happen," Chance says with a gleam in his eye.

Matt looks like he's ready to punch Chance. I guess there is still time for that event to happen.

Chance puts Darcy on the couch beside Emma and fluffs the pillow behind her. Darcy is still giggling like a sixteen-year-old girl meeting the Jonas Brothers. Chance sure charms the ladies.

As I observe the people around the fire pit, I realize I've found that happiness Julian asked me about months earlier. More happiness than I thought possible.

"Hey guys," I say to get everyone's attention. "I have some news to share." Everyone quiets and settles down, all eyes on me. "I got a call today from Harlan Rockwell. He works with some big country music names these days." I take a deep breath. This isn't baseball or hockey we are talking about. "Anyway, they bought one of my songs, and Danny Stone will record it for his next album."

Since we settled in Nashville, I've leaned into my guitar as an outlet when I'm stressed, especially on the road. I can't deny that the love of my life is my muse. I give Leigh a new love song almost weekly. Most nights, she snuggles in her reading nook while I work out the lyrics and tunes that she inspires. There aren't enough words to express my love for this girl. Mine.

Leigh looks at me, shocked. She knows I write songs, but I didn't tell her I've recorded a few demos since we've been in Nashville. I wanted it to be a surprise.

She looks stunned. "Which one? Will you play it for me?" she asks. That was precisely the response I'd hoped for.

"Absolutely, sweetheart. It's one you haven't heard yet." I reach for my phone and not my guitar, surprising her. I hit play on my recorded demo, and the opening bars are picked up on the Bluetooth speakers around the yard.

Everyone is listening to the song, my guitar playing a melodic tune while my words tell the story of hope, heartbreak, and love. Tears fill her eyes as she realizes it's our story. When the last verse starts, I get down on one knee and hold a ring out to her. I let the words speak for me.

I've known it from the moment I saw you. You were meant for me. Always and forever. Be mine.

"Marry me?" I ask as the song comes to an end. The backyard is silent, and I start to second-guess my idea of proposing in front of everyone.

Her eyes fill with unshed tears. "You wrote a song about us?" she whispers. Did she miss the fact that I'm on one knee with a ring?

"Yeah, I did. You make me want to sing and tell everyone how much I love you, Ashleigh Rutledge Decker. So what do you say? Will you be mine? Forever?"

She kneels in front of me. "Of course, trouble. I've always been yours." Her arms wrap around my neck, and she kisses me with reckless abandon.

Our friends and family let out a collective sigh and shout congratulations.

I pull away so I can put the ring on her finger. It's a round solitaire surrounded by rubies. It reminded me of a baseball - the game that brought us together.

I can't wait to tell her how her father and I designed the ring together. I may not be a Reaper, but he has welcomed me into the Decker family with his blessing.

This is the beginning of all our dreams coming true.

WHAT'S NEXT FOR THE DECKER CONNECTION?

Get ready for a Decker Connection brother's best friend story!

Sliding into Home: Matt and Darcy

Overwhelmed doesn't begin to describe my life. I'm in over my head remodeling a multi-million-dollar beach house. It's the only thing standing between me and college graduation. Then the guy I've crushed on since middle school offers to be my assistant. Did I mention he's my brother's best friend? Yep. Matt Hartman, swoony boy next door and professional baseball player, is working side by side with me this fall. It takes everything I have to keep my feelings for him contained, until, well, I don't. Can I put his friendship with my brother on the line for a relationship with me?

I've hit more milestones this year than most do in a decade. I graduated from college, got drafted into Major League Baseball, played on a triple-A team in my hometown, and now, for the first time in my life, I'm enjoying my off-season. But am I? When I'm presented with the opportunity to help Darcy Davidson with her senior project, I gladly volunteer my services. It's something to fill my time, and besides, my best friend's sister needs help. That's all it is, right? Then why do I want to be so much more than her assistant?

ALSO BY CHERYL CAMPBELL

Living the Suite Life: Alexander and Dani

Stress and pressure come with the territory when you're the youngest General Manager in the MLB. Add in my self-appointed role as the protector of the Decker Connection, my tight-knit group of siblings and friends, and it's no wonder they say I'm grumpy.

I'm facing down a public relations nightmare after one of my players assaults someone at a local food festival, and this PR problem is about to push me over the edge. Then I meet this full-of-sunshine, rainbows from storm clouds, heart-full-of-kindness, single mother, and I'm in more trouble than I ever imagined. There's absolutely no saving me from falling now.

The Final Draft: Julian and Harper

Julian Decker's billion-dollar sports agency represents the top athletes in the world. His charm, success and sexy blue eyes have landed him on the hottest bachelor list for the past five years. He's a hopeless romantic, with money, fame, and a rotation of beautiful women on his arm each week. Some would say he has it all. But things aren't always as they seem. Behind the flashing lights and camera clicks, Julian has deep-seated trust issues and a secret he keeps hidden, even from his closest friends in the Decker Connection.

Harper Cartwright is tired of being known as "the hockey player's sister" and is ready to forge her own path. With her master's degree in hand, she's headed to New York to learn from the best and make her author dreams come true. It's a whole new ball game for her. A new city. A NHL goalie roommate and his adorable dog. An intense and demanding writing program. She has a lot on her plate. Harper's handling all these life challenges until she encounters Julian Decker, a handsome playboy with a panty-dropping smile. His intense pursuit of her has Harper excited and wary, especially after she discovers his secret.

LET'S CONNECT

Cheryl loves connecting with readers and talking about the Deckers. Join her in the conversation. Follow for sneak peeks and behind the scenes fun.

And don't forget to leave a review on Amazon 😃

Cheryl Campbell Facebook Cheryl Campbell Author

Cheryl Campbell Instagram @Cheryl_Campbell_Author

Cheryl Campbell TikTok @cherylcampbellbooks

CherylCampbellbooks@gmail.com

Want to hear The Trouble at First playlist? Check it out on Spotify.

Trouble at First Playlist on Spotify